Death in Copper Town

CHAPTER ONE

I'D BEEN EXPECTING a quiet summer writing traffic tickets in the small mining town of Mingus, but all that changed the morning the fire chief called me.

"Hello, I'm trying to reach Deputy Quincy."

"I'm Peg Quincy. Go ahead."

"We may have a problem."

As he described the situation, it quickly became apparent that problem was an understatement. His hotshot crew was fighting an out-of-control campsite fire on Black Mountain. One of the men spotted a body in an old mining excavation several hundred feet below their mop-up activity.

That excavation had to be the now-closed copper mine William Clark had carved out years ago on the outskirts of Mingus. That location was smack dab in the middle of my jurisdiction, so I went to investigate.

When I arrived at the open-mine pit, locals and tourists milled about the chain link fence securing the front entrance. Layers of sulfur-yellow rock had been blasted back like an inverted ziggurat, forming a semicircular cliff hundreds of feet high. Oil-slick water pooled in the center of the semi-circular opening. Behind that, next to the cliff, was a dark crumpled mass.

A sunburned tourist in Bermuda shorts pointed through the fence. "Is that a body? I've never seen a dead body before."

Neither had I. Maybe seasoned veterans could view a corpse with no problem, but I was a rookie, barely a month out of the police academy and on temporary summer assignment in this small Arizona mining-turned-tourist town. I hadn't even been in town a week, and now this.

I pressed my lips together and talked my stomach into staying where it belonged. Then, while I awaited the arrival of the mine employee to unlock the fence gate, I canvassed the crowd. Nobody had seen or heard anything out of the ordinary.

A late-model Lexus braked to a stop, spattering my uniform pants with mud. It was Roger Heaton, the vice-mayor of Mingus. He opened the door of his Lexus and stepped into the same mud puddle he'd splashed onto me. Too bad.

"What's going on?" he demanded.

My red hair bristled at his sharp-edged manner. His damp handshake probably came from nerves or ulcers, but I still didn't like his attitude. My six-foot height had two inches on him, which ought to count for something. Maybe not.

"Body in there." I gestured. "I'm waiting for access from the mining company."

"Need help? Or you got it under control?" His voice dripped with condescension.

Sharply aware of my position as the only law enforcement officer on duty, I swallowed my pride. "Thanks. I could use you to stand at the entrance to control ingress when we get the gate open."

A few moments later, the mining official arrived, puffing at our mile-high elevation. "Sorry, I'm late." He wore a khaki shirt with a pocket protector, but no I.D. badge. Perhaps he was an engineer for the mining company.

"We usually keep this area fenced and padlocked," he said. "Don't want any amateur prospectors breaking a leg in here." He stared at the shape inside the fence.

I've noticed two types of people—those that are attracted by death, and those that are repelled by it. The engineer must have been the second, for after he opened the gate he didn't stick around long.

With Roger Heaton fending off the curious spectators, I paced the parameter of the death scene. The dead man lay sprawled face down, with his head canted at an unnatural angle, and one arm pitched beneath him. He wore a stained white shirt, soiled khakis, and cheap loafers with no socks. The neutral colors of his clothing contrasted against the dark red and blue gravels of the mine tailings.

I gagged at the foul mixture of smells—the man hadn't bathed for a while and had soiled himself in death. And a third odor was instantly familiar. A smashed bottle of Scotch lay next to the body: Cutty Sark, my mother's brand of choice.

The man appeared to be in his late twenties, with dark hair worn long in front, but ragged in back, as though he'd cut it himself. Death had robbed the face of all expression, the features gray from blood drainage after death. I glanced up at the mountain cliff, already in late afternoon shadow. Did he trip and fall under the influence of too much alcohol? It might be an accident, then. That would make the case easier to close.

I shot digital pictures of the corpse from all angles and then centered in on a head shot. No one I had interviewed thus far had knowledge of how or why he got there, so photos might be essential in making a positive identification.

When the medical examiner arrived, he concurred with my initial findings. "I'll have to do an autopsy to be sure, but it looks like a simple accident to me."

"Approximate time of death?"

"He's not been here long. From the liver temp, probably sometime after midnight."

"Okay if I roll the body?" I asked.

"Sure, I'm done for now. Let me give you a hand."

It was the first dead body I'd ever moved. We put our weight into it, and the body plopped over, rigor mortis already setting in. Heavier than I'd expected.

The fall had mushed the side of the man's face into a bloody mask. It didn't look human, and the view made me light-headed. I clenched my jaws together again. No way was I getting sick in front of all these witnesses.

I slipped my hand into the dead man's shirt pocket. Then searched the pockets of his pants looking for any sort of ID. Nothing.

The gestures felt like a violation of the man, somehow. The body was cold, no warmth left and I hurried my motions.

From the condition of his clothes, the dead man might be homeless, belonging to no one. Or maybe he had a family—I tried to imagine kids waiting someplace for a father who'd never return. Hard to think about that. I shifted back to the present.

Unless he had served in the military or been arrested, there was a good chance he might not even be in the national identification system. Nevertheless, I made a note to press the medical examiner for a quick fingerprint scan. If that didn't turn up anything, we'd have to go the dental identification route and hope that he was local.

Green flashed from the hand that had been wedged beneath the body. Bending down for a closer look, I discovered a fragment of silk in a striking emerald hue. I photographed it, tagged it, and put it in an evidence bag for the lab. Nothing else appeared in the immediate vicinity of the body, and the hard gravel surface surrounding the body revealed no footprints.

I glanced upward. If the man had fallen from the campsite above, there might be signs of a scuffle. If so, this case could change from a simple accident to a homicide. I'd best go up there and check it out. Did I want the complication of a murder investigation? Part of me, the conservative side protested, "no way," while the ambitious side shouted, "hell, yeah," inside my head.

After the medical examiner left with his loaded van, I relocked the mine fence to secure the area and stuck the key the mine official had given me in my pocket. I sat in my squad car finishing my notes and then made some follow-up calls.

The fire chief was apologetic. "I'm sorry, Deputy Quincy, if we disturbed stuff up there. We just wanted to put the fire out, before it started to spread. Too late to do anything about it now, I guess."

Too late for the dead man, anyway. What had the man been doing up on Black Mountain? Was his death a tragic misstep or something more sinister?

The fire chief gave me road directions to the burned campsite above the pit. I said I'd be by later to interview the firefighters.

When I called the sheriff to report the dead body, he wasn't happy.

"No trouble for years, and then you show up." His voice roughened. "I'm attending a commissioners' meeting this afternoon, a budget meeting. Do your investigation of the accident and write the report. I don't need complications up there."

His budget concerns weren't my problem. Inexperienced or not, I'd take a close look at the situation before I ruled it an accident. Sometimes that habit of standing my ground got me in trouble. I still carried the scar over one eyebrow from when my mother's then-boyfriend took offense at my smart mouth. But in this case, I was closer to what happened in Mingus than the sheriff was. He'd just have to trust me.

Slamming the door of the old Crown Vic, I cranked the engine and did a U-turn, then headed out of town. Navigating a series of sharp switchbacks on Highway 89a, I climbed from the mile-high elevation at Mingus to the top of Black Mountain, over two thousand feet higher.

When I reached the cut-across road at the top of the mountain, I turned right. The squad car bounced on worn shocks as I drove down the dirt trail to the burned campsite. A yearling mule deer raised its head at my approach and then returned to browsing on purple thistles nestled among the Ponderosa pines that thrived at this higher elevation.

At the far side of one meadow, I saw an old pickup—it looked like my grandfather, HT Tewksbury's, truck. I narrowed my eyes for a closer look. Fuzzy dice on the rear-view mirror and one fender, primer gray—his truck all right. What was he doing up here?

I looked around the clearing, but there was no sign of him. Instead, two strange men emerged from the shadow of the pines. The first was dark-eyed with black hair pulled back in a knot at the base of his skull. He looked to be Italian, or maybe part Native American. It was hard to judge his age because of his small stature, perhaps a skinny seventeen.

The second man was a big hulk of a guy, his height diminished as he leaned forward, one arm supported by a steel crutch. He appeared to be in his mid-fifties, with longish gray hair and the blotchy complexion of a heavy drinker. Both men looked uneasy at my approach. However, when I pulled to the side of the road and got out to meet them, their attitudes changed.

"Hey Peg! I'm Armor Brancussi, a good friend of your granddad." The big man projected a forced cheerfulness. "And this here is my nephew, Ben Yazzie."

"Where's my grandfather?"

The two men exchanged glances.

"I'm borrowing his truck for the afternoon," Armor said. "He lets me do that sometimes."

Ben picked up the story line. "We're just looking for *peresia*. It's a plant." He launched into a description of the desert herb: how it served as a styptic to stop bleeding and as an aid in childbirth. His uncle stood silently behind him.

My B.S. antenna cranked up a notch at the lengthy explanation. Was the young man dodging the real reason they were up here? Might it have anything to do with the dead man on his way to the morgue? I needed to interview them, but I also wanted to examine the site of the man's fall before dark set in.

Signaling for them to wait a moment, I pulled out my phone and called my grandfather's house. He wasn't there, but his housekeeper Isabel confirmed the truck loan. That settled it. I'd go up to the campsite first and question these two later. Mingus was a small town. I knew where to find them.

I waved a hand in the boy's direction, cutting his explanation short. "I need to get to the top of the cliff that overlooks the old copper mine."

"You'll want to head this way." Armor pointed to the left fork in the road ahead.

"But it looks like the fire truck went there." I extended my hand to the right where tire tracks were clearly visible.

Armor shook his head, challenging my statement. "Landslide up there. This way peters out a quarter mile in. Go left."

I took their phone numbers and addresses and said I'd be in contact. Then I walked back to the squad car. Shifting into low gear, I turned left. The old chassis groaned as I crept down the rutted lane and across several washouts. The car tilted one direction and then the other, almost high centering. The Crown Vic hadn't been made for this type of terrain, even in its good years. The oil pan grated across one sharp rock and the brush closed in on either side of the car, as the road narrowed. Rough chaparral brush scraped desert pin striping on the side panels of the cruiser.

Finally, the path vanished in front of an old cypress tree. To the right, the view opened up across the Verde Valley. I stopped the car and yanked on the emergency brake for good measure. Then I switched off the ignition and rolled down the window. The odor of burn and char filled my nostrils. The campfire site had to be close. I got out of the car and walked over to the cliff for a look. The town spread below me, the old mine forming a rough open patch at the far end. I triangulated on it to locate the edge of the cliff where the burnout should be located.

It looked to be about five hundred feet ahead of me. Gingerly dodging prickly pear and yucca, I walked to the top of a large knoll. I once again peered over the edge of the cliff. I was close. Far below me, the police barrier tape stretched out in a yellow square and the last of the sun glinted off the tailings pond.

Up ahead, smoke marks on still-standing tree trunks increased. It looked as though the fire had spread outward from the campsite, igniting the lower manzanita brush and then leaping upward to char the shaggy-bark junipers.

The crew had countered by drawing backfire lines in the dirt and clearing the underlying duff. They had managed to hold the fire to the size of a large vacant lot. I broke into an open area and in front of me lay the makeshift campsite. No fire or smoke remained, but the ground was trampled and sooty. The bare outline of a tent flapped in the breeze, mostly destroyed by the fire. No sign of a vehicle. Had the man hiked to this location?

A few feet beyond the tent, the cliff dove straight down several hundred feet to the gravel pit below. The soil was crumbly and disturbed near the edge of the cliff, but that could be from the men fighting the blaze. I peered over the edge, holding onto a juniper branch. The earth sank beneath my feet and I jumped back. A long way to fall. I picked up a handful of dirt and rubbed it between my fingers to cut the stickiness of juniper pitch.

It wasn't an official crime scene yet and might never be if the commissioners' budget had anything to do with it. Indeed, the fire crew had trampled much of the crime scene, if it were such. Still, I was curious. My life goal in joining the sheriff's department was not pounding the street writing tickets. I was destined for bigger things, like homicide detective.

What better way to prepare for that future than gain a little surreptitious practice, out of the watchful eye of my superiors? The good angel urged caution, but the dark angel was performing a victory dance. Here, in the solitude of this late afternoon forest, I could practice my ultimate goal of becoming a CSI expert with nobody looking over my shoulder.

I performed a visual grid search of the area near the ruined tent. Nothing obvious. Then, using the tent as a pivot point, I walked a spiral search pattern out from the center. It was a dusty business. My boots crushed the black ash sending up clouds of flume, and I coughed as the particles entered my throat.

Some of the prickly pear and bear grass, missed by the fire, created a patchwork of green in the midst of the black scar. But other than a few scraps of clothing, almost everything of human origin appeared destroyed in the blaze. I returned to my car and retrieved the evidence kit I'd bought myself as a present when I graduated from the Police Academy and gathered what fragments of cloth I could.

Then I spotted a single, pointed-toe boot print hidden in the shadows beside a large rock. Cowboy boots weren't regulation footwear for a hotshot crew. There was ample evidence of their hobnailed wear throughout the burn site. I traced my memory: the dead man had been wearing loafers. And the print seemed fresh, made within the last day or so, which would mean it could have been set down just prior to the fire.

Had there been two people at the campsite? Perhaps someone meeting the dead man had left this footprint. The earth had been sheltered from the rains by the overhanging boulder, but shifting storm winds could destroy potential evidence.

I hadn't taken an impression in the field before, but the steps of evidence collection came back to me from the Academy lectures. First, I used my camera to take pictures of the general location of the print relative to the tent fragments. Then I placed a scale next to the print and photographed it at both a low oblique angle and then from directly overhead. The tedious work that underlay creating an evidence framework quieted my mind.

Thunder growled in the distance and I picked up the pace. I'd only seen how to make an impression of a footprint in a demonstration, but it didn't look hard. Just mix up some dental stone to the consistency of pancake batter, they said, and pour it into the depression. Simple easy.

I returned to the trunk and dug out the jug of emergency water I carried there. Tipping some of the water into the bag of powder, I squished it a few times to moisten. A tongue depressor deflected the stream of liquid to prevent distortion as I poured the mixture into the print. How long did it take to harden? I checked the bag. No directions on that critical element. I'd have to wing it.

I squatted on my haunches to wait and tried to recreate the scene in my mind. Had the dead man been drinking alcohol? No evidence of more empty bottles or cans up here, but he could have visited a bar and then come up here to sleep it off. If he had walked all this way, wouldn't that sober him up? Would me, I know.

Still, a misstep in the dark was a definite possibility. Perhaps the dead man had been making a campfire to spend the night when a thief showed up. Why a thief? I played the scenario out in my head. What would this man have that would be valuable enough to kill for? No personal possessions remained intact after the fire. If the man had backed away from an attacker, the result would be the same, death at the bottom of the fall. The pine trees surrounding me were silent, offering no answers.

I touched the dental stone mixture with my finger. Oops! Too soon. My fingertip left an ugly mark on the warm surface. I smoothed the indentation, hoping the lab wouldn't notice my beginner's mistake. A few minutes later it was ready. By the time I had enclosed the now-hardened impression in bubble wrap and stowed it in the squad car with the rest of my gear, the threat of storm had passed, but the sun was going down.

The burn site turned ominous and dark in the gathering dusk. The adrenaline rush I'd felt at the murder scene earlier receded as well, leaving me cold and empty. Time to head for Mingus.

The tree shadows receded from the headlights as I reached the spot I'd met the two men. My grandfather's pickup had disappeared and they were gone, too. I continued along the dirt road to the paved highway. When I got there, an old Jeep Wagoneer blocked access to the main road.

My irritation rose. Any idiot could see this side road had been traveled recently. Why park in front of it? Sighing, I unclicked the seat belt and got out.

CHAPTER TWO

I SHINED MY FLASH at the Jeep's window and then tapped on the glass. A large man popped into view. I jumped back and reached for my gun.

Holding a hand in front of his eyes, the man lowered the window. "What the hell! Shine that light away."

I shifted the beam. "No camping here, sir. License and registration, please."

He shook his head and reached in his wallet for his license. Dug around in the glove box for the registration.

"Wait here." I walked to the Crown Vic to call Melda, our dispatcher. She relayed that the man was one Flint Tanner from Oklahoma City. No wants, no warrants. I walked back to the Jeep to return the documents.

"Officer, I wasn't camping, just sleeping a little."

"Sorry, Mr. Tanner, we're having problems with fires in this area. You'll have to leave."

"I've been driving for fifteen hours," he protested, scrubbing the bristles on his chin. "Just let me sleep a little and then I'll go."

Maybe I could have let him stay, but given the events of the day, I wasn't up for negotiating a settlement. "Sorry, time to leave."

He made one more attempt. "I have a job here—with the mining company. I'm a geologist."

The hair on the back of my neck rose in an irritated prickle. This yay-hoo was a giant fallen log blocking my way home. "I don't care if you're King Tut. You have to move."

He raised both hands in submission and shifted the Wagoneer into gear. I followed him into town at his law-abiding two miles under the speed limit. Weariness settled on my shoulders as Tanner's Jeep went one direction and I headed the other at the outskirts of Mingus. Would he circle back to the mountain to finish his beauty sleep? I would have. But I was too tired to stick around and see. Tonight the hills would have to take care of themselves.

I navigated the final steep curve into the old mining town perched so steeply on the side of Black Mountain. Houses on one level looked down at the roofs on the street below. The town had been nicknamed Ghost City after the mines closed and the miners left. In some ways, Mingus reminded me of the Tennessee foothills where I grew up, but I was learning this tough town had a character all its own.

I turned onto the side street where my grandfather lived and parked behind his pickup. The truck was twenty years past its prime, just like its stubborn owner. Spider-web cracks in the windshield glinted in the moonlight, and the truck hood felt cold to my touch. Armor had made it back to town some time ago.

I stood for a moment staring up at constellations, sharp-edged in the high desert air. What was I doing here in Mingus? I had lived in a blue funk for months after I'd committed my mother to the sheltered care facility. Then one day HT called and invited me to Arizona. He'd made a deal with the sheriff to get this temporary assignment for me. HT said I needed a break after settling my mother's affairs.

Maybe he was right. My mother wasn't dead, but might as well be with the dementia. And moving to Mingus had seemed a way out of the depression that clung to me like Tennessee morning fog. But now I was having second thoughts. I'd been estranged from this branch of the family for years. Getting to know HT again would be a difficult venture at best.

I strode into the kitchen and filled a glass at the old sink, washing the dust and grit from my throat.

"HT, you still up?" I spoke the words into the silent house.

"Out here, Ellie, on the front porch. Come and sit a spell."

I frowned. Was his calling me that an intentional slight or just the beginning of memory loss? Ellie was my grandmother's name. I'd been christened Eleanor Pegasus Quincy. Eleanor for the estranged grandmother, before she was, and Pegasus as a sop to my Greek-reading father, long absent from my life.

HT's persistence in calling me by my grandmother's name irritated like a cocklebur in a too-thin sock. She had disowned my mother and me when my father left because she blamed us for her beloved son's disappearance. After that, I refused to answer to the name Eleanor, and chose to go by Peg, shortened for obvious reasons.

I walked out onto the porch and perched on the front step. The porch swing tilted back and forth behind me as HT shifted his weight on the landing above. Close to seventy-five now, my grandfather had gray, unkempt hair and a drooping cowboy mustache that didn't disguise the deep lines in his face. The overalls he favored hung too loose on his frame—maybe he missed my mother, too.

"My name's Peg, not Ellie," I countered.

"Could've fooled me. You've got that stubborn look and red hair just like your grandmother."

"I'm not her."

"Yeah, I know. I may be old, but I'm not senile yet." Then he dropped the topic before it turned into full conflict. "I heard about the trouble up at the mining pit."

I nodded. "I didn't expect to deal with death right off."

Needing to release the tension of nerves strung tight as wire on a new fence, I told him about the dead body and my reaction to it. Then I confessed the awkwardness of the conversation with the sheriff and how the lawman kept stressing I was a fill-in until they found someone more qualified, implying that I didn't know what I was doing.

"We all get nervous, girl. Happened to me when I was out on a job." HT chuckled.

I bit my lip. The job you were on was cracking a safe, not catching criminals. My grandfather's checkered past and his time in prison blocked any true communication. The gap between us seemed immense, and I withdrew into myself again. "I'm going to bed. You need to come inside, too. It's getting cold out here."

I climbed the stairs to the loft where I was bunking. The lyrics of an old song echoed in my mind, something about the game of life being hard to play, being up to the individual to accept the challenges dealt. I sighed. This time around, I intended to take the hand dealt, to prove myself in this small town of Mingus, no matter how difficult that might be. Bunking with my grandfather was only temporary. Soon I would leave this house and find my way in the world.

* * * * * *

THE NEXT MORNING, I awoke to a scrabbling noise on the roof and banged my head on the low-angled ceiling of the loft. Damn! I could feel a knot rising. I pushed down the claustrophobia that tight spaces always gave me and stretched leg muscles cramped and stiff from the tension of the day before.

A new town, a new life. For me, anyway. That dead guy had lost his chance. I jerked a comb through hair stiff with sweat and twisted it back into one thick braid. Then I pulled on my last clean uniform. I closed the door behind me and pounded down the outside stairs to the kitchen.

HT lived in one of the original boarding houses built for the miners. A full balcony surrounded each of the upper two floors, with an outside set of stairs leading to the ground level. There used to be an outside privy for the miners, too. Thank goodness, HT had since installed inside facilities for guests.

HT's housekeeper was fixing breakfast as I entered the kitchen. Isabel was a middle-aged, Hispanic woman, solid both in stature and belief. She rented the second floor of HT's house, or maybe she just took advantage of his generosity, but they seemed satisfied with the arrangement. I knew she worked for other families in Mingus as well, house sitting, doing some light cleaning.

She and I hadn't gotten to know each other much yet, and I made an effort to be cordial this morning. “Something smells good.”

“These eggs are for HT,” Isabel announced. “Fix your own.”

No breakfast service for me, it appeared. I poured myself a cup of coffee and walked over to the kitchen table.

HT looked up at my approach. “Good morning, Ellie. I could use a spot of jam for my toast since you're up.”

That name again! I pressed my lips together at the sound of it. Between HT’s mistake and Isabel’s abrupt greeting, I found my good mood evaporating. “HT, we need to talk.”

He followed the direction of my glance. He finished a bite of toast and took a sip of his coffee. Then he spoke. "*Pegasus—*" He emphasized the name. "Isabel's family has been in Arizona for hundreds of years. She is more a native than I am."

"No, that's not what I meant. I want to…"

Isabel abruptly jerked off her apron and left the room.

I pushed to my feet. "I'll get breakfast downtown."

With a childhood like mine, I hadn't gotten many how-to-make-friends lessons. But somebody like Isabel didn't make me feel welcome, either. I walked out to the squad car and slammed it into gear.

* * * * * *

THE WEATHER CALMED me on the short drive to the office. After the rain the day before, the clouds clung to the foothills across the valley like strands of coarse wool. This being mid-July, likely we'd have more rain this afternoon. Monsoon season in Arizona began about the Fourth of July and for the rest of the summer you could set your watch by the late-morning thunderheads building to gully-washers in the afternoon.

An acrid tinge filled the air. Another forest fire? Fires had leveled Main Street three times during the mining heydays. Even now a century later, empty lots contained only grass and groves of the invasive Ailanthus trees. During the pollution days of the mining smelters, the Chinese "tree of heaven" was the only tree that would survive in Mingus. Now, with the smelters closed, it formed groves in every open space.

The town was built on a steep series of zig-zag roads clinging to the side of the copper-ore bearing mountain. The lots were small to start with, and this configuration meant you would holler at one end of the town and be heard at the other.

I parked the cruiser and walked to the front entrance of the sheriff's annex station on a sidewalk cracked and tilted from abandoned mining tunnels beneath it. The oak door creaked as I opened it, and I glanced at the gold lettering on its window that read "Cyrus Marsh, Deputy Sheriff." Cyrus had died and I was his replacement.

It gave me an eerie feeling to walk past that sign every morning, and I made a mental note to change it. I felt awkward being the lone law enforcement officer in this small town and reminded myself that it was only a summer assignment. I'd be gone soon enough.

The station contained four rooms arranged in a square: a small foyer, an equally small kitchen area to the right, and then off a small hall to the left, my office and the holding cell. Any long-term prisoners were transported to the jail facilities in Camp Verde, about a half hour's drive across the valley. Formal arraignment used to be in Prescott, over the mountain, but with the new county jail near I-17, most prisoners found their way there.

The aroma of freshly brewed coffee welcomed me as I entered. Maybe my missing clerk had returned. I'd inherited him from Cyrus Marsh's tenure, but when I first arrived in town a week ago he wasn't in the office. There had just been a note saying he was down in Phoenix for training.

Instead of my clerk, the Native American kid from the mountain yesterday played video games on the computer in the reception area.

"What are you doing here?" I barked.

He jumped at my entrance and swiped the game away, replacing it with a screensaver of Utah arches. "I have a key," he said. "I'm Ben Yazzie, your clerk."

This kid? He looked barely out of grade school, and anyway I didn't trust him after the episode on the mountain yesterday. I opened my mouth to voice that thought.

Ben Yazzie stood, shoved glasses back on his nose and pushed a hank of black hair out of his eyes. "I got a perfect score on the SAT test. I finished college at seventeen. I'm studying to be a Navajo Hot Shot. You know, a firefighter?" He paused to check my comprehension. "I have a photographic memory and I know everybody here in town. Anyhow, I need the job and I make good coffee."

I bristled, ready to engage in argument about how he was wrong. He didn't belong here; I sensed that in my gut. On the other hand, being so new, I had a lot to learn. Having somebody acquainted with the town might be useful.

Best let him stay for a few days until I saw how it would work out. "Coffee?" I asked, to save face.

Entering my office, I sifted through a stack of pink telephone messages on my desk, written in a black angular script. It appeared that the small town had noticed my arrival. The first message was from a Johnny Evans, identified as the manager at the Community National Bank. What did he want? If there'd been a bank robbery, I'd have heard from our dispatcher.

That left something personal, perhaps. I didn't even have a bank account yet, so it couldn't be my perennial problem with overdrafts. I'd given up using checks and usually relied on cash, when I had it. My statements accumulated and I opened them all at the end of the year. The system worked well, usually.

I tried the bank number but just got a busy signal. I'd try later.

On the next slip, Ben had scribbled "Tal Garrett" and a phone number but no message. Garrett was the mayor of this small town—was there trouble?

"What does Garrett want?" I hollered.

Ben opened the door and set a steaming mug of coffee on my desk. Cream, no sugar. How'd he know I liked it that way? My first impression went up a notch.

The kid shrugged. "Don't know."

"What's Garrett's reputation here in town?"

Ben frowned. "That Garrett started buying up land when the mines closed. He'd spot a piece of property and dive down like an old turkey buzzard." His hand made a swooping movement. "He thinks he owns us."

"Does he?"

Ben shrugged. "He had something going with Cyrus Marsh. Maybe he wants to reestablish connections with the new law in town."

Cyrus Marsh. I'd read through some of his old reports and wasn't too impressed. He filled the forms with "parties of the first part" and "notwithstanding, the alleged perpetrators..." The town had been shocked when he dropped dead from a heart attack, providing the job opening I now filled. Still, Marsh had been here for twenty years, and the town had grown used to him. I'd best move slow to change his way of doing things.

Before I could call Garrett, the door jangled. My grandfather entered, and behind him, Armor Brancussi, the man from the mountain. I greeted them in the foyer by Ben's desk.

"This here's my buddy, Armor," HT said. "You met him last night. What he don't know about this town ain't worth knowing." He waved a vague hand in my direction. "Armor, meet my granddaughter."

Done with formalities, he gave my clerk a piercing look. "Ben, where's the coffee?"

The boy scrambled to find more cups.

HT seemed brighter and more alert in Armor's presence, as though he absorbed energy from his friend.

Armor reached around his crutch and his big hand engulfed mine. "Glad to meet you properly. Your granddad has been talking about you."

I looked at the Harley insignia on the pocket of his leather vest. "You a biker?"

"Used to be. Will be again when I get this hip fixed." His expression darkened. "I hit a slick spot and took a little tumble off my bike."

"Don't be so modest." HT took up the tale. "He ramped up to eighty, hit an oil slick, bounced off the guard rail, and skidded across the highway, right under that semi coming the other direction..."

He paused for breath and punched his buddy in the shoulder. They both grinned at the war story.

Leaving HT and Armor to finish their coffee by Ben's desk, I went back to my office and closed the door. The old chair creaked in protest as I sat, and the piece of duct tape patching the leather seat bit into my rear. Trying to ignore it, I reviewed the events from yesterday. I could declare this case an accident and move on, but first I wanted to know who the dead man was. I dialed the medical examiner's office to see if they had anything yet.

"Look, you got lucky," the doc said. "I had a new intern start this morning, and we moved your dead body up in the queue."

"And?"

"Well, I can't tell you his identity. We passed the fingerprints along to the crime lab. Wait a minute, though, and I can give you a quick report on what we did find."

Papers rattled in the background. "Cause of death, massive trauma. Multiple lacerations to the face and body, consistent with a fall. Multiple broken bones, ditto. Ate a meal of beans and corn chips with salsa during the last couple of hours before death."

"Drugs?"

"I was getting to that. The tox screen came back positive for cocaine. And the man had an alcohol reading of 2.0. Easily enough to cause balance issues."

Where did a guy in his disheveled state get drugs? A dealer? My mind filed it away for further investigation. "So was the fall accidental?"

"I don't see any evidence that it wasn't. But it's your call."

Great! I'd need more information to do that. I hung up and dialed the crime lab. I'd been cultivating a relationship with a guy there who was still new enough at his job to be enthusiastic about dead bodies.

"No word on the fingerprints, yet," he said. "Soon."

"What about that scrap of green cloth?"

"An old silk. I'm doing more research on that. But no usable fingerprints on it. Sorry."

I was down to my last option. "What about the boot impression?"

"Ah, you've got something unusual there. Our database identified it as a Lucchese Classic. Custom-made boot, right down to the lemonwood pegs. Not too many of those boots around in a size 12. I'll fax you the report."

I sighed. We didn't have a working fax machine. Ben told me he'd put in a requisition several months ago to replace our busted one, but hadn't gotten a response. I guess I shouldn't have been surprised, given the size of our office. But at every step, I was reminded of the remoteness of this small mountain town. Its dearth of resources mirrored my own lack of experience. "Just send it snail mail." I gave him the address and hung up.

The information on the boot print was good news, maybe the break I needed to advance the case. I dialed Patrick Shaw, the fire chief, to double check that nobody on the fire-fighting team had worn cowboy boots.

There was a pause while he thought. "Nope. I insist on those steel-toed lace-ups. All I need is for one of those guys to drop a chainsaw on his foot and sue us."

"Did one of them bring something back from the fire? A souvenir, like?" Maybe they'd found something that I'd missed.

"Nah, the fire was pretty involved when we got there. Not much left except the remains of the tent. You saw that."

Another dead end. "If you think of anything else, call me."

My phone rang again. "Didn't you get my message?" A loud voice exploded in my ear. "I need you over here, right now. My property's been vandalized." He hung up before I could answer, but the caller ID matched the one on the pink slip there on my desk: Tal Garrett.

My jaw set, irritated at the man's tone. Problems with authority my mother always used to say. It wasn't that, exactly. I just liked to be on the giving end of orders.

Reluctantly I headed for the door. Whether I liked it or not, Garrett was a consumer of our services, just like everyone else in this town. I needed to respond to his request.

Out on the street, a fire engine rushed past in a gust of dusty air. Ben dashed out the door ahead of me, slamming a hard hat labeled "Volunteer" on his head.

"Fire! Back later." He hopped a fence and raced down an alley to catch the truck on the next zigzag down the hill.

I still doubted this kid was suited to a desk job. But then, neither was I.

Straightening my shoulders for the interview ahead, I walked down the street to confront Tal Garrett's ill temper. His office was on the next block, within easy walking distance, but nobody could tell me how fast to walk. My pace slowed to a rebellious saunter.

CHAPTER THREE

BEING THE MAYOR of a small town like Mingus was only a part-time job. Tal Garrett's regular office occupied the second floor of the old Adams Hotel. But boarded-up windows on the two stories above the office gave mute testimony to rough economic times.

Like other mining towns in Arizona, when the mines closed, the town had almost died. Then, over the years hippies moved into the ruined buildings, looking for a sanctuary. After them, the rich folks from Phoenix arrived to renovate the old Victorian mansions for summer homes. Artists followed, with their plein air festivals and street fairs. They all stayed. Mingus was still small as towns go, and yet divided at its core.

The front door to Garrett's office was sandwiched between a Western art gallery and a biker bar. I opened the door and climbed an interior stairway, the steep wooden steps echoing beneath my heels. A rich maroon carpet softened my footsteps when I entered a mahogany-paneled reception area. A woman with black hair pulled into a severe bun looked up as I entered. Past middle age, she had the tightly wrinkled face of a chain smoker beneath heavy pancaked makeup.

"Have a seat. I'll see if Mr. Garrett is free."

The waiting room presented an image of prosperity and competence. On the coffee table were copies of Architectural Digest, Luxe, Civil Engineer's Quarterly. On the vanity wall behind the couch hung photographs of a portly man with a shock of pure white hair, usually posed with other smiling dignitaries.

In one photograph, Garrett wore a hard hat as he shoveled a ceremonial pitchful of earth, his face carefully turned for a good camera angle. I peered closer. The photo had no legend, but the San Francisco Peaks created a jagged silhouette on the horizon—the proposed development for Mingus?

Ben had filled me in on the ambitious plans, and the controversy they created within the town. One faction was all in favor, but another hated the idea of a California-style suburb that would clash with the historic brick buildings from the mining era.

"Deputy Quincy. So nice that you were able to drop everything and come over."

Tal Garrett had put on even more weight since the photos—too many power lunches. He was shorter than I was and wore an expensive gray sharkskin suit and black wingtips. An Annapolis class ring weighed down one pinky finger. I did my best to be impressed, but wasn't too successful. I never did get along well with politicians. On the other hand, maybe my kind wasn't too popular with him, either.

His grip tested mine, and then, courtesies satisfied, he walked back into his office, assuming I would follow. "We have some matters to discuss," he said.

Garrett's office took up the rest of the second floor of the building with windows that looked down on Main Street. A single sheet of paper rested on the glass-topped table. I flashed to a memory of my own World War II relic of a desk with its stacks of reports.

Must be nice to be that organized. Maybe the sheet of paper was his shopping list. That thought buoyed me.

"Sit, sit," he said impatiently, gesturing at the couch in front of the desk.

What was I—a cocker spaniel? If I sat on that couch, my eye level would be several inches below his. I'd have to look up at him as he spoke. It reminded me of getting in trouble when I was a kid in grade school. I always hated that tiny chair in front of the principal's big desk.

Not this time, short fellow. I looked down at Garrett. I did not sit on his couch.

After a moment of silence, he conceded the point. “Oh, all right. Here, have a chair.” He motioned for me to join him at a conference table next to the window.

He settled heavily in the chair beside me and looked out the window to the sidewalk below. There, HT and Armor perched on a bench, passing judgments on the people starting to fill the sidewalk below.

“See what I have to put up with?” Garrett gave me one of those perfunctory almost-smiles that aren't friendly. “Oh, I'm not talking about your grandfather, of course, or maybe I am. Those two give the wrong impression to the folks visiting Mingus.” He leaned closer to me, intimating we were both people of the world who knew how things should run.

I edged my chair back a bit, rejecting the offer of mutual understanding. I was positive that my idea of a good world order didn’t jibe with his. “You wanted to see me?”

“Yes, I did. Your grandfather and his friend there pulled out my survey stakes and moved them five feet east. Go look! You can still see the holes. I paid good money for that survey.” Garrett's face reddened as he remembered the slight.

“This would be for that new development east of town?”

Garrett gestured proudly to an elaborate model on a table in the corner. “Franklin Belleview Acres.”

“What’s the Franklin stand for?”

“My older brother. Killed in the service of his country. This is his ring.” His voice softened. “I told him I’d make him proud someday, and by God, that’s exactly what I intend to do.”

For a moment, I could almost relate to this man, still wanting the approval of his older brother.

Then his platitudes resurfaced. “The town will prosper when that development goes in. Those two say they want to leave things as they are. Well, I can tell you without tourist money and proper development, this town will die.”

“Your intent is to tear down the historic district?”

He stiffened. “Of course not. Most of it would remain. A good coat of paint and it’ll be fine. But we need to level the roads, add some good shopping…”

Which he would undoubtedly own. I'd heard this rationalizing of self-interest before.

"What about the lower-income people who live here?"

He bristled. "It's time for some of them to move on. We need to clean up the image of the town."

I shrugged. Not up to me to pass judgment one way or the other. I kept my expression neutral and returned to the topic that brought me here. "You said some survey stakes were moved. Got a proof?"

Garrett hedged. "Not exactly, but it's obvious they were. " He rose abruptly and bellowed to his receptionist. "Nina, bring me that ground-breaking photo."

He snatched it from her and jabbed at a corner of the print. "See, right here. *That's* where the stake should be."

I looked closely at where his well-manicured fingernail was pointing, but I didn't see anything. "Have you tried talking to Armor and HT?" Always a good idea if folks handled things like this directly, face-to-face.

Garrett's face turned red. "It's not your place to tell me how to do my job. I'm the mayor of this town, and as such, I'm responsible for the citizenry."

The obvious insinuation was I needed to butt out and let him do his job his way. But in this case, I couldn't. I was the law in this small town, and now I was involved. "I'd need more proof than this. Got any witnesses?" I asked again.

"You're a temporary employee," he blustered. "You don't understand how things are done here."

Ah, that meant nobody had seen the deed being done.

Now Garrett attacked me directly. "There's something fishy about your hire. A young girl with no experience. I agreed to your hire against my better judgment, and you can be replaced if you don't work out here," he warned. "*Easily* replaced."

Anger flushed my temples. Time to leave before I told Garrett exactly where he could put his threats. I stood. "If you can bring me something more specific, I'd be happy to talk to HT and Armor for you." Since you can't do it yourself, asshole.

I nodded to the secretary on my way out and walked down the stairs to the street. I rotated my shoulders, trying to shed the unpleasant experience. Because, much as I disliked Garrett, I needed to find a way to work with him, or my job in this town would be that much tougher. I added stake pulling to the growing list of issues I needed to discuss with my grandfather.

Not for the first time I wondered why conflict seemed to flare like a campfire full of pitch logs whenever I was in the neighborhood. Better start getting used to it, an inner voice warned me. If the trouble ever stops occurring around here, you'll be out of a job.

Ben was holding the phone receiver when I opened the front door. He transferred the call to my line. I went into my office and closed the door.

It was my *real* boss, Sheriff Abner Jones. "Quincy, I just got a call from Tal Garrett. First, it was that man's fall, and now you're being uncooperative with City Hall." He seemed to relish recounting my flaws.

It was "Peg" when I was hired, and now it was "Quincy." Not a good sign. I wondered what influence Garrett had on the sheriff and then I remembered it was an election year. Garrett was the type who'd be a big contributor. Money talks.

"Garrett's right," the sheriff said. "We have those homeless nuts coming through the woods all the time. Close the case. Move on."

No, these are *people,* sheriff, as much a part of your constituency as Garrett and his crew.

"I'm still not sure it was an accident," I said. "The call from the medical examiner's office ruled the manner of death inconclusive. I'm waiting for a possible hit on the fingerprints, and then I want to do a little more investigating before I close the case."

"If it turns out to be something more than a slip-and-fall, I'll send Sanchez up there to handle it. Don't try to play out of your league."

"I'll get right on it," I said. He hung up and I heard a snicker from the other room.

"That guy, he's got a loud voice," Ben said. "You really want to work for him? Maybe you want to leave this little town. We got nothing to offer you here."

He might be right. Why beat myself up over this? Like the man said, just call it an accident and move on. I wasn't being paid to think, it appeared. Better use of my time would be to write a few traffic tickets to mollify the Commissioner Gods and pay my salary, since that was what was expected of me. I paused. On the other hand, it was getting toward lunchtime.

Ben was way ahead of me. As I walked toward the door, he handed me a head shot of the dead man he'd Photoshopped into the facsimile of a recognizable person. My clerk said Mingus didn't have a Mexican food place, but recommended three in Clarkdale, just down the hill.

"I'd start with Taco-King, and then try Mi Casa or El Cajon," he said.

I must admit I felt a sudden hankering for a good burrito.

* * * * * *

THE ROAD CURVED in great arcs through century plants and prickly pear, descending rapidly from mile-high Mingus to Clarkdale on the valley floor. In the mining days of the early 1900s, Mingus provided the ore from deep underground mines and shipped it down to the smelter in Clarkdale via a narrow gauge railway. The mining corporation had torn down the huge smelter chimney fifty years ago, but the small town, built by magnate William Clark for the mining families, remained.

Unlike the executives' Queen Anne mansions high on the hills, the miners' houses of the lower town were small and squat. Like Lego houses in a row, each brick structure had one door, a window on each side of that, and a tiny porch in front.

I arrived at the town square with its neatly clipped grass and turned into the parking lot at Taco-King. I turned off the engine, unfastened my seatbelt, and walked in.

The fast food place was jammed. My uniform took me to the front of the line, past the giggling teenagers and little kids doing loop-de-loops on the customer line barrier bars. The pimply-faced manager who didn't look much older than his customers glanced at the victim's photograph without expression. He shook his head. "Man, this is half our clientele."

One Mexican food restaurant down, two to go.

El Cajon was just down the street. No cars in this parking lot and no customers in the restaurant. New cook or bad food? Still, it was on my list. The restaurant door stuck as I tried it. No maintenance, either.

But maybe the dead man hadn't been so picky. The hostess gave me a pretty smile as I showed her the photo, but said she hadn't seen him. The headwaiter just grunted. No tips for him. I left cards with both of them and tried the third restaurant, Mi Casa.

This restaurant occupied an adobe building painted burnt orange and draped with strings of colored pennants. In the dark cavernous serving room, serape table runners decorated the tables of rough-hewn wood and Mariachi music blared from ceiling speakers.

This restaurant looked the most promising of the three Ben had provided me, and I was hungry. A gum-chewing server with blond, straggly hair led me to a table, dropped a menu in front of me, and took my order for iced tea. A few minutes later, she placed the pebbled plastic glass on my table and stood pencil and pad in hand. I ignored the menu and ordered the combination plate. Safe bet in a strange Mexican restaurant—always order the combination plate. She scribbled down my request and strolled to the back window to clip it to the circular rack. Said she'd send the manager over.

While I waited, I sipped the tea and watched the patrons. A solitary woman in the corner read a book and picked at a green salad. One multi-generational family filled the banquet table—kids in strollers, young parents, and one old gentleman who arrived with a retinue of attentive relatives. A birthday celebration?

I hated to pull out a photo of a dead guy at a birthday party, but a couple of construction workers lingering over a lunch of Dos Equis beer and nachos looked more promising. I half rose to visit them, when a woman stopped by my table.

"Hello, I'm Mrs. Wilson, the manager." She was a person of generous proportions. Her uniform pulled a little at the buttons and black-rimmed glasses crowned her mop of hennaed hair.

She sat in the chair next to me. I showed her the picture and explained my mission. She shook her head. "I heard about this tragedy. No one deserves to die like that. But sorry, I don't know him." She turned the picture face down on the table and tapped it with her finger, thinking. Then she gestured with her hand to the woman in the corner. "Talk to Nancy. She's one of our regulars."

The construction guys had vanished. Nothing like a cop close by to send folks back to work on time. The salad lady had sensed my presence, too. With a startled look my direction, she closed her book and scurried out of the restaurant. I threw some money on the table and followed her.

CHAPTER FOUR

I CAUGHT UP WITH THE WOMAN in the parking lot. "Please, may I talk to you?"

She threw me a hassled look. "I'm late for yoga."

"This will just take a moment." A huge spreading cottonwood tree provided shelter for a picnic table, and I suggested we sit there.

When I introduced myself, she shook my hand in a no-nonsense manner. "Nancy Brun." Hard lines drew parentheses between nose and jaw. She might be late forties, with short brown hair tending to gray. She wore a blue cotton blouse, rough-spun gray trousers, and Birkenstocks. When she spoke, it was with a precise Germanic accent. "The manager is wrong."

"What do you mean?"

"That man *was* here." She shifted on the wooden bench and brushed an ant off her arm. "Here in the parking lot several nights ago when I was coming in. May I see the picture?"

I handed it to her. She studied the photo carefully and then returned it to me. "Yes, that is one of the men. I am sure of it."

"What were they doing?"

"Arguing. Shouting at each other. I come to this restaurant to enjoy my food and to eat in peace." She frowned. "We don't need arguing here. Fighting."

"What did they say?"

"Cursing. One man saying how the other didn't understand. That he was a…"

She hesitated, and I got the sense she was trying to translate some unusual anatomical expletive into English.

"That's okay," I said. "I've heard them all before anyway. Can you describe the two men?"

"One was tall, dark hair. The other, shorter, more slender, like that one." She gestured at the picture. "The parking lot was dark, and I saw them just for a minute. They pushed and shoved and then something heavy dropped to the ground. With a clunk. Then one man picked it up and they ran off. I didn't want to get involved, you understand."

"Remember anything else?"

"No, I was glad they left. It was eight o'clock and I was hungry. I went inside and that was the end of it."

I gave her a card. Nancy Brun walked away with a determined step and pulled out of the lot in a sensible Buick. This woman's statement echoed what I'd heard before—folks just didn't want to get involved. I wondered if the dead man would still be alive if someone had given a damn.

I sat at the table to record notes in my notebook, adding the information on the fight to the crime lab's news on the unidentified boot print. A case is built on details, and I was gathering a few. The boot print indicated a second person at the campsite and this reported argument meant conflict. If the dead man was involved, his fall might relate to this fight. This case was looking less and less like an accident.

Dark anvil clouds defined the horizon. Rain, this afternoon, for sure. My stomach growled, but it was time to head back up the mountain to Mingus. I stopped at the hostess stand and canceled my order. Maybe I could make do, like I usually did, with food on the run. I returned to the drive-through at Taco-King and ordered a burrito.

I tucked napkins in all the usual places to stave off drips and drops of hot sauce. When I reached the switchbacks, I poked the remains of the burrito back in the takeout sack. The aroma tantalized me, but I didn't want red smears on the uniform. Hard to explain in a town where a man had recently died.

* * * * * *

VOLUNTEERS REFOLDED THE HOSES on the pumper truck as I neared the fire station. Ben must have returned to our office because I didn't see him among the crew. I pulled in to talk to the fire chief. Patrick Shaw was a little older than I was, slender-built and tall. He wore baggy firefighter's pants supported with red suspenders.

"I'm Peg Quincy. We talked on the phone."

Patrick flashed a big grin, still adrenalin-charged from the fire. Then his face sobered. "Again, I'm sorry about messing up that campsite. If I'd known what was going on..."

My chin tilted up just a bit so that I could meet his hazel eyes. Taller than me. One point in his favor.

He ushered me into his office and shoved magazines off a chair for me. I sat down, pleased to see his desk was as old and battered as my own.

"Is everybody in town a volunteer fireman?" I asked.

"Just about. I get a small salary, but not enough to quit my day job. I own Jimmy Bob's Donuts down the street. Nothing better after a good fire than donuts and coffee."

"You call a fire *good*?"

He raised his arms defensively. "You gotta understand this about firemen. We respect and even admire the creative power of fire.

"I hate the destruction, sure," he said, "but I've been fascinated by fire since I was a little kid. Some firefighters are even reformed youth fire-starters. Not me, of course." There was a twinkle in his eye. "But fire is this living breathing dragon that you battle."

He jerked a bit in his seat, restless. "I'm still hyped from the fire. Mind if I work while we talk?"

He led me into the high-ceilinged barn, a space swept and clear, except for the truck they'd just brought in. "Need to clean the crud off before it sets," he explained.

He pulled big sponges out of a cabinet, filled a bucket with water, and set to work on the front fenders. "Thanks for letting Ben take some time off. There was a fire safety workshop I wanted him to attend."

"Isn't Ben small to be a firefighter?"

"Well, he's slight, but he's not done growing yet. Motivation counts for a lot. He really wants this." Patrick soaped one big fender and then hosed it off.

"Was this last fire a big one?"

"No, we snuffed it before it took off. Good thing the winds had died down a bit."

"Man caused?" I asked.

"Not sure. Maybe lightning. Dry strikes before the monsoon season begins frighten me. The pine duff is tinder before the humidity rises. Then dry lightning can start a nasty fire."

He polished the chrome around the headlights and started on the grill. "And worse yet are the Wildies."

"Wildies?"

He shrugged. "That's what I call them. Not homeless really, just drifters, like. They stand on the street corners in Phoenix during the winter with these hand-lettered cardboard signs: 'Will Work for Food.' Then they hitchhike up here to camp in the woods during the summer. Most are harmless, mind their own business, but some can get high on meth and that sometimes makes them careless with campfires."

"What's your biggest nightmare?" I asked, handing him a towel to catch the final water drops around one huge black tire.

"After a wildfire that kills folks? Probably a serial arsonist. We haven't had a fire starter around here for a while, but with all the small fires we've been putting out lately, we may have one in the neighborhood. An arsonist lights a fire just for the excitement of watching the yellow pines burn."

He dumped the sponge in the empty bucket and stood back to admire his handiwork. "Did you ever see anything prettier in your life?"

I agreed to be polite. My love life was so vacant that even a red fire truck was exciting. Or that might be just the tall fireman reflected in it.

Patrick held out a big hand. "Come back anytime. You're a good listener."

Officer Friendly, that's me. Yet the compliment was nice counterpoint to the darkness of investigating the death in the mining pit. I smiled as I headed back to the office. Damned if this town wasn't starting to grow on me.

* * * * * *

WHEN I WALKED BY the bank, a car occupied a place of honor in a manager's spot, "JVE" on the personalized plate: Johnny Evans. The pink message slip sitting on my desk nudged at me. I'd put off returning the bank manager's call, but I needed to deal with whatever he had in mind.

I entered the bank and stopped at the receptionist's desk. The nameplate read, "Vanessa Heaton." Perhaps Vice Mayor Roger Heaton's daughter? The young woman's turquoise sheath dress clung to a model-slim body and fluffed blond hair fell in perfect waves down her back. Three rings decorated the edge of one ear lobe, a stylish declaration of youth. She was about twenty, one of those women who was beautiful and knew it.

Vanessa looked up with a small frown as I neared her desk and stopped filing one perfect red nail. "Yes?"

"Johnny Evans?"

"You have an appointment?"

"No." I stood there, letting my uniform speak for itself.

She sighed. "You can wait in his office. Don't touch anything."

Right, like who appointed *her* hall monitor. I glanced back as I entered the manager's office. Vanessa had commenced typing, one finger at a time, on an old IBM Selectric typewriter. Perhaps the atavistic action entertained her on a dull afternoon when her thumbs were tired from texting a boyfriend.

The banker's office had taupe carpet and mushroom-colored drapes. An abstract watercolor in shades of umber and sienna hung on the wall. This guy was into brown. A bronze nameplate reading "Mr. Johnny V. Evans III" sat on top of a mahogany desk. Johnny, not John. On the other hand, the insistence of "Mr." as a title. Almost as though there were two sides to the man, one attempting to appear casual while the other demanded attention and respect.

The desk bore no family photos or knick-knacks, but a picture book of antique weapons rested on a side table. I reached for it and flipped through the pages. A great-uncle of mine collected old flintlocks, and I recognized several models.

"Hello, I'm Johnny Evans. Sorry to keep you waiting."

I rose to greet a thin man in his early forties. He had thinning sandy hair and pale brown eyes hidden behind thick horn-rimmed glasses. The too-long sleeves on his tan seersucker suit partially concealed slim, white hands.

I assumed he would offer to shake my hand, but instead he reached across his desk for an enormous bottle of hand sanitizer and pumped some into his palm. He rubbed his fingers together briskly. He gestured at the book in my lap. "I see you've found me out." His reedy voice enunciated each word.

"What?"

"Antique weapons. The passion that I share with Tal Garrett." His mouth twisted at the man's name. "Have you seen his collection?"

"Collection?" I felt like a parrot echoing his words.

"Yes, Garrett has a gun room. All of these antique rifles and breech-loaders. Row after row of them hung on the walls. Amazing, really."

He straightened his desk blotter a fraction of an inch. "Of course, at least three of the flintlocks on the south wall are reproductions. But he wouldn't know that."

How long was this going to continue before he got down to business? Social communication was an agony for me. I learned to read non-verbals during a childhood spent with a parent who drank too much. And I had an uneasy feeling that Johnny Evans did not want to see me on a law enforcement matter.

Finally, he assumed a serious expression, and I thought, here it comes.

"I wanted to talk to you about that house your grandfather lives in."

"What about it?"

Evans looked down at his desk. "Well, this is awkward, really, to talk about. Your grandfather is behind on his loan payments."

"How far behind?"

He gave me a polite smile, his eyes distant behind the thick lenses. "Almost six months now. I talked to him several times but got nowhere. If he doesn't start making payments soon, we'll have to foreclose. There are rules, you know." He shook a finger at me, half in jest, half not. "People can't break the rules. Then where would we all be?"

My jaw tightened. "I'll talk to him. Anything else?"

"No, that's it. Again, welcome to Mingus. We're thankful to have you here."

As I rose, my sleeve caught the lip of an antique urn on the bookshelf. Evans rushed to straighten it. "Careful. You are dealing with family there."

"What?" This tense, rigid man was getting on my nerves.

"That urn holds my mother's ashes. She died this past year."

What do you respond to a statement like that? I settled for, "I'm sorry," even though I'd never met the woman. I gave the urn a cautious pat and edged back in my seat.

Johnny Evans stood above me, staring at the stone jar. "A blessing, really," he mused. "She'd been blind, and then started losing her hearing that last year. Nothing left." He touched the urn gently with his white fingers. "At first I put her in the safe at home. But that didn't seem right, so I brought her in here to keep me company. I'm torn. If I put her in a church crypt, I am false to my atheist beliefs, and if I scatter her to the winds, she'll haunt me even more than she does now. So there she sits, *a memento mori*."

He touched the urn once more. Then he turned back to me, all business. "You talk to your grandfather, now."

I shivered in the bank's air conditioning as I walked back to the front foyer. Vanessa's desk was vacant. Maybe she had run out of interesting things to type with those lacquered nails. The plate glass window reflected Johnny Evan's office behind me. The man was sanitizing his hands again.

* * * * * *

BACK AT MY OWN OFFICE, I returned to a review of Marsh's files to familiarize myself with the happenings in the town. One folder had what looked like a mustard stain on one corner, and another had waffled edges as though rain-soaked. I wasn't a neat freak, but the unkempt files mirrored the office's ambiance, slapdash and haphazard. It was something, at least, that I *could* change while I was here.

I tugged a matchbook from under the desk leg only to have the table wobble. I wedged the matchbook back in. Cracks splintered down the plastered brick wall, and a draft blew through a gap at the bottom of a side window.

I gave up on the décor and addressed the problem that had been tickling the back of my mind since I left the bank office.

"Ben, come here for a minute." He walked into my office and slouched in a chair in front of my desk.

"What do you know about Johnny Evans?" I asked.

"His mother's dead. He likes to play video games."

"With you?"

Ben shrugged.

"Does he seem a little strange?"

"Don't know him that well," he stalled.

I guess video games don't count. Giving up on that topic for the present, I tried again to tap this fount of all town knowledge. "How long has Isabel, HT's housekeeper, lived in Mingus?"

"As long as I have."

Only half-jokingly, I asked, "Is she a witch?" She was certainly giving me the evil eye.

That opened the gates. "No, Isabel is a *yerbera*. Don't you know the difference?"

"Enlighten me."

"A witch is a bad person who can kill you with a glance, but a *yerbera* is kind of a *curandera* who knows plants and how they can help people. Isabel gathers herbs up on Black Mountain to make tinctures and salves. She is teaching me the ways of her people so that I can help mine."

"I'd like to go with you sometime."

"Whatever." Ben reverted to teen monosyllables and I gave up. Maybe another time.

My phone rang and Ben reached over to answer it. "Mingus Sheriff's Station." He listened a moment and then handed me the receiver. "It's Melda. There's big trouble at the Heaton place."

CHAPTER FIVE

"DOMESTIC DISPUTE," the dispatcher said. "Vanessa Heaton called it in. She said her folks were arguing over a gun."

"Are both parties still at the house?"

"I'm not sure. Vanessa was shouting and their dog was barking in the background and then the phone went dead. I tried to call back, but all I got was a busy signal."

"Any backup?" It was always better to go into one of those situations with a partner. I knew that from my Police Academy lectures.

"I'm sorry, Deputy Quincy, there's only you. Usually it's quiet up there in Mingus. We haven't had any complaints at all since poor Cyrus…" Her voice broke.

The recently departed Cyrus Marsh again. Marsh had known everybody by their first name, probably even the coyotes and lizards. Small towns like this could be trouble, especially for strangers like me. I transferred the call to my cell and walked back to the cruiser, listening as I went.

"Can you find the house?" Melda asked.

No GPS or computer in this squad car from the Dark Ages. I jerked a worn map from the glove compartment. Frustration added to my anxiety. No backup patrol in this little town's meager budget and a squad car with over 200,000 miles on the odometer. Even now, it sat there idling and grumbling while Melda recited directions.

"Turn right on Rose and then left on Elder?" I repeated the directions to remember them, losing the route in one torn fold and then finding it again on the other side.

"Yes, it's the only house on the left side of the street, about half-way up the block. A three-story brown Victorian with purple trim. You can't miss it."

Black Mountain's brooding presence loomed over me as I pushed the old cruiser through steep, shadowed streets. The shocks gone, the wreck of a cruiser lumbered like a camel on the mountain roads. Brisk crosswinds pushed it one way and then the other. Weather was coming.

When I reached Elder Street, I glided to a stop at the end of the block to assess the situation. The tick-tick-tick of my overheated motor echoed in the silence.

Roger Heaton seemed to be a man under pressure when I met him at the scene of the man's death. In addition to his part-time city role as vice mayor, he was part of Tal Garrett's development sales team. Working for that man would be like trying to breathe in a clamped-down pressure cooker.

It was possible that Heaton might take his stress out on his wife, or Vanessa might be the lightning rod for an angry family battle. I envied my predecessor's twenty years of experience in this town. He'd have known how to handle this family better than me.

I had no problem with conflict, but domestic disputes could be volatile, even dangerous. Cops would rather go mano-a-mano with some street thug than handle a situation like this one. Raging spouses sometimes killed cops who tried to intervene. I didn't want to be one of those unlucky fatalities.

I reviewed what I'd learned at the Police Academy: Maintain control. Separate the disputants. Never turn your back and stay out of rooms like kitchens that had sharp, pointy objects in them.

All seemed quiet at the house down the street. Whatever was happening, the combatants hadn't taken the dispute outside. The only way to find was to knock on the door and ask.

I drove the cruiser to the restored Victorian mansion and parked in the front drive. My shoes slid on the damp grass as I crossed the lawn. The stiffening breeze blew strands of hair into my eyes, and I brushed them away. I needed clear vision for this operation. There was a light in a ground floor window—the kitchen?

I breathed in and out once to steady myself and straightened my shoulders. Showtime. Before I could lose my nerve, I strode up on the porch and knocked. Then I moved to the side of the door out of the target range of possible weapons inside.

The front door jerked open. Mrs. Heaton was a short woman, in her late thirties. She might be attractive at other times, but today she had mussed platinum-dyed hair and disheveled clothing. She stood defensively in the open doorway. "Officer, I am so sorry. Everything is fine, really."

"Ma'am, we had notice of a domestic disturbance at this address. Is your husband here?"

"No, he's gone down to the store for some…" She hesitated. "…some ice."

I took a deep breath. With no angry spouse present, the odds suddenly improved. "May I come in for a moment?"

She sighed and stepped back for me to enter. A small dog crouched behind the woman's ankles, yapping excitedly. Mrs. Heaton turned to her daughter standing behind her. "Vanessa, take the dog into the back bedroom."

"And stay there a moment, please, Vanessa," I added. "I'd like to talk to each of you separately."

The girl shrugged and disappeared with the yappy dog in her arms.

Mrs. Heaton moved into a large living room and I followed her. Two plush sofas in burgundy framed a prow window. Blue-velvet wingback chairs rested on an expensive Aubusson carpet near the window.

"Would you like something to drink?" the woman asked, slipping into an obligatory hostess role.

I ignored the chill in her voice and sat down in one of the wingbacks. "Thanks, water would be great."

Accepting refreshments had created a bond between strangers since medieval times. More important, the delay allowed me to gain more information. My lack of practical experience weighed on me. I'd just have to learn as I grew into this job and hope nobody else died in the meantime.

A picture hung on the wall in a cock-eyed fashion and one of the sofas canted a bit from plumb. An accent pillow had dropped to the floor as if tossed by an angry hand. I picked it up and stroked its plush surface before returning it to the stack on the sofa.

Two glass-front cases dominated a corner of the room. I walked over to examine their contents. One contained a series of expensive scale model racing cars. The other displayed row upon row of miniature liquor bottles. Both masculine proclamations—I own this place and don't you forget it. Next to them was a big leather recliner that didn't match the almost feminine décor of the main part of the living room. That would fit with what I had seen of Roger Heaton.

Hearing Mrs. Heaton approaching, I sat down in a wingback and waited. Mrs. Heaton handed me the glass of ice water and settled into the chair opposite.

"Please call me Alice." She folded her hands in her lap like an obedient child.

"Alice, what were you and your husband arguing about?" I took a sip of water.

"A gun." Alice made a dismissive motion with her hands. "It's not what you think. My father left me a pair of old dueling pistols. They haven't been fired for years, but they are very valuable. They were set with gems, one topaz, and the other ruby. I called them the family jewels. I planned to sell them to pay for Vanessa's college fund. And now one is gone!" Her blue eyes filled with tears.

I made what I hoped were sympathetic noises and offered her a tissue box on the coffee table. She pulled two and put one in her lap. With the other, she dabbed each eye in turn, careful not to disturb her mascara.

"Alice, did your husband hurt you?"

"Of course not. Roger wouldn't hurt a fly."

"But your daughter called us."

"Well, she made a mistake." Mrs. Heaton shifted uneasily on the chair. "What you really need to do is find that thief who stole my pistol."

With no witnesses willing to testify, and no visible signs of physical harm, my options narrowed. I followed her lead on the theft, knowing I'd eventually return to the original purpose of my call.

"Might I see the remaining pistol?" I wondered why the thief stole only one, not the pair.

Alice retrieved a deep-brown leather case from the other room. She undid the small clasp and opened the lid. Inside were two velvet-lined cavities. One was bare, but the other held a green silken bundle, green silk that appeared identical to that in the dead man's hand.

Alice unwrapped the antique weapon with care. The long-barreled pistol looked authentic, with an octagonal barrel in a Damascus finish, a carved walnut grip, and an engraved lock plate. "My father said they were worth half a million as a pair, that they'd been used in a famous duel. He told me never to separate them. And now one is gone." Her eyes moistened again as she presented the pistol to me.

I turned the old weapon over in my hands. Inlaid into the grip was a brilliant yellow stone.

"That's topaz, for success and good fortune. The other pistol had an inlaid ruby, for wealth and prosperity. My father let me hold them sometimes, for good luck. I called the topaz one my sunshine and the other my fire."

What sort of father would give a young child a weapon like this to hold? I could only guess at Alice Heaton's upbringing.

I'd get Alice's permission to take the cloth for analysis. If it matched the scrap in the dead man's hand, I could connect the dead man with this theft. That still didn't get Alice Heaton's matching pistol back, but it was a start.

I made a second pass at the domestic violence issue. "Do you and your husband fight often?"

Alice shook her head. "Nothing like this. You have to understand. Roger is under a lot of stress finishing a project at work. I shouldn't have pushed it. But these pistols are important to me, too."

"Are they insured?"

She blushed. "Roger meant to talk to our agent, I know he did. He's usually so careful about those things. It's my fault, really."

I wasn't sure that was the case. She was doing a lot of apologizing for the absent husband. "So, no insurance. You want to file a burglary report?"

She hesitated. “I need to talk to Roger first. I never do anything without checking with my husband. He wouldn’t like that.” She smiled, but her eyes looked haggard.

“If you won't file a robbery report, let me take a picture of the topaz-inlaid pistol you've got left. I'll do some checking around. And, I'd like to borrow the silk wrapping on this one, if I may. It might help identify the missing one.”

It was likely that the stolen pistol, inlaid with ruby, had already been sold to a disreputable dealer or transported to another state. But I’d make inquiries, and have forensics check out the fabric.

“Whatever you feel is best.”

I returned to the cruiser for my camera. I put the green silk in an evidence bag and shot some identifying pictures of the remaining pistol to help trace the missing one. Then I asked Alice to summon her daughter, Vanessa.

There was some murmured conversation in the hall and a sharp yip as the dog was transferred from daughter to mother.

I stood when Vanessa entered the room, assessing her doll-like perfection. She had appeared shaken when I first saw her at the front door. Now the sophisticated veneer was back in place and she frowned at me with newly glossed lips.

“I hoped they would replace Deputy Marsh with somebody younger…”

Oh, I'm younger. Just the wrong gender. I'd dealt with Vanessa's type since high school: Spoiled and impossibly vain. I tucked one untidy strand of red hair behind my ear, self-conscious of my sweat-damp uniform. “You know anything about this missing pistol?”

The girl looked blank for a moment. “No, of course not. What would I know about some old gun?” She tossed her hair and struck a pose on the opposite couch.

I had two issues here: the domestic disturbance complaint and the missing antique weapon. My curiosity about the theft would keep. I returned to the initial purpose of my call. “What were your folks arguing about?”

“I don’t know. Most married people fight, don’t they?”

She was evasive. But the question still in the air was whether or not she’d trust me enough to tell family secrets. Probably not. My job still required that I pry them out of her if I could. "Has the fighting ever become violent?"

The young woman tossed her blond curls in denial. "No, my dad always leaves first. I don't know why she provokes him. That's not the way you get what you want from a man."

I smiled tightly. "And how *do* you get what you want?"

Vanessa just looked at me. "Well, any woman knows…"

She was back to playing games. I'd not get anything out of Vanessa Heaton tonight, but I'd be back. I closed my notebook and stood. "If you think of anything that might help locate the pistol with the ruby stone, please call me."

I offered my card, which she took gingerly between two fingers as though it were contaminated.

"Say goodbye to your mother for me. I'll check in again soon to see how she's doing."

I strode out into the cooling air, the adrenaline of anticipated danger gone. Backing my car out of the drive, I turned toward the road to the sheriff's station, then changed my mind and headed toward my grandfather's house instead.

On the way, I called Ben and told him I was shutting down for the afternoon. Maybe the second pistol would turn up, or I'd find another link to the dead man. One thing was certain—I had not heard the last of the Heatons.

* * * * * *

AS I DROVE DOWN the hill toward my grandfather's house, the storm confronted me head-on. Lightning broke in horizontal cracks across the sky and gusts buffeted the cruiser. I pulled into HT's drive and shut off the engine. It was good to be home. A light in the window blurred behind the heavy rain as I rushed onto the porch and into the kitchen.

HT was standing at the sink doing the supper dishes alone. Isabel must be at one of her church meetings. A good opportunity for us to talk. I opened the door, unhooked my equipment belt and dropped it to the floor in the corner. Then I pulled out a towel and started to dry the cups he set in the rack.

"How's the investigation of that man's death going?" he asked.

I told him about the boot print I'd discovered on the mountain.

HT sniffed. "Probably not worth much. Everybody in this county wears boots."

Maybe so, but I resented his easy dismissal of the work I'd done. He was my grandfather, but when he started to think for me, I took exception. I wasn't a child! I breathed deeply and changed the subject before disagreement escalated.

"Actually I did want to ask you about something," I said. "When I was up on the mountain, Armor kept directing me the long way around to the burn site."

HT chuckled. "Oh, I imagine that was just to keep you away from The Patch."

He dropped a stack of silverware into the basket, and I grabbed a handful to dry. "The what?" I asked.

"Armor's marijuana patch. He's very protective of that. I'm surprised he let you get that close."

"You knew about it and still lent him your truck?"

"Well, how else is he going to get up there? Anyway, the whole town knows about his little garden."

"Even Cyrus Marsh?" I asked.

"*Especially* Cyrus Marsh. I think they had a deal going. Ol' Cyrus would wait until the crop was ready and cue Armor he was coming up for a raid. Low and behold, when he arrived, the plants, all but one, would be harvested and long gone."

"And the one?"

"Well, you couldn't prove it by me, but I think that was Marsh's cut." He handed me the cast-iron skillet to dry.

"Well, I'm not Marsh," I declared. "That marijuana plot's got to go."

"Go slow on that, young lady. Armor's in a heap of pain with that leg. The weed's all he's got to keep him going." He dropped a cleaned pan in the drainer. "The world isn't all black and white, you know, Ellie."

"I know that. And my name's *Peg*." Damn it, why did I start to feel about five years old when I was around this man?

I moved on to the next topic on my list-of-stuff-to-talk-about with HT. "I ran into Tal Garrett today, too."

"That bag of wind."

"Yeah, well that bag of wind said you pulled up some survey stakes."

"I just moved them back where they belonged. I've lived here long enough to know what's his property and what's not."

"Did you ever think shifting those stakes puts me in the hot seat?"

He was silent. Did that mean he agreed? Or even heard me? I sighed and moved on to problem number three. "And then I went to the bank and talked to Johnny Evans."

"Yeah?" he said in a cautious tone.

"He says you're behind on your loan payments. What is this, HT? They'll take your house away. Banks don't go on a handshake anymore. They want cold hard cash."

His voice roughened with anger. "And exactly where am I going to get 'cold hard cash'? You want I should go rob another safe? You saw where that got me."

His shoulders rigid, he stomped out of the room.

For five long years, since he'd been convicted and sent to prison, I'd had no contact with this crusty old man. And now this.

I was ready to give up on the whole project, my mother's last cogent wishes be damned. There was no way that I could befriend this judgmental, irritating, son of a bitch. And I was beginning to believe I didn't even want to try.

I hung up the dishtowel and turned out the lights. The stars mocked me as I climbed the outside stairs to the loft. Leave, they said. Get out while you still can.

CHAPTER SIX

THE NEXT MORNING, Alice Heaton called me. She said she wanted to clarify some statements she'd made the night before and asked me to come over. I welcomed her invitation. I wasn't a social worker, but if there was a potential domestic violence situation, maybe I could point her towards the help she needed. Even in our small community, there were resources she could use.

My mood lifted as I drove to the Heaton's old Victorian mansion. The morning was warm and sunny, and my heightened arousal at last night's domestic dispute had vanished. This follow-up call fell into the category of routine business, and for that, I was grateful.

As I walked up steps to the Heaton house, now ablaze with sunlight, the aroma of fresh coffee and just-baked bread greeted me. My mouth watered in anticipation. I'd never been a cook, but I appreciate good food.

Alice opened the door. Her hair was combed, but one eye had the makings of a nasty shiner. The woman appeared more stable than she had last night, a good thing.

"Come in, Deputy Quincy. I've been expecting you." She led me into the living room, and I sat in the recliner.

Alice's eyes widened in apprehension. "You're in Roger's chair, but I suppose that's okay. He isn't here and he won't know."

She disappeared into the kitchen and soon returned with coffee and cinnamon rolls. After serving me, she sat, primly crossing her legs at the ankles. My grandmother used to say a lady never crosses her legs at the knee. Maybe Alice had a similar authority figure in her past.

The rolls were flaky and light, filled with cinnamon, frosted with that white icing that sticks to your fingers. I pulled off a piece and popped it in my mouth.

Alice smiled at me. "My grandmother's recipe."

Nailed it. I knew there had to be a grandmother in there somewhere. Always a pleasure when one of my Sherlock deductions actually panned out. "Delicious," I said, giving her a generous smile. They *were* good.

Alice took the empty dishes back to the kitchen and returned to sit on the couch across from me.

I reached for my notebook and sat there, waiting.

"I don't know where to begin…"

"Why don't you start with the pistol," I suggested. Always start with the easier subject. Only the story of the weapon wasn't, it turned out.

"Well, it wasn't stolen. I lied about that." Alice swallowed. "I gave it to my son."

"Your son. You and Roger have another child?"

"I guess I need to start at the beginning. I was pregnant when Roger and I married. When I got the courage to confess it wasn't his child, Roger was furious. He accused me of tricking him into marriage so I'd have a free ride." Tears streamed down her face.

The Police Academy lectures taught that domestic violence sometimes began with the first serious argument. I took a guess. "Did he hit you?" I asked.

"It wasn't much of a hit, just a slap. And he apologized after," she said in his defense. "He was just upset. It was my fault, really. He said he wasn't going to raise another man's *bastard*." She flushed when pronouncing the word. "He ordered me to get an abortion."

"But you didn't."

"I couldn't. Taking another life is a mortal sin. I hid the pregnancy as best I could and went to stay with my aunt—she's dead now, bless her soul. When the baby was born, I gave it over to an adoption agency."

She sighed. "I was desperate back then, and Roger seemed to offer a way out. I've learned to love him—he's a good man, in his own way. At the same time, I've been tortured with guilt at abandoning my son and turning him over to another woman to raise."

She sniffled. "I would have polished his little shoes and walked him to school that first day of kindergarten, and gone to all of his school plays. But all these years I've waited, patient. When my son turned twenty-one, I wrote to the adoption agency, like they said I could."

Her thumb rubbed the knuckles of the other hand, soothing herself as she relived the moment. "I waited for that day. I composed that letter twenty times over in my mind. I almost had it memorized by the time I sent it."

"And he responded?"

"Last month I got his letter. I was so excited." Alice frowned a little. "He wasn't what I had expected, but he had potential, I could tell."

"And then what?" I prompted.

"Well, my Sonny said he wanted to go back to college. He planned to attend law school, just as soon as he finished his undergraduate credits. Just imagine, my son a lawyer! I was so proud."

"Let me guess. He was a little short of cash?"

She wadded a tissue into a tight little ball, and then unwrapped and smoothed it against her knee. "I knew my son was honest. A mother knows those things. That's why I gave him the ruby pistol?"

Her voice rose at the end of the sentence, seeming to ask for validation. I didn't give her any. Not my place to judge her actions.

"I hated to break up the set of pistols, but I have two children and it's important to share what I have equally. My Sonny needed money and he said he could sell the pistol to raise some."

She sighed. "I dream about being invited to his law graduation. Maybe he'll get me a corsage and I'll sit in the front row. We'll all be a family and these years of secret keeping will be worth it." Her face brightened, and expressions of hope replaced those of regret.

I checked my notes. "But you told me the ruby pistol was stolen."

"Yes, and that's what I told Roger, too. You won't tell him, will you? If my husband found out, he would yell at me, accuse me of lying to him."

My own mind shifted into rapid gear. Maybe I was basing too much on the green scrap of cloth in the dead man's hand; however, it appeared to be an exact match for the wrapping of the pistol Alice had shown me the previous night. And that would make the dead man Alice's son.

I tucked the thought away and returned to Alice's explanation.

"I can't let Roger get too angry. If he left me, what would I do? I can't even balance my checkbook." Her voice tightened with stress.

I didn't do too well in the bank account area either, but I managed. To Alice, financial security seemed reason enough to remain in an unhealthy relationship. I couldn't see it, but that worked for her.

I patted her hand. "Does Roger know about your son?"

Alice sighed. "That's what our fight was about. He found the letter from Sonny. I thought I put it away, but there it was on the counter when he came home from work." Alice stopped to think. "That housekeeper, Isabel, must have put it there. I don't trust her, she looks at me funny."

Could have been Isabel but I doubted it, given what I'd seen at HT's house. Even though I didn't get along with the woman, she seemed honest enough, not the sneaky type.

"Back to your son," I said. "Do you know where he is now?"

"I haven't heard from him since that night. He told me he'd call when he had the money from the pistol sale. Something's wrong. I know it is. He's never coming back to me. I'll never see him again."

Alice's voice raised an octave and then faded. Something about her erratic manner alerted me.

"Nooo." She moaned and slumped over.

I caught Alice just as she lost consciousness. I eased her back on the couch and put a pillow beneath her feet. In a moment, she coughed and then opened her eyes.

Just then the front door opened and Roger Heaton entered the room.

"My meeting was over early and I came home to pack for the Phoenix conference…"

He stopped talking when he saw Alice lying on the couch. He looked at her and then at me.

"What are you doing here, Quincy, and what's wrong with my wife?"

"I'm afraid she's had a shock."

"Not that fainting thing again? There's nothing wrong with her. She does that to win attention," he said harshly.

But when he turned to Alice, his voice softened. "Are you all right, sweetheart? Here, let me help you to the bedroom. You'll be better soon."

Alice allowed herself to be led from the room, leaning against Roger's arm.

He returned shortly. "I've given her one of her sleeping pills. She'll be fine when she wakes up. Sorry you had to be a witness to one of her fake spells."

"Are you sure she's all right? Your wife seemed quite upset. Do you think perhaps she needs to talk to someone?"

"A shrink, you mean? Oh, we've seen our share over the years. Alice has usually recovered by the time we arrive. She can put on a fine act, just like she did for you."

I wasn't convinced it was an act, but moved on. "I've been meaning to talk to you, Roger. Where were you last night between say, ten p.m. and two a.m.?"

"I was right here all night. Alice can vouch for that."

"Actually, you weren't." My tone was flat and definite. "I was summoned here for a domestic disturbance call last night. When I arrived, only your wife and daughter were here."

Roger's face reddened, and his eyes bulged. "My wife had no business calling in the cops!" Then he took a deep breath. "Look, Officer, I know you're just doing your job, and I appreciate that. We all do. My wife and I had a small disagreement last night. I went out for a walk to calm down, okay?"

"Anyone see you?"

"No, I just walked. I like to do that at night sometimes. It helps me relieve stress and gain perspective on work."

Roger seemed defensive, but he was under pressure and according to him, had a mentally ill wife. I tried to take his words at face value. He said he cared for his wife, yet the two of them seemed to collude with each other's dysfunction. Beyond the scope of my understanding.

He glanced down at his status-expensive watch. "Anything else? I'm due in Phoenix and I need to pack."

I wasn't ready to leave yet. "What about your wife's first child, a son?" I made a point of consulting my notes.

"She dredged up that ancient history?" He snorted. "I forbade Alice to have that child, and she took care of it. End of story."

His arrogance prickled the hairs on the back of my neck. Forbade. What was this, the Dark Ages? "There's a possibility that the dead man in the mining pit may have been your wife's son."

"Oh, I doubt that." His contradiction was firm. "Don't get me wrong. I feel regret for that man's family. However, you need to understand the nature of my wife's illness, Deputy. Alice lies compulsively. She does not have a son. Vanessa is our only child. We adopted her when we found out my wife couldn't have children."

Either he was telling the truth or he was a better liar than his wife. Too soon to tell which Heaton to believe. Perhaps neither.

Roger ushered me out of the house and onto the porch. "I resent your implication that I had anything to do with that man's death. I may have stepped out for a moment, but otherwise I was here, all night. I don't need an alibi because I was never there at that mining pit."

He crossed his arms and glared at me. "And stay out of our personal business. Alice doesn't need to be bothered by further calls from you."

The door slammed firmly behind him, leaving me alone on the steps.

* * * * * *

THE OLD CAR STALLED on an uphill grade as I returned to the office. I turned off the cruiser's air conditioner to generate more power, and the car interior immediately turned into a sauna. Bigger police stations bought the new wheels while Mingus inherited the older cars after they worked their way down the line. I choked back a mixture of resentment and uncertainty. Was this summer replacement job a similar dead-end spiral for me?

As I entered Main Street, my stomach growled. I'd missed lunch and I still wanted to check Armor's whereabouts the night the man died. If I stopped at the biker bar where Ben's uncle worked, I could grab some food, talk to him, and then head back to the office. I parked and went in.

The bar had an old-time saloon décor. A chair rail divided one wall, with flocked maroon wallpaper on top and dark bead board underneath. A mural of ladies in can-can skirts danced above the bar. A large painting of a well-endowed nude in a feather boa decorated the side wall, and a jukebox filled the air with the "Streets of Laredo." I smelled fried onions as I pulled up a stool to the long mahogany bar. No better smell on earth when I'm hungry.

"What can I get you?" Armor asked, wiping the counter with a damp rag.

I studied the cracked plastic menu edged in black tape. "How about a…" I strained to see the print in the darkened room. "…a Spook Burger. Pickles, onions, and some horseradish on the side, if you have it. And some iced tea."

"Coming right up." He scribbled the order on a green slip and handed it over the back counter to the grill man. Then Armor pulled a glass from a rack and filled it with iced tea.

"What's the story behind your name?" I asked, passing time. That cook better hurry or I'd be chewing on the bar soon.

Armor settled on a stool and leaned his crutch against the bar within easy reach. "The Brancussi part is easy. I'm as Eye-talian as they come. I've got some stories I could tell you about the old neighborhood. But you want to know about the Armor part."

I nodded, pouring sugar into my tea.

"I didn't earn it in the war. I was too young for 'Nam and wouldn't have gone anyway. Hell, you'd find me hightailing it to Canada for sure. No, Armor is for my belly. Feel that sucker." He punched himself in his ample gut with satisfaction. "It's like motorcycle armor that protects you when you ride. But I ain't doing much riding lately." He shifted on the stool and grimaced. "Need to move a little. This damn leg tightens up when I sit too long."

"An operation might help?"

"You got fifty thou to spare?" His tone was bitter. "Look, I'll be honest with you. I'd sell my soul for one more good ride down Yarnell Hill. But it ain't going to happen, anytime soon." He thought a moment and rubbed his chin. "Or maybe it will, you never can tell."

The cook rang the bell, and Armor slid the hamburger plate in front of me. Then he opened the bar refrigerator and extracted a jar of horseradish, handed it to me with a flourish. I opened the lid, grabbed a knife, and slathered some on my burger. The first bite was pure pleasure, greasy and sharp, the bun toasted and warm.

"You live close?" I asked.

"Whew, how do you stand that smelly stuff?" He waved a hand in front of his nose. "Yeah, right here in fact. The owner lets me sleep in the room behind the kitchen. That addition used to be the crib where the 'girls' worked when the place was roaring in the 1900s. Just think of it. I'm sleeping in a whore house." He chuckled a little.

"And Ben?"

"Well, he bunks with me, sometimes. Your granddaddy talked ol' Cyrus into hiring him. Thanks, by the way, for keeping him on. Ben needs the money. I've been trying to talk him into getting a real job, but he's hung up on that firefighting thing."

"He told me. A Navajo Hot Shot?"

"He's half Italian, half Navajo. His daddy—my brother—was living in LA, fell in love with this Navajo lady. He was as wild as they come, but he was devoted to that woman. They raised Ben in the big city—the kid didn't even know he was Native until they up and moved back to the Rez one day. The wife, she needed to visit her roots, I guess."

He held up the pitcher. "More tea?"

I covered the glass with my palm. "This'll hold me. And then what happened?"

"My brother and his wife were doing okay building a new life there together. They started home from a Navajo sing one night and got to weaving a little on the road, you know? And then that old red steer walked right in front of his pickup. Shebang that was it. Killed by a cow." His fist banged on the counter. "Can you imagine? A goddam cow!"

"What happened to Ben?"

"Well, he stayed on for a while. Lived with his Navajo grandma, herding her sheep, living in her hogan. When she died, he came here to live with me. No other family around, just the two of us now. End of story." He stood and shifted uneasily on his good leg, seeking to end the conversation.

"I've got a couple of other questions for you."

"Shoot."

"What were you doing on the mountain the night that man died?"

The warmth he had shown when talking about Ben vanished. "I got a right to be up there, just the same as anybody else."

"And between ten and two that night?"

"I was right here, serving my buddies the drinks they'd paid for. You can ask any of twenty people sitting at the bar, just like you are right now." His voice turned cold. "Now, if you'll excuse me, I got work to do." He moved away leaning heavily on his crutch.

One of the downsides to being the Law. I was finding that I could alienate a whole townful of people faster than writing a speech for the PTA.

* * * * * *

BACK AT THE OFFICE, Ben asked for the afternoon off so he could join Isabel in the high meadow collecting herbs. Work was slow and I said okay. I was in a magnanimous mood. Besides, he promised to bring me a bouquet of wildflowers.

I reflected on my conversation with Armor, his uncle. The boy probably needed more mothering, something HT's housekeeper Isabel seemed ready to provide. Come to think of it, the idea of fresh air appealed to me, too. After a while, I closed the office and swung by HT's house to change into running gear.

I walked quickly through the small downtown district filled with tourist cars packing up for the trip back to Phoenix. The I-17 freeway would be clogged with them heading back to the metropolis, sunburned and happy, filled with fudge from our local shop. Fudge! I shook my head, resisted the temptation, and headed to the hills above town, instead.

I planned for a run but found more than I bargained for at the top of those hills.

CHAPTER SEVEN

ONCE OUT OF TOWN I picked up the pace, running along natural trails that the mule-tailed deer had used even before the Native Americans arrived. The higher elevation soon had me breathing hard, but I relished the constant adjustment of trail running, dodging the rocks and cactus spines.

Running gave me time to think, and I needed that space to put the events of the recent past into a matrix that made sense. I knew I'd have to call the death of the fallen man soon—accident, murder, or suicide. But for now, I stayed in the moment.

The brittlebush had died back in the summer heat, but brilliant fruit called tunas decorated the edges of the prickly pear like oversized grapes. I watched out for the black-tailed rattlers that warmed themselves in the sun. There weren't too many, but it only took one in a bad mood to ruin a person's day.

Pausing at the top of the ridge to catch my breath, I glimpsed Ben and Isabel in the meadow below. Isabel held pruning shears and Ben carried a big woven basket for the herbs they were gathering. The rocks surrounding the meadow created a peculiar echo chamber, like an ancient cathedral where a whisper at one end could be heard clearly at the other. Their conversation was bell-clear, as though they stood right next to me.

"What about this datura stuff?" Ben asked.

"Just a little is good for headaches," Isabel said. "But more than that can blind or even kill you."

Her shears clipped just the tips of the crucifixion thorn as she moved down the path. She'd told me that it was good for making tea to calm the stomach after "bad water" or "bad food." After the burger at the biker bar, I could use that remedy. I gave a soft burp. It couldn't possibly be the horseradish.

Isabel reached out a cautioning hand as Ben touched the orange globemallow blossoms. The plant was nicknamed "sore eye poppy" because of the fine hairs on its stems. I heard other voices approaching, and so, apparently, did Isabel. She halted work, listening.

Tal Garrett and Roger Heaton emerged from the junipers at the edge of the meadow below, the bitter odor of Garrett's cigar drifting ahead of him. Isabel whispered something to Ben, and he took off at a half run. She turned in the opposite direction toward the men, like an ancestral wolf protecting her cub. I ducked behind a large boulder to eavesdrop.

"Use your imagination, man," Garrett said. "We can put in an Olympic-sized swimming pool and a clubhouse. They'll love it."

He must be speaking of the buyers for his new development.

"But what about town residents?" Roger Heaton asked. "How's that going to benefit them? And what about the destruction of those old historic buildings?" It was a side of the vice mayor I hadn't witnessed before.

"You ask too many questions—unimportant questions. I pay you to sell houses and developments. Leave the thinking to me." Garrett's voice roughened. "Those old wrecks need to be torn down. Half of the buildings in town are sliding down hill anyway. They're dangerously unstable. Instead, we could put up some fast food places to feed the tourists. And a supermarket and a decent drug store. The townies will fall in line soon enough when they see the money come rolling in."

"This is just a game to you, isn't it," Roger said. "Moving players around on a board." His tone seemed to indicate his frustration being one of the chess pieces.

"Life *is* a game. You need to relax a little, Heaton, and learn how to play. Just look at this view. Can't you envision the houses, row upon row of them, looking out on that million-dollar view?" Garrett's gesture was expansive, including the entire valley spreading far below the meadow.

I squeezed tighter behind the boulder as they moved closer, their voices becoming more distinct in the rock's echo chamber.

"I have to disagree with you, but…"

Garrett's responding chuckle was false, even to my ears. "Roger, maybe you need to turn that thinking to your own problems. Any thoughts on repaying that debt you owe me? I'm a patient man, much more patient than those folks at the Casino."

Gambling debts. Interesting. Roger had a few secrets of his own, then. My brain started to play the what-if game. What if the dead man stole a valuable pistol that Roger had intended to sell himself? What if the fall was accidental in an ensuing argument? Roger could be a vital link to solving the mystery. I plunked him in the definite/maybe category of suspects.

"Listen up," Garrett said. "Go to the commissioner's office first thing in the morning. Pay out some bribes if you need to. This deal needs to go through *now*, before the mining company gets wind of what we're trying to do."

His voice dropped as he drew close to where Isabel stood. "What have we here?"

There was the sound of scuffling and then a sharp cry.

"Let go of my arm." Isabel's voice raised in alarm.

Time to intervene, before the situation escalated. Isabel could probably handle it on her own, but it was two against one. I rose to my feet to even the odds a little. Stretching out stiff muscles, I walked down the hill towards the group.

"Deputy Quincy. Not in uniform. That mean you're off duty?" Roger asked.

"A cop is always on duty." Funny how that was true. I drew up to my full height and looked down on the men. "What seems to be going on here?"

"My property," Garrett blustered. "This woman was trespassing."

"And you were doing what to her?"

I turned to Isabel who was rubbing a red welt on her arm. "You okay? Want to file charges against this man for assault?"

Isabel shook her head. But under her breath, she muttered and canted her head. "His land start *there,* not here."

"Are those the sunflowers Ben promised me?" I pointed to the basket.

She took my hint. "Yes, but they need water. I'll take them to HT's house now."

Isabel disappeared into the trees. I turned to Garrett. "Since I'm here, why don't you show me those stakes you say Armor Brancussi and my grandfather moved."

The two hadn't moved the stakes much, maybe five feet. Just enough to prick Garrett's sense of importance. The man yanked one out of the ground and shoved it into the original hole, scuffed some dirt around it. The stake fell over in a slow tumble as if it didn't belong there. I felt a moment of satisfaction. Law enforcement folks are supposed to be neutral, but I disliked Garrett's treatment of Isabel. The man needed a serious comeuppance.

"Time we got back to the office," Garrett declared. "Nothing more here for us." He dropped his cigar stub and crushed it underfoot.

"Careful," I countered. "Fire danger high up here. Better take that with you."

"Roger?" Garrett's tone of command was plain.

Roger shot me a look of frustration as he leaned down to pick up the cigar butt. Hard to live under another man's boot. I wasn't excusing his behavior, but maybe Alice became the target for the underlying tension he felt toward his boss.

After they left, I jogged down the hillside in the gathering darkness, cautious of rough patches in the trail. My mother's drinking had forced a stressful black-or-white existence on me, but this town presented a more complex view of life. Law enforcement was more than writing traffic tickets and issuing reports. Over the past several days, the underbelly of dark secrets that seemed to percolate from the deep mining tunnels underground swirled about me.

No black and white here, just a lot of maybes. I still had lessons ahead of me in this life-long process of growing up, and Mingus seemed more than willing to be the teacher.

* * * * * *

THE NEXT MORNING when I opened the loft door to the outside staircase, a bouquet of flowers greeted me on the sill. A simple pottery jug contained calendulas, Queen Anne's lace, and some brilliant pink roses from Isabel's garden. Their cinnamon-sweet aroma drifted past my nose as I picked up the jug and placed it on my nightstand. Tucked into the bouquet was a simple card. "With much gratitude, Isabel."

Still smiling a few moments later, I carried the flowers with me as I walked down the hill to the sheriff's annex.

Ben bent and sniffed the bouquet as he set down my coffee mug. "Nice. That Isabel knows how to make beauty."

I agreed. The presence of the flowers brightened my office as I dealt with small-town matters. My first call that morning was from a widow complaining about javelinas in her fruit orchards. According to Ben, she called every summer about this time.

The javelinas, our local "wild pigs," were like migrant farm workers, moving from one ripe crop to another. The herds were extended families from newborn babies to the boars with magnificent sets of tucks. They could glean an orchard in a matter of minutes. The animals were especially fond of ripe peaches, but they mostly ate the fruit on the ground—climbing a tree was too much work. Smart pigs.

But no way was I going to tackle those wild peccaries—they were welcome to this lady's peaches. I listened to her talk for a while and then suggested that she call the county animal control unit. They wouldn't come out either, but it shifted the problem off my docket.

Then a gallery owner called requesting an investigation of a burglary. I walked down the hill to his store and asked the standard questions. What was missing? Did he find any signs of forced entry? A jimmied lock?

He was indignant. "The door wasn't locked. Nobody locks doors here. This is Mingus."

I wasn't impressed. Maybe he needed to lock his.

Ben had news when I returned to the office. "The crime lab called. A hit on the fingerprints." He held the message slip just out of my reach.

I grabbed for it. "Give me that."

I walked into my office and dialed the number. "Quincy, here. Message said you had something on our dead guy here in Mingus."

"Yeah, just a minute, let me find the file," he said. "Man's name is Druce Kevern. Spent some time in the Florence Penitentiary for robbery. Prints on file for that."

"What's his last-known?"

"Turns out he lives—lived—right in your backyard, out Rimrock way."

Rimrock was a small town located on the east side of the Verde Valley, or, "the Valley" to locals. That massive depression, formed by the shifting of the earth's crust over a million years ago, defined the center of Arizona. Home for most of the free-flowing water in the state, the green valley is replenished by one major river, the Verde, and numerous tributaries—Sycamore Creek, Oak Creek, Clear Creek—and cutting Rimrock in half, Wet Beaver Creek.

I put Ben in charge of the office and headed out to the address the lab tech gave me. Near Wet Beaver Creek, precious water provided the means to build an exclusive country club community with manicured green links and tall cottonwood trees. On the other side of Wet Beaver Creek, a drier climate of high desert was home to a group of independent, off-the-grid freethinkers.

The neighborhood turned rougher there, as I turned off the pavement onto a primitive dirt road. Weed-filled yards contained piles of trash lumber and dust-covered vehicles with expired license plates.

Druce Kevern's last-known residence was a single-wide trailer parked under an old catalpa tree. A sagging wooden fence enclosed a small yard overgrown with sticker bushes. Pulling a couple of cockleburs off my pant leg, I stepped up on a cinder block serving as the front stoop and knocked on a rusty screen door.

A skinny woman in her late fifties appeared behind it. Although it was mid-afternoon, she wore a terrycloth bathrobe and held a half-smoked cigarette in her hand. "Yeah?"

"Is this the residence of Druce Kevern?"

The woman looked at my uniform and then at the squad car in the driveway. "Come in." She pushed open the screen door and turned toward a living room filled with kids' toys. A dirty green couch with a sprung seat sat against one wall with a wooden chair on each side. A small round-screen TV blared out a reality show rerun. She switched it off.

“I'm Druce's mother.” She waved vaguely at the toys. “Don’t mind the mess. I do child care now and then to bring in some cash since Druce is moved out.”

“Maybe you better sit down, Mrs. Kevern.” Resignation deepened the lines around her tired eyes. She sat heavily on the couch and gestured to one of the wooden chairs. I dug into my pocket, pulled out the picture of the dead man, and handed it to her.

The woman studied it for a moment, then, expressionless, handed it back. “That's Druce, all right. How’d it happen?”

“A fall, up on Black Mountain. You all right, ma'am?” She showed no obvious emotion, but her face had turned stiff and her posture was rigid. “Anyone I can call for you?”

She took another drag on her cigarette. “I'm fine. Don't bother me none.” She stubbed it out in a saucer on the scratched end table.

“Don't get me wrong, Officer. Me and Druce, we made our peace over who he is and what he does, a long time ago. But I always worried he might end up like this.”

“You said he no longer lived here.”

“Yeah, when they released him from prison this last time he sweet-talked himself into a work-study program in Phoenix. Didn’t last there long. Druce was never too good at stickin' to anything that smelled of work.”

“You got the name of the place?”

She grabbed a stubby pencil, scribbled a name on the back of an envelope, and handed it to me. “Don’t have the address. In the Phoenix phone book, probably.”

I tucked the envelope in my pocket. “Was your son despondent? Any indication that he might want to hurt himself?”

“Druce was always on the lookout for the next big deal, but I never saw any intent of killing himself. Least he never said anything like that. Think he was too much of a coward to do himself in.”

“What about drugs or alcohol?”

The woman's eyes shifted. “You ain't got a search warrant. Ain't no drugs here.”

Whether she used or not wasn’t my business today. I brushed her hand with what I hoped was a calming gesture. “We should be done with the autopsy soon. Where would you like your son's body sent?”

"You keep him." The woman gave a harsh laugh. "Look around you. I ain't got no money for burying."

Mrs. Kevern stood abruptly. "You can see yourself out." She rushed from the room with muffled sobs.

I closed the front door quietly and walked to my car. I doubted the telling ever came easier. No good way to tell a mother her son wasn't coming home again, ever.

Driving back to Mingus, I pondered my next step. If I wanted to investigate Kevern's job history, that meant traveling to Phoenix, about two hours south of Mingus. But if I called my boss and told him what I was doing, he'd want to know why. And if I declared it was a murder investigation, he'd just assign it to Sanchez. He'd already told me he'd do that.

I thought some more. Maybe there was a third alternative. I dialed the sheriff's number before I lost my nerve.

He answered on the first ring. "Well, you got that case closed yet?"

"Soon. Just a few more items to clean up." I took a deep breath. "I'm calling on another matter. Need to request a personal day off."

"A day off? You just got there."

"I know," I said, "but some business down in Phoenix I need to take care of." Not a lie, exactly. Not the entire truth either. I ignored that final thought and continued. "I'll leave early and should be back the same day."

He sighed. "Don't make me regret hiring you." He paused for a moment. "Okay, go. But take your own vehicle."

My ruse immediately became more complicated. I didn't have a car. Now I'd have to ask HT if I could borrow his truck. I hated to be beholden to anyone, but I needed to know exactly what Druce was doing before he died in my jurisdiction. I owed that much, at least, to the weeping mother in Rimrock. Ignoring my internal warnings about deceiving and tangled webs, I marched straight forward into trouble.

CHAPTER EIGHT

"NOW DON'T GO ABOVE SIXTY," my grandfather ordered the next morning, fussing over his old truck like a parent with a sickly child. "She's not used to those freeways and all. Why aren't you taking the cop cruiser?"

"I can't. Don't ask." The evasion made me wish I could be open with both my grandfather and the sheriff about my reasons for the trip, but a lie takes on a life of its own.

Temperatures had cooled in Mingus, but Phoenix still hit triple digits this time of year, and HT's truck had no air conditioning. I opened both windows and the rear vent and the heat responded in shimmering waves off the black asphalt. Sweat trickled down my spine as I followed HT's directive and set the speed at a steady 60. It would be a long, hot drive to Phoenix.

When I-17 South neared New River Junction outside Phoenix, the lanes clogged with RVs and boaters from Lake Pleasant. As I swung out to pass a slow-moving delivery van, HT's pickup stalled and its temperature gauge swung into the red danger zone. I coasted to the right side of the road and turned off the engine. I let three cars and a garbage truck pass, then walked to the front and lifted the hood.

An overheated radiator belched steam into the air and singed my eyebrows before I could jump back. Any other time there'd be a highway assistance van or a friendly patrol car swinging in to help, but the cars kept zipping by.

I had just pulled my cell from my pocket to call roadside assistance when a Jeep Wagoneer pulled in behind me. A man got out and walked to the pickup. I shaded my eyes to assess his intentions. Friend or foe?

He gave me a quick wave. “Why, Peg Quincy. Surprised to see you here. Car trouble?”

It was Flint Tanner, the sleeping man I’d rousted from Black Mountain.

“I met your grandfather this morning and he said you were heading this direction. Need a lift?”

“You know my grandfather?”

Flint nodded. “We go way back, but I didn’t know you were related until I talked to him this morning.”

Living and working in the same small town, you never knew whether the guy who invited you to his backyard barbecue might be someone you arrested the next week on a traffic violation. Maybe I’d gotten off to a wrong start with this guy if my grandfather knew him.

“Radiator?” he asked.

“Looks like it. Old truck. Getting ready to call a tow.”

“Might just need a cool down and some water.”

“That, too.”

We stood looking at the steam still rising from the pickup’s engine.

He was possibly right, but how long would it take to cool off the engine? The temperature zoomed higher by the moment until even the cactus in the median looked wilty. A Jeep with a working engine was parked directly behind me, and my mission of discovery awaited.

“What’s your day look like?” I smiled my most ingratiating smile.

He looked doubtful, so I sweetened the deal. “I can pay you to give me a ride.”

After making that rash offer, I mentally reviewed my slim bank account and almost empty wallet. No way would the sheriff’s department reimburse trip expenses since technically I was on personal leave. Maybe he'd take plastic?

“Buy me lunch and I’ll do it. My day’s clear once I deliver this report to my mining company’s office on Central Avenue.” He returned my smile. “Anything for a friend.”

A misinterpretation on his part. I needed a lift, no Best Friends Forever relationship. But I let it pass. A ride was a ride.

"You're on." I slammed the hood, rolled up the windows, and locked the doors.

Leaving an unattended vehicle on a city freeway was chancy. I could return to find the tires missing, or the truck gone. I stuck one of my cards under the windshield wiper with a scribbled note, "Back soon." Maybe that would forestall potential thieves, if they could read.

I walked to the Jeep and hopped in the passenger side. "Thanks, I appreciate this."

"No problem."

Flint let the jeep engine idle a moment. The air conditioner roared a blast that iced my forearms. Pure heaven.

I snuck a look in his direction. In the daylight, with a fresh shave, this Flint Tanner reminded me of my ex. He was impossibly handsome, sure of himself. The man sported a black Stetson, white T-shirt and freshly pressed blue jeans.

He also wore boots—pointed-toe cowboy boots. I bent down to tie my shoe and stole a look. Too bad they didn't label boots with initials like those expensive purses. Then I could scope out the brand.

"You a fan of good boots?" he asked, noticing my observation of his shoes.

Damn! I thought I was being subtle. I straightened up and fastened my seatbelt, aborting my attempt at covert activities. "I swear by my Adidas running shoes. What makes boots so special, anyway?"

He signaled and merged into traffic. "Some people say it's the leather. An amazing variety—eel, moose hide, even ostrich with all them little bitty polka dots." He braked for slowing traffic ahead of us. "But for me, it's the workmanship. A sixth-generation boot maker can make a custom last, and then your boots fit perfectly and serve you a lifetime."

"What's your favorite brand?" I asked.

"I thought you didn't like boots."

"Just making conversation."

He shrugged. "These are my work Justins. Got others at my apartment, though. Glad to show you, anytime." He wiggled his eyebrows.

I sighed. This was a business trip, not a singles bar, and I was in no mood for a pick-up line. Served me right for smiling at him. I didn't respond, and we spent the next half hour in silence, as we headed down the freeway.

Once in midtown Phoenix, Flint dropped his report. Then we hit the 202 loop to the east side of Phoenix and exited at 40th street. Twenty minutes later, we wove through a complex of one-story medical and dental buildings that covered a large city block. Our destination was a company called Fresh Beginnings, and we made it in time for the late morning appointment I'd scheduled with the manager.

The Bermuda grass edging the complex was yellow and brittle in the summer heat. In the fall, gardeners across the city would plant winter rye under a thick layer of black manure. Now, at the end of the summer, we were spared the odor of cow dung but also missed that brilliant green that October would bring.

Flint spotted the building number I'd given him, and he pulled in to park.

"Wait here," I ordered. "I'll just be a minute." My plan was to make this quick and get out of Phoenix as soon as possible.

"It's too hot," he protested.

"Okay, come in, but you're not part of the transactions."

"Absolutely not. I'm just your taxi driver. Won't make a sound."

His shadow engulfed mine when we walked toward the building. He had a good three inches on me. Once I would have enjoyed that height and masculinity, but my short-term marriage had dissuaded me from the princess-forever dream.

Phil. I thought I'd met my prince charming in him, but my ex morphed into the beast from hell after the ceremony. He started to drink heavily and became physically abusive besides. I spent several nights in the hospital before I wised up and called it quits. Now, my relationships were short-term and physical, nothing serious. Focusing on my career kept life much simpler.

That goal might be difficult now that this hunk entered my world. Was I ready to try again? Might this Flint Tanner be worth the effort? I shelved that question for a more opportune moment. Business first.

* * * * * *

I OPENED THE OFFICE DOOR and stepped onto a thick, moss green rug that muffled my footsteps. Hudson River School paintings hung on the walls and a discreet sound system offered a Mozart horn concerto. This atmosphere reeked of Old Money and that made me vaguely uneasy. I took care not to brush the white linen upholstery with my sweaty palm when I walked by. No telling what it cost to clean that stuff.

The receptionist picked up the phone and soon the manager, a Mrs. Bradford-Smythe, opened an inner office door to join us. She wore a mauve designer dress with a tasteful string of pearls. Her graying hair swept into a chignon, and a whiff of perfume wafted my way. I recognized it as one my great aunt had worn: Chanel Number Five. Expensive. That figured.

The manager headed toward Flint like iron filings toward a magnet. A significant minute later, she noticed me, too. I didn't count just because I wasn't some handsome guy wearing a cowboy hat? I wiped the scowl off my face.

"Why don't the two of you come into my office?" she purred.

"Thanks, I'll wait here." Flint picked up a magazine and settled into a white linen chair like he owned it.

She led me into her office and offered me a seat. Pictures showing cheerful couples holding smiling infants covered the walnut-paneled walls, and real stand-up plants, not silk ones, softened each corner. A discrete sign, "Fresh Beginnings," decorated her desk.

She nodded at it. "Yes, that's us. We've kept a low profile after all the abortion clinic bombings. Terrible, just terrible."

"But you don't do abortions."

"Just the opposite. We offer an exclusive adoption service. Our clients pay handsomely for exactly the right little one."

"Pay? Is that legal?"

The woman seemed insulted that I would ask. I felt bad suggesting it.

"What our clients pay are the costs of the birthing," she said. "Plus our fees—just to cover expenses, of course—and an honorarium for the mother's adjustment after she gives up her dear child." She shifted some brochures on the desk, neatening her already tidy office.

"As part of our service, we keep a file in perpetuity for each child. In perpetuity," she emphasized. "At age twenty-one, a child is free to contact the birth mother." She smoothed her skirt with a well-manicured hand. "Of course, few of our adoptees ever want to do that. They're happy with their new parents."

"But it works the other way, too? If a birth mother wanted to contact her child when they reached adulthood, she could?"

"Well, of course. We're not monsters. We want everyone to be happy."

Niceties behind us, she pierced the atmosphere with gimlet eyes. "And what exactly brings you to see us today, Officer Quincy?"

"I'm investigating the death of a man who once worked here, Druce Kevern."

"Oh, no! What happened?"

"We think he may have"— I chose my words carefully— "fallen to his death. It might be an accident or possibly suicide. We're still gathering information at this point. Did Druce give any indication of being depressed?"

"He was very happy here. All our employees are. We are a happy company."

She'd be singing Kumbaya next.

"Druce." She sounded thoughtful. "I had hopes for that young man. He was one of our work-study hires, planned to return to school."

"His responsibilities here?"

"Opening the mail, answering routine correspondence, that sort of thing." A crease wrinkled her brow. "But we had some complaints. We had to let him go after three weeks."

My ears perked up. "Complaints?"

"I am not at liberty to discuss that. Confidentiality issues with client information, you understand."

A handy-dandy subpoena could fix that. I made a note. "Do you have a home address for Druce?"

"Of course, but I don't think he lived there after he left our employ. I heard he moved someplace up north. But I'll get it for you."

She returned with a note written with an elegant hand on cream vellum and handed it to me like an invitation to the White House. I contrasted it with the dirty envelope Mrs. Kevern had written upon— two hours away from here and two worlds apart. This note indicated that Druce had lived at The Manfred Arms in the Sunnyvale district. That would be our next stop.

Flint leaped to his feet when I entered the reception room. “After you, Boss Lady. Where next?” He swept off his hat and reached for the doorknob. I pushed ahead of him and opened my own door.

Out in the parking lot, he unlocked the Jeep for me and I climbed in. But this was Phoenix. In the short time we’d been in the office, every surface, even the leather seat, turned stovepipe hot. I squirmed, trying to get comfortable.

He turned to me. “I'm hungry. Are you hungry? I know this great French restaurant.”

I’d have loved a good meal in a cool restaurant. But my flat bank account and my desire not to mix business with pleasure suggested a different course of action. “No time. McD's will have to do. We'll eat as we go.”

We hit the next drive-through, and I ordered the combo. I reflected on the injustice of life chewing on a dry burger, no horseradish, as we drove to the west side of town.

On his side of the Jeep, Flint Tanner negotiated the crowded freeway, whistling a country tune, a definite distraction to my work concentration.

We turned on Glendale Avenue and ventured into an area of Phoenix hit hard by the real estate slump. Developers overbuilt and sold to owners who then defaulted on mortgages they couldn't afford when the balloon payments came due. The remaining owners maintained their properties, but next door, dead grass stems poked up from the caliche and front doors with smashed panels banged in the hot wind. Graffiti marred adobe walls, signaling that the gangs had claimed what the default owners had abandoned.

I shuddered. “I'd hate to raise a family in this area.”

“Me, too, but some of the small towns in East Texas where I came from were as hard hit by the recession.”

“I grew up in the mountains of Tennessee,” I volunteered. “Some of my relatives still live in the coves and hollows there. I miss that green, moving west to the desert.”

East Texas was almost next door to Tennessee—we could be country cousins, almost. I could sense my growing interest in the man sitting beside me. Concentrate on the job, not the man, I reminded myself. Business, first. And afterward, my wicked mind asked? Never mind.

Flint slowed the Jeep as we neared the complex where Druce Kevern had lived. In the parking lot, a rusting Toyota sat on blocks, its hood up. Three guys leaned over the engine. A small mesquite blocked some of the sun for them. Almost qualified as a shade tree.

"I'll drive around the back side first if you don't mind," Flint said.

I nodded. Given the questionable neighborhood, I'd have taken the same step. The back of the complex was quiet, though, and after circling, Flint parked again in front.

"I'll come with you," he announced.

I didn't object. Two were better than one in this neighborhood. We followed the sign pointing to the manager's office. I pushed the bell and waited, brushing away flies that approached more eagerly than the manager did. Inside the building, a football crowd cheered amidst TV commentary.

"Just a minute." There was a rattle of a security chain, and a man opened the door. "Sorry. Summer exhibition game with those Cardinals. Thought maybe their luck had changed." He was a smallish man with a bony nose and a thinning comb-over.

"Did they win?" Flint asked.

"Nope, lost again." The manager surveyed us. "Renting? How about a nice two-bedroom on the second floor. Has a view of Shaw Butte, almost."

Great. Now apartment managers took us for a couple. I'd make my own decisions about that, thank you. I introduced myself, showed my badge, and asked about Druce Kevern.

"Druce was quiet, unlike some." The manager looked with disapproval at the group out front. "Haven't seen him around lately. Past due on his rent, too. Hope he didn't skip. Got a warrant?"

He looked at us and shrugged. "Doesn't matter, always like to cooperate with the law." He slipped into some Crocs and grabbed a huge key ring from a hook by the door. "Follow me."

We wound our way through an interior concrete passageway, and then up an outside stairway to a balcony edging the second floor like a cheap motel. The manager halted in front of a corner apartment and swung the ring around trying to locate the right key.

The door stuck when he pushed it open. "Monsoons," he said. "Ups the humidity and the doors swell. I'll be downstairs. Second game coming up. Maybe the 49'ers will have better luck." He switched on the fan and left.

The apartment smelled musty. It had needed paint ten years ago and still did. In the living room, one Venetian blind hung at an angle. Another had quit trying and lay in a heap on the floor. A dusty couch and small TV on a rickety thrift store stand completed the decor.

I moved to the kitchen and opened the refrigerator. It contained a box of half-eaten pizza, the crust shrunken and rigid. That and a jar of pickle juice. A pile of beer bottles that had missed the bucket shot surrounded the trashcan.

I went into the bedroom with Flint tripping on my heels. The closet doors were open. Coat hangers dangled from one another like a cheap mobile. Dirty clothes mounded in a smelly heap in one corner. Gingerly I poked through them. No telling what lived there.

"Hey, what have we here?" asked Flint. "I didn't know they made these anymore." He pointed to an old Remington typewriter on a decrepit table. A plastic patio chair faced it, and beside it sat a wastebasket full of crumpled paper.

I reached into the basket and grabbed one wad. Pulled it apart and started to read. "Dear Mrs. Jance, it is me, your son, Bryan. I have wanted to contact you for such a long time. . ." I pulled out another paper ball. "Dear Mrs. Heaton, it is me, your Sonny. We have never spoken, but I feel I know you. I am currently in a work-study program so that I can finish my law degree. I so want to meet you!" There had to be half a dozen false starts in the wastebasket.

"Our Druce has been a busy boy," I said.

"No kidding," said Flint. "What was he doing, scamming these poor mothers?"

"That's what it looks like." I should have anticipated something like this. Druce's mother said her son was a schemer, but inside, I hoped she was wrong. Apparently not.

Druce Kevern used his job to gain access to mothers who had given up their sons for adoption. The paper scraps in the wastebasket were proof that he'd been setting up introductions to them so he could run a con. I wondered how much money he reaped with his hard-luck story of going back to school.

How could these birth mothers be so gullible? It came down to love and need, I thought. Most cons had a grain of truth at their core, preying on people's desires. Alice Heaton was living example of that.

I was surprised Druce lasted at the agency as long as he had. I wondered if Mrs. Bradford-Smythe had any idea of the magnitude of trouble coming her company's way when these birth mothers realized what Druce Kevern had done.

And they *would* find out, I'd make sure of that. I smoothed the rest of the letters and placed them in a rough stack to turn over to local authorities. Let the chips fall where they may, these women deserved to know their "sons" were not all they had expected them to be.

I glanced around the apartment but didn't see anything else of import. The more I discovered about Druce Kevern, the less I liked him. However, no one deserved to die at such a young age, even a crook like him. I checked my watch. Time to leave if we wanted to beat the Phoenix rush-hour traffic. It could be brutal once the hi-tech plants let their employees leave at the end of the day shift.

"Let's go," I said.

We stopped at a Circle K where I bought five jugs of water for HT's beast of a truck, and a huge Diet Coke and a box of Jr. Mints for me. Flint flipped through the auto magazines while he waited for me.

He watched with an expression of amusement, as I propped open the Circle-K door with my elbow and swiveled around, loaded down with water jugs like a pack mule. Made no offer to help. That's the problem with being an independent woman—the door swings both ways. When we neared the Jeep, he tossed me the Jeep keys.

I grabbed for them, dropped the jugs, saved the Coke, and missed the keys. They thudded at my feet. I stifled my impulse to growl at him. It was just too damn hot. I bent to retrieve the keys and clicked open his passenger door without comment.

All the initial teasing between us at the adoption agency had vanished. I was no mind reader, which meant I had trouble figuring out what men expected. Was he ticked off because I'd been poor company? I sniffed under one arm. I could use a shower after all the Phoenix heat. Maybe that was it.

"Know the way back? I'm ready for some shut-eye," he announced.

He pulled his hat down over his eyes and snored softly while I pushed through the stop-and-go traffic that turned the freeway into one huge parking lot. A stress headache built against my temple. I could have used a nap myself.

A half-hour later, I spotted the truck on the other side of the freeway. Still there with all four tires intact. I signaled for the next exit beyond the truck, crossed over, and re-entered the freeway going back toward Phoenix.

I pulled in behind my grandfather's pickup, grabbed two of the plastic water jugs and sprung open the truck hood. The thirsty radiator drank those and looked around for more. When I started the truck, it hiccupped once and then settled down to a syncopated rumble. Good so far. I turned it off and returned to the Jeep. Opening the passenger door, I flipped the keys into Flint's lap.

I rattled off my ready-made speech. "Thanks for taking the time to help me. You went out of your way, and I appreciate it. Maybe I can return the favor someday."

As far as I was concerned, that was the end of it.

"Oh, are we there already?" Flint unfolded his long legs and exited the Jeep in one easy motion. He found a break in traffic, walked to the driver's side and then paused. He met my gaze across the top of the Jeep. "Anytime, Quincy." I could have sworn that he winked at me as he opened the door and disappeared into the Jeep.

I drove the now obedient pickup to the next exit, U-turned once more and began the five-mile grade up Black Canyon. I should have stopped at a repair shop to check the radiator, but I was too hot to care. Flint followed for a distance, then passed my staid sixty-miles-per-hour and zoomed out of sight. He'd be in Mingus before I even hit the Camp Verde turnoff.

I tried to be philosophic about it. Cops sometimes had to talk to dozens of witnesses, had to sift through hundreds of facts, before that one surfaced to turn a case. This Phoenix trip might have given me that one.

I rolled down both windows, unbuttoned an indecent number of buttons on my shirt, and braced against the stiff bench seat for the slow miles to reach home.

CHAPTER NINE

DARKNESS FELL BY THE TIME I reached Mingus. The big dipper was a resplendent counterpoint to a crescent moon just breaking the opposite horizon. I pulled into HT's drive, shut off the ignition, and headed for the house.

A porch light winked out as I walked toward the building, plunging the walkway into blackness. I climbed the outside stairs by feel, one hand on the railing, making a note to tell HT about the bulb in the morning. Shoot, if I could find a spare one, I'd replace it myself.

As I reached the third-floor landing, I stumbled over a soft form that yelped in pain. Now what?

I pulled out my flash and illuminated a small brown dog who shook floppy ears and backed away whimpering. Its ribs showed clearly, and its eyes stared at me, perhaps fearing a second kick.

"Hey little guy, it's okay," I said, holding out my fist for it to sniff.

HT opened his bedroom door on the ground floor. He peered up at the light, shading his eyes. "Peg, that you?" he hollered.

I leaned over the balcony. "Yeah, sorry for the noise." The light of my flash accented his wrinkles and stubbly cheeks. How old he looked!

I swung my flashlight to point at the dog. "What is this?"

"Oh, that. It's Ben's new dog. A Rez reject."

"What's it doing *here*?"

He looked nonplussed in the light's glare. "Ben's bunking with us. He and Armor got in a fight."

"He's bunking *where*?" Something told me I really didn't want to know.

"Well, he's sleeping up in the loft with you right now. We'll figure out something in the morning."

"You're darned right we will. I'm going to bed." I stalked to the loft door tripping over the dog the whole way. When I opened the door, he pushed ahead of me and hid behind a blanket-covered Ben, asleep on the floor.

I kicked off my shoes and stumbled into bed, not bothering to undress. HT and I would go head-to-head on this loft-sharing arrangement, soon.

* * * * * *

WHEN I AWOKE the next morning, Ben and the dog were gone. I pulled my red hair into a quick braid and splashed my face with cold water. I didn't look forward to the conflict ahead, but HT and I had to come to an understanding. I was not sharing this living space with my clerk and a smelly dog. This just was not happening.

HT and I were still tiptoeing around the financial argument we'd had the other night. Nothing was resolved. The real estate taxes were still due, and I had no idea how to find money to pay them. It should be *his* problem, not mine, anyway. That made the upcoming conversation about the squatters in the loft even more painful. One more barrier between us.

I clumped downstairs and shoved opened the kitchen door. HT sat at the table, his attention focused on a hummingbird feeder just outside the window. "Look at those little guys. They're feisty and hungry."

"Like Ben and that dog, right?"

"Ellie, they won't cause no trouble. He didn't have any place else to go."

I sighed and let the misbegotten name go unchallenged. "I can't bunk with a damn teenager. The kid *works* for me, for Pete's sake. And that dog. What's he calling it, anyway?"

"Bitzer."

"What sort of an idiot name is that?"

"Well, Ben says it's because the dog's a bit of this and a bit of that, just like he is. Fix you a cup?" He reached behind him for the coffeepot.

I sat down, accepting his peace offering. Not that I was forgetting the flea-bitten dog in the loft—*my* loft—or the boy who owned him. Someone was leaving, and it wasn't going to be me.

"How did the trip down south go?" he asked.

"Radiator needs work."

"I was meaning to caution you about that. Did you add some water? That usually does it. Truck's getting old. But it's got some good miles left in it yet, just like me."

I just grunted, remembering the long hot drive. I told him about the truck breakdown and Flint Tanner's rescue. "He said he knew you."

"Does. His daddy, Jake Tanner, used to be a cop around here. Lost track of them when they moved east. Glad to see Flint back. I liked his daddy. I like him."

He pushed back his chair and put his hand on my shoulder. "Come sit with me a spell."

I grabbed my coffee and joined him on the porch swing. I rocked my body, setting the swing in motion leaving one foot anchored on the porch, as my grandfather had taught me when I was four before the family troubles started.

The swing tilted gently back and forth creating its own breeze. Isabel's garden smelled of roses and mint. The valley spread below us, going all checkerboardy with the gathering clouds. My eyes followed a red-tailed hawk climbing the thermals, and I breathed deeper. Work waited, but it felt like entering Eden to linger here for just a moment.

"So you met Flint. Then what happened the rest of the day?" HT asked.

I described the visit to the adoption agency and the trip to Kevern's apartment.

"Kevern, you say." His tone grew contemplative. "What first name might that be?"

"Druce. Druce Kevern."

The swing jerked to a halt.

"I'll be damned. After all these years."

"What do you mean?"

"Druce Kevern was the guy who set me up to take the rap on that burglary job that got me sent to prison. Always working the angles, Druce loved to scam folks." HT's voice held a bitter note. "Probably scamming me, too. I trusted that kid, wanted to give him a chance. Big mistake."

Then he told me the whole story. How my grandfather had gotten wind of a bookmaker with a stash. He figured if he stole from a thief, there was a good chance the burglary wouldn't be reported. HT made plans to visit the house when the man was out of town. Druce begged to come along, and HT let him. What he didn't know was the cops had the house under surveillance.

"Druce just panicked," HT said. "He shot the first uniform through the door and ran. I didn't even know he had a gun."

HT chose to stay, stemming the flow of blood from the cop's arterial wound until the emergency techs arrived.

"They said I saved his life." HT's voice held wondering pride, even now.

I was starting to get the drift. "And that officer, might his name be Abner Jones?"

"Yeah, that's him. Head of the sheriff's department now. He recommended leniency for me, but the judge disagreed."

And with that, HT spent five years, five long years, in jail. My mind raced ahead. The job offer that came unexpectedly at exactly the right time, *my* job offer for this summer position in Mingus, was the quid pro quo between lawman and crook. They were even.

So now I knew. I got this job, not because of my qualifications, but because of favors between two old enemies. And that put me even further in the debt of my grandfather. I didn't like that fact, and I'd deal with it at some point. There was no way to sugarcoat Druce Kevern's cowardly actions that led to my grandfather's imprisonment.

But the young man was dead, and that death was my responsibility. The argument with HT would have to wait for another time. I had a job to do. I dressed in my uniform and headed into work.

* * * * * *

I ADMIT I WAS WOOL-GATHERING when I reached the station door and turned the handle. My foot followed automatically, and rammed into a door that refused to budge. My big toe exploded with pain. "What the hell—"

The wood had swollen with the higher humidity and stuck, just like the door at Druce Kevern's apartment. I shoved harder and the door suddenly released, hurtling me into the office.

Ben's head jerked up from the computer screen. "Morning, Boss."

Surely, the town's sole law enforcement officer deserved better than this run-down office. We didn't have to exist like homeless wildies. Besides, my toe throbbed in agony. Resentments about having to settle for whatever dregs were left in the sheriff's department boiled to the surface.

"Who are we renting this place from?" I shouted at Ben. "They need to get a move on and fix this door. Install a decent dead bolt lock, too, while they're at it." I stormed into my office and slammed the door.

There was a quiet knock a few moments later. "Come," I barked.

Ben offered me a cup of coffee and then retreated from the line of fire. His manner reminded me of the dog on the stairs. Did he fear me? First, that Flint guy dumped me, and now my clerk cowered like I was a many-headed monster. It seemed that the harder I tried to exercise good people skills, the clumsier I became.

I turned to an easier topic for me, the death of the man on the hill. My thoughts twisted and shaped the facts of the Druce Kevern case into yet another what-if. That's what I was good at. That's what got me into the Police Academy and that's what helped me pass all those God-awful exams.

I'd learned to trust the click of those mental tiles sliding into place, like that plastic puzzle with numbered tiles. Four rows of four possible, with one space left over for good measure. They didn't start in numbered order but were randomly stacked.

By using that one empty space you could move tiles this way and that, and then shift that whole row backward and then up. Finally, the tiles would line up, numbers one to fifteen with one space left over. Solving a case was like that if you had all the pieces. I was still missing a few on this one.

I had to discover if someone else was on that cliff the night Druce fell to his death. The lady at the café had identified Druce and described a fight between two men. Roger Heaton denied talking to Druce, but his alibi was shaky.

And then there was the problem of my granddad's pickup. Its tire tracks were all over that mountain, and Armor had illicit operations up there, by HT's admission. Maybe Druce had just ventured into the wrong place at the wrong time.

The boot print. That was a missing tile in the puzzle, too. My clerk had worn nothing but neon green sneakers since I'd seen him. Boots didn't seem his style. But *somebody* had worn them, and it wasn't Druce Kevern.

HT's surprise at hearing Druce Kevern's name seemed genuine. Or was it? How well did I know my grandfather, truly? I had to face the fact that anyone could commit murder, given enough incentive. HT'd been confined to a six by eight cell those long years, waiting to touch green grass and hear birds sing again. Could that experience create a desire to punish, even murder, the coward who caused it?

I shied away from that unwelcome thought. No need to go down that path just yet. HT was my closest relative now that my mom had entered the dementia twilight. I needed to trust and rely on him, no matter what his past had held.

The phone rang and I put down my coffee mug to answer it.

It was Melda, the dispatcher. "Vanessa Heaton just called. She says her mother is threatening to kill herself."

"Is there a crisis counseling service as a backup?"

"Sorry, you're it. Vanessa asked for you. She said you gave her your card."

I swore under my breath as I ran out the door and climbed into the squad car. I knew all too well where I was going from my previous visits. The old Crown Vic was still accelerating when I reached the hill to the Heaton Victorian.

I opened the car door at the drive and Vanessa ran to me. "My dad's on a business trip and I didn't know who else to call." Her blonde hair was tangled and she had a rip in one sweater sleeve. She breathed heavily, her mascara smeared as though she had been crying.

I walked her to the porch. "What's going on inside?"

She took a gasping breath. “My mom isn’t taking her pills. She didn't sleep last night or the night before. She's muttering something about that guy who died.”

“Druce Kevern?”

“Mom says she killed him.” Vanessa shivered. “She didn’t do that, did she? And now she's talking about killing herself with the remaining dueling pistol.”

I patched through to Melda to give my status. She said the EMTs were on their way. Then I retrieved my bulletproof vest from the trunk of the car and shrugged into its stiff weight. I wondered if Alice was a good shot and whether she’d consider me an enemy, too. I hoped not.

The door squeaked when it opened, and I had the irrational thought that 3-in-one oil would fix that. “Alice, I'm coming in. I don't have a gun.” Well, at least not a drawn one. I’d never talked down a suicide before, and I sent a small prayer skyward.

“Go away.” Her shriek echoed through the empty house.

I found Alice backed into a corner of the living room, waving the dueling pistol inlaid with topaz unsteadily. She wore an old negligee and her feet were bare. Her hair stuck out in spikes and her eyes were unfocused and staring. But she was alive.

“I'll kill myself,” she threatened. Her voice was raspy, as though she'd been screaming.

“Not a good idea. Think of Vanessa. She needs you.” I tried to keep my tone low and soothing.

“Nobody needs me. I want to die.”

I jerked as the door behind me opened. Vanessa poked her head in, her voice breathless. “The ambulance is coming, I hear the sirens.”

I didn't need two unstable females on my hands. I waved her back with an impatient gesture. “Go sit in the squad car.”

The girl retreated and I turned to face Alice.

With a sudden motion of her free hand, she grabbed a vase of roses and threw it at me. I ducked and it hit the side wall with a smash. Shattered glass and water ricocheted into my path. I advanced, the glass crunching underfoot. Alice backed away, a wild look in her eyes.

I had to calm her down.

"Alice, can you understand me? I'm here to help. I won't hurt you."

The pistol wobbled. "Go away. I don't want to talk to anyone."

"You've got Vanessa worried. You don't want to worry Vanessa, do you?" I slowed my words, as though speaking to a small child.

Alice looked puzzled. "Vanessa? What is she doing here?"

"Vanessa is your daughter, remember?"

"I don't have a daughter. I have a son, and I've killed him!" The woman was in her own brand of hell.

"Alice, are your feet getting cold?" I said, trying to distract her.

Alice looked down at her bare toes. I took a short breath and crept to the middle of the room. A few steps more and I could grab the gun.

"Alice, I want you to listen to me. Are you listening?"

She nodded.

"Set your pistol down on the floor. Please."

Alice looked at the gun and slowly turned it toward herself.

I dove for her and wrestled the heavy pistol barrel away from its target. Alice's fingers clenched on it and we struggled. Then she let go and collapsed on the floor, crying uncontrollably. I set the gun far out of reach and gently pulled her to her feet, moving her in the other direction.

It was over.

She collapsed in my arms and I half carried her to a couch. "Hey there. It's okay." Stabilizing the woman was my first concern. The pistol would keep.

I shifted Alice's feet onto a pillow. "Soft now, you're going to be fine." I gently stroked her hair, calming her as I would a horse that had bolted at some imaginary terror.

"I killed him. I killed him," Alice moaned, shaking her head from side to side.

My own vision widened from the narrow black-and-white tunnel my stress created, and I started to think again. Maybe Alice had killed Druce Kevern, and maybe she hadn't. The woman's mind was broken, and until it was put right, the truth would remain locked inside.

The EMT crew knocked and then came in. Vanessa followed close after. I caught my breath in jerky starts. Had I been holding it?

The lead tech approached Alice. "Did you threaten to kill yourself?"

She nodded sullenly.

"If we leave you here, might you try it again?"

Again the nod.

The corpsmen stepped to a corner and conferred.

Then they addressed Vanessa. "This your mom?"

She shrugged.

"Well, we think your mother is a danger to herself. It might be best if she went into protective care for a twenty-four hour period. Are you okay with that?"

"Fine. Whatever."

"Can you walk on your own, Mrs. Heaton?" Getting her assurance that she could, they aided her down the steps and into the waiting emergency van.

After they left, silence filled the room. I walked over and picked up the dueling pistol. The gun was heavy in my hand and still seemed to carry Alice's warmth. Whatever its original owner had intended, the gleaming topaz in the grip had not brought this family good fortune.

Or maybe it had. When I checked the barrel, I discovered it held no charge. Alice had been threatening to take her life with an unloaded gun—She'd been safe all along.

But I didn't know that, and probably neither did she. The threat had been real. And next time the gun might be loaded. The woman needed help.

In the moments that followed, I did what I could to restore order. I needed some physical release, and picking up the shattered bits of crystal and flowers helped put closure on the event for me. Vanessa followed my lead in a half-hearted manner, sweeping the remaining glass shards into a dustpan and straightening the couch.

The situation had been tough for me, but I wondered about the girl beside me. Did it even bother her that her mom had just about died?

"You going to be all right?"

She shrugged. "I got hold of my dad," Vanessa said in a tired voice. "He's on his way home."

"Anyone you can call to stay with you until he gets here?"

Her mouth twisted bitterly. “You don’t understand—this is my life.”

I put a tentative hand on her shoulder but she jerked it off. I could have left it at that, but the girl’s well-being worried me. So I tried one last time. “Look, at least let me take the pistol into custody. Keep it safe for you.”

She glared at me, her eyes filling with tears. “You can melt it into slag for all I care. It's caused nothing but trouble.”

I carefully replaced the pistol in the leather box. Then I walked down to the squad car and put the case in the trunk. I stripped off my sweat-stained protective vest and dumped it in, too.

I hadn’t been in mortal danger, but my body didn’t know that. Merely navigating the switchbacks to return to the station became an effort as my revved-up adrenaline drained away.

The Heatons. What misfortune, when a family’s meaning and purpose focused on the combination of Alice’s mental state and Roger’s drinking. Did they even consider the accumulated effect it must have had on their child? I wasn’t sure how I could help Vanessa, or even if I should try. At least with the gun out of the house, she’d be safer.

Yet, somewhere in the midst of this family tragedy, there was a connection. The missing dueling pistol inlaid with ruby and the decades-old adoption issue tied Druce Kevern to these people, too.

The tiles moved and shifted in my mind, but no order emerged. I could sense it was in there waiting for me if I could only find the missing piece.

I put the Heaton topaz pistol in the office safe and clocked out early, leaving Ben in charge. Stripping off my uniform in the bathroom at HT’s loft, I changed into running shorts, T-shirt and my Adidas.

I jogged for three miles, climbing hill after hill above the town. In the distance across the valley, the red hills of Sedona glowed in the setting sun and then disappeared into the blue haze of twilight.

Finally, tension released, I returned to HT’s house. My grandfather, at least, was alive and well. The disagreements we’d had seemed small in comparison to the events of the day. And I’d find out what happened to Druce Kevern. It was just a matter of time.

CHAPTER TEN

THE NEXT MORNING, I drove to the Cottonwood Medical Center, half an hour from Mingus, to check on Alice Heaton's condition. The desk clerk looked up Alice's name on the roster and directed me to a lock-down facility at the far end of the first floor.

I'd never been in this part of the hospital and took several wrong turns before I found the right corridor. The ward nurse squinted through the wired entrance window at the ID that I presented to her. The release clicked and she pointed to a square pressure plate to the left of the door. I pushed it, and the door slowly opened.

The nurse was in her forties, thin and quiet on crepe-soled shoes. She checked that the lock was secure after me. The dim interior hallway lent gravitas to the ward as I followed her. Dark to keep the inmates quiet? The faint odor of disinfectant mingled with the smells of institutional meals awaiting breakfast delivery to the rooms.

We passed one room where a man tipped a bowl of oatmeal over his head. "Oh, Hank," the aid snapped. "Why'd you do that? Now I'll just have to clean you up and start all over again." From another room, a woman called out, "I want to go home. Please help me, please help me, please." Her wails of abandonment echoed down the hall.

The nurse glanced at me to see my reaction. "This is a community mental ward. The saddest are the dementia patients. Sometimes families just park them here for a few days to have a break at home. We try to help whenever we can."

I thought of my mother and wondered what her world was like now, living in a ward like this. It horrified me to consider she might not know where or who she was most of the time.

The nurse stopped by her station to flip open Alice Heaton's chart. She read for a moment, her lips moving slightly as she deciphered the doctors' scrawls. Then she instructed me to check in with the psychiatrist on duty, a Dr. Cravets, to get more details before visiting with Room 123. She'd just read the chart with the woman's name plastered all over it, but already Alice had become a number. Now I remembered why I didn't like institutions.

The doctor looked up when I entered his office, a spare man with gray, buzz-cut hair. "Take a seat," he said, clearing a stack of charts off the chair by his desk. He looked tired, as if he'd been up all night.

"I've come about Alice Heaton."

"I thought somebody might be by. It took us a while to get her calmed down last night. Something about a gun and her children. She was babbling a lot that I didn't understand."

"She threatened to kill herself," I said.

He looked up sharply. "How?"

"A gun. Unloaded."

He nodded, apparently not surprised. "That's a new one. Glad the weapon wasn't lethal. Alice is no stranger to our ward. When she's on her meds, she's fine. Off them is another story. She can get manic, delusional."

"Would she ever lie?"

"Oh, frequently, I presume. Don't we all?" The doctor smiled briefly.

"Do you feel she'd ever get violent enough in one of her delusional states to hurt someone?"

"Herself, you mean? Anything is possible. She's threatened suicide several times, but it's hard to predict if she'd actually go through with it. Never successful so far, thank God. I think it may be a way to manipulate her daughter and husband when things aren't going her way. And those words are just my personal, not professional, opinion at this point. That and five dollars will get you a Starbuck's latte." Again, he smiled.

I tried to pin him down a little. "Could Alice be capable of hurting someone else?" I wanted his professional opinion on her potential to hurt her son.

"Hard to say. She could, I suppose, in one of her manic moods." He called the nurses' station for her chart. Flipping up the metal cover, he reviewed his own notes. "She's responding to the anti-psychotics. Unfortunately, the mood stabilizers take longer. I'd like to keep her a few days for observation, but given the insurance guidelines, she's due to be released this afternoon. As long as there is somebody at the house with her, she should be fine."

He set the chart down on his desk. "Look, I've got to finish rounds. If you discover anything in your investigations that might help in her treatment, let me know."

He rose, the interview over. Locking his door behind us, he zipped down the hall, clipboard in hand. I wondered how many hours a week he put in. Being the only shrink in the hospital, sometimes it might be 24-7. He was already at the end of the hall disappearing into another room by the time I returned to the nurses' station.

The floor nurse directed me to Alice's room halfway down the ward. She was sitting up in bed, reading a current copy of Martha Stewart's *Living* magazine. Made sense, that the doyenne of perfection and good taste would be her idol. Alice had combed her hair, and she wore pink fleece pajamas, not the skimpy hospital kind. Roger sat hunched in a straight-back chair beside the bed.

He rose when I entered. "Deputy Quincy, I thought you might be in this morning, so I waited. Alice has something to tell you."

Alice set down the magazine and looked up brightly. She appeared alert and cogent. The meds must be working.

"First, I want to thank you for intervening yesterday. I hadn't slept for two nights, and I must have been overreacting because I was so tired." She stopped and glanced over at Roger.

He nodded slightly in encouragement and gestured for her to continue.

"It was my fault the pistol was left out so that it could be taken by that thief. I'm to blame. I was careless, but I didn't kill anyone." She started to cry.

Roger took up the narrative. "What my wife means is that she set in motion some unfortunate actions that might have affected someone." Alice started to shiver uncontrollably and Roger stood abruptly. "You're upsetting my wife. You need to leave. You can talk to her later." He put a hand under my elbow and nudged me toward the door.

"Take your hand off me." I detest being touched by strangers.

He dropped my arm, immediately conciliatory. “Of course. I didn't mean anything. May I see you out in the hall, please?” He closed the door firmly behind us. “I didn't want to upset my wife. I—we all—have been through a lot. But if you want to talk to her again, I must insist our attorney be present.”

“We can arrange that.” I was in no mood to give him an inch.

“And the pistol you took from my house?”

“The one inlaid with topaz. With Vanessa’s permission.”

“With my daughter’s permission,” he admitted. “It’s worth a lot of money, even if only one-half of a set. I’d like to pick it up soon.”

It wasn’t part of a murder investigation—yet. “Give me your assurance that you’ll keep it where Alice can't touch it, and I'll release it to you this afternoon.”

“Oh, I'll take full responsibility.”

I just bet he would. Somehow, the value of the antique pistol seemed more important to him than his wife’s welfare. But, then, what did I know?

He opened Alice's door to rejoin her, leaving me standing there.

Disk-shaped ceiling mirrors monitored my progress toward the locked exit of the ward, their distorted images lending an air of unreality to the scene I’d experienced. With a metallic click, the nurse released the lock on the heavy security door. I pushed it open and walked through. My steps hurried, I retraced my way to the main hospital entrance and out into the morning sunshine.

I felt lighter, as though I’d been released from prison. Was this how my grandfather had felt, leaving his cell for the last time? I was starting to understand, a little, his mixed reaction to Druce Kevern’s death.

* * * * * *

BACK AT MY OFFICE, a jumble of brown pellets decorated the corner of my credenza.

Ben wandered in and poked at the pile with a pencil. “Looks like rat shit,” he said.

“Yuck. Don't do that.” I took a piece of paper and scraped the mess into the wastebasket. “Where did it come from?”

"It's probably from Herman. I thought we had him under control, but maybe he's made another nest since Cyrus left. He's a *neotoma albigula.*"

Ah, a packrat. I knew that one from biology class. One of those nature movies the science instructor had tucked away to entertain us on rainy days. When I wasn't passing notes to my best friend Becky Jean, I'd tune in occasionally. Especially when something squirmy like rats was involved.

According to the film, packrats built their middens, or nests, in the midst of cactus, because the thorns deterred predators like coyotes from reaching them. The rats were avid collectors, which meant the middens contained a wide variety of found objects. Because successive generations of pack rats might use a single midden, anthropologists sometimes studied them to delve into the early history of an area.

We didn't have a lot of prickly pear cactus in Tennessee where my high school was, but I'd dodged mountains of the stuff on my hill runs since I'd come to Mingus. In fact, there had even been patches of it up at the burned campsite.

I thought for a moment. Revisiting the burn site to look for what pack rat middens might contain offered another chance at evidence collection. Moreover, it got me out of the office and into the clear mountain air for a few hours. A lot more fun than writing traffic tickets.

I needed some special equipment to dig around in cactus piles, so I left Ben to deal with the office packrat problem and walked over to the firehouse. I wasn't above benign coercion. Patrick Shaw might be bothered enough about disturbing a possible crime scene to lend me some gear.

Sure enough, he outfitted me with a Pulaski, that combination hoe and pickaxe, for pulling the packrat middens apart, a good pair of boots a volunteer had donated to the unit, and a dust mask as protection against the hantavirus rodents might spread.

"*Humans* can catch that?"

"Yeah, but not likely. Anyway, it's usually carried by deer mice, not pack rats." He loaded all the gear in a box and carried it to the squad car for me.

Great. Now I was becoming an expert in rodent control. Somehow, his assurance did not bring me comfort. Maybe I needed one of those white Haz-Mat suits. Nah. I doubted they had a lady's version in my size anyway.

I drove to the top of Black Mountain and took the right fork in the road this time. As I arrived at the burn site, the meadow turned dark and then light as storm clouds passed in front of the sun. I checked my watch: two o'clock already. I'd need to hurry to finish before the afternoon rains poured down on my investigation.

Ben had told me packrats usually ventured no farther than about ten meters from their lair, so it was likely if they took anything from the campsite, it would be close.

Taking the tent as a center point, I walked in an expanding spiral. The first prickly pear clump I encountered was empty, except for a Gambel's quail that took sudden zooming flight at my approach.

The second prickly pear was dying. White fuzz attacked the cactus pads, evidence of a cochineal bug infestation. Funny to find cochineals, those bugs used to make the brilliant red dye for Roman cloaks, here in Arizona.

The base of the third cactus held a maze of twigs, feathers, and cloth, glued into a solid mass by a hard brown substance: *Amber-rat,* dried packrat urine. I'd found a pack rat nest. What I'd hoped.

Perhaps the midden might hold something of interest to my case. I returned to the squad car to suit up for the expedition. The fire chief's cautions echoing in my ears, I changed into a long-sleeved shirt, put on standard-issue cop gloves, and the filter mask. The mask immediately clung to my nostrils as I breathed in and sweat beaded on my forehead.

The filters blocked most of the dusty cloud billowing from the pile, but then my eyes started to water. Ashes exploded upward from a nearby cactus patch as I poked at it and I sneezed. Did this work fit into my job description? If so, I needed a raise—big one.

I used the Pulaski to clear the area around the cactus and then started to disassemble the midden. The pads broke off easily when I pulled on them with my gloved hands and soon a big stack of them rose to the side. I switched again to the shovel and thrust it into the pile, splintering the hardened brown goo.

Then I started to encounter pack rat treasures: one Nehi bottle cap and bits of small animal bone. A used condom rested on top of an old shotgun shell, the blue paper hull tattered and wadded around the brass primer. Plastic hulls had replaced paper in the eighties so this nest had to be decades old.

I leaned on the Pulaski, taking a breather with sweat dripping from beneath my hat and my shirt damp in the growing humidity. Thunder rumbled and I returned to work with renewed determination. Once the rains started, the rest of the exposed nest would disintegrate in a hurry.

I sifted through the debris as quickly as I could, dribbling bits and pieces through my gloved fingers. Then I spotted a glint of metal in the midst of the cactus barrier. Maneuvering carefully around the thorns, I cleared an opening around a small gold-colored object. A beautiful gold crucifix dangled on a bit of broken chain, irresistible to any well-meaning packrat.

I fished out my cell phone and took a picture before I carefully untangled it from the twigs. I pulled a set of tweezers from my pack and wiggled the small bit of metal free. I'm no antique dealer, but this piece looked ancient—maybe hundreds of years old— and well worn, like it had been touched often. The Christ figure was smiling, also unusual. I wrapped it in cotton and placed it in a small evidence box.

No telling how long it had been there. This gold piece might have something to do with Druce Kevern's death, or it might have rested for thirty years in the midden like that shotgun shell. Maybe worth fingerprinting.

You had to sift a lot of chaff to get to the wheat, my Police Academy instructor always said. In this case, which would the crucifix prove to be?

CHAPTER ELEVEN

I'D BARELY RETURNED to the office and put the crucifix in the office safe when Mrs. Kevern called.

"Did you find Druce's boots?"

"What boots?" I asked. "Describe them." The elusive footprint at the campsite. Maybe it belonged to Druce Kevern, after all. But if so, where were the boots?

"They was this bright purple. Druce was real proud of them, showed 'em off the last time he was up here. I was thinking what you said about his funeral and all."

"Yeah?"

"If we could sell them boots, maybe that would pay for the services."

Where did this "we" come from all of a sudden? Last time I looked, I wasn't in the shoe auction business. "Were they Lucccheses?"

"That sounds like what he told me. Druce bragged he'd bought 'em for next to nothing, but that they was worth a lot more. I said well if you can afford to buy them fancy boots, maybe you can help your mother out a little here." I could hear her take a drag on her cigarette.

"Sorry, nothing like that at the apartment in Phoenix. I'll keep a lookout." I grabbed the Kevern file and thumbed through it. "Something else, though. When Druce got 'let go' down at the work-study agency in Phoenix, you know where he moved to?"

"He didn't come home to take care of me, that's for sure. I told him he couldn't stay here, anyways, less he paid me rent. He said he didn't have any money, but that he was going to get some soon. If he had enough money to buy them boots, he could have paid me rent, don't you think? That's what a good son does for his mother."

Mrs. Kevern's voice turned querulous, almost whiny, and I had a sudden sympathy for her dead son.

She thought some more. "Oh, yeah, I remember. When he came back from Phoenix he called to tell me he had a new job at some halfway house, a ranch sort of place here in the Verde, working with horses."

I thumbed through a worn copy of the Yellow Pages while I talked. HT had told me of a horse farm where they worked with young men with problems. Found an entry under "equine." "Might that have been the House of New Directions in Camp Verde?"

"Yeah, that sounds like it. I don't think he lasted long there, neither. His parole officer was looking for him, too." Her voice brightened. "Now what about them boots?"

"Well, if we find them, I'll let you know."

"Oh, okay." She turned vague and disinterested since the boots were no longer a possibility for financial gain. I wondered if Mrs. Kevern had intended to sell them for Druce's funeral or for money for herself. I'd heard of combat soldiers divvying up the clothing and personal items of a dead comrade. Perhaps this was no different. Survival.

The manager at the halfway house, Regina Smith, answered when I dialed the number. When I told her that Druce Kevern was dead, she seemed shocked but accepted the bad news as if she'd been anticipating it. I'd find out more when I talked to her in person. We set an appointment for the following day.

* * * * * *

THE NEXT MORNING, I found the New Directions Ranch at the end of a long dirt road outside Camp Verde, about an hour from Mingus. A primitive fence surrounded the property, the uprights fashioned from notched juniper branches and the old barbed wire hanging loose in spots. Turning left at the crudely lettered sign for New Directions, I bounced over a cattle guard and drove past yet more velvet mesquite, catclaw acacia, and a lot of brown dirt. The squad car threw up a dusty cloud when I braked for rocks in the road, and my sinuses clogged.

A young man raking a paddock opened an inner compound gate for me. Three large dogs wearing red bandannas circled the cruiser as I pulled in, and I slowed to a crawl to miss them. To my left was a corrugated metal barn and a riding arena fenced with welded galvanized pipe. Chickens clucked in the yard, and an earthy compost smell drifted through my open window.

A large, rawboned woman in her mid-sixties greeted me on the porch of the run-down ranch house. She wore a faded orange polo shirt with the ranch insignia above the right pocket. Her jeans hung on skinny hips, and she cinched her waist with a leather belt decorated with a big rodeo buckle. Manure splotched her low-heeled work boots, and a sweat-stained felt hat hid tangles of sun-bleached hair.

"Deputy Quincy, welcome to the House of New Directions. Call me Regina." She gave me a firm handshake, once up and down, and then led me inside.

We passed through a living room with a worn brown leather couch, one cushion patched with duct tape. The room had several wicker chairs misshapen from heavy use, a coffee table made from a chunk of aged juniper, and Navajo rugs scattered on the painted cement floor.

Regina led me past half a dozen young men prepping the noon meal in the kitchen—a big bowl of salad, pasta. My always-hungry stomach growled at the aroma of freshly baked rolls.

In Regina's office, a rude iron cross hung on the wall and a smiling Buddha perched in one corner. The King James Version of the Bible, the Koran, and the Book of Mormon occupied a nearby bookshelf.

"Please sit," Regina said. "We are faith-based, but no particular religion. All do the Lord's work. But you came here to talk about Druce. What a waste of a young life. He was so intelligent."

She picked up a pack of cigarettes from her desk. "Mind if I smoke? I don't seem to be able to kick the habit." She lit one up and dropped the match in the ashtray. "I limit myself to three a day. Some of the kids here are fighting that same addiction demon. I don't make a very good role model."

She shrugged. "Druce washed out of his work-study in Phoenix and landed here at the ranch. We're known as the place of last resort. But he didn't stay here long, either. This isn't a lock-down facility, and unfortunately, that means if the boys want drugs they can find them. It becomes a vicious cycle: if a teen is using, he often won't take the legal psychotropic medications that will even out his behavior.

"And you think Druce was using?" I asked.

She nodded. "He was full of enthusiasm when he got here, very convincing. I believed him. And then he changed, started lying and stealing things."

"Stealing things?"

She touched her throat, and her fingers paused. "I'm missing a crucifix that my sister gave me. A piece that she had picked up in Italy, had to be over a century old. Unusual, really, in that the Christ figure was smiling, transfigured. It disappeared about the same time Druce did."

It was likely the crucifix I had discovered in the packrat midden. Yet I wanted to be sure before I mentioned it to Regina. I'd not get her hopes up until the crime lab reported back any findings. So I took a confirmatory route. "And you think he took it?"

"I believe so. If it gives—if it gave—him joy, then I let it go willingly." She paused for one last drag and then stabbed out the cigarette with an abrupt gesture. "It seems so hard to believe he is truly gone. Druce lived in this fantasy world. One minute he was going to be a cowboy and live by the Code of the West. The next, he wanted to be a real estate magnate.

"What he wanted most of all was for people to notice him, to treat him like a real person. I was quite fond of him. He had that effect on most people, I think, except his parents."

"I've met his mother."

She laughed shortly. "Isn't she a piece of work? His dad wasn't much better. Before he was killed in a meth lab explosion, he either ignored Druce or beat the crap out of him. My sister works for Child Protective Services. They got called out on a regular basis. Kids that come from abusive homes like that start life two steps behind the others. Some kids catch up. Druce never did."

"He was only here a short time?"

She nodded. “He wasn't following our rules. We don't have many, but the ones we do have are pretty strict. We're responsible for not only the safety of the boys but also the horses and other animals here. But Druce rebelled against any type of authority.”

“How did that play out?”

“Well, it was the cause of his leaving here. One day I cautioned him about the dangers of fire, and he set one in the stable hay three hours later. I told him he had to leave. His parole officer came by to collect him the morning after the incident, but by then he’d disappeared. That was about two weeks ago.”

“You sound regretful.”

“He's one of those that haunt me. Maybe somebody else could have reached him, even though I couldn’t. In a way, I don't blame him for running away. He didn't belong back in prison.”

“What was his job here?”

“Let me show you. Come.” Regina led me into the yard. The three dogs, eager for company, escorted us to the barn. Even with my long legs, I had to quicken my pace to keep up with her.

“These young men come to us angry and resentful,” she said. “Normal talk therapy won't bust through the strong defenses they've set up.”

“But a horse can?”

“Exactly. That’s why we call it Equine Assisted Therapy. A horse isn't a pet like a dog or a pussycat. It's a big animal you can't push around. And being a herd animal, the horse is exquisitely sensitive to non-verbal behavior.”

A young man in chinos and a black T-shirt worked a bay wearing a halter but no saddle in the arena ahead. A volunteer leaned against the rail, observing the boy and horse.

“What’s he trying to do?”

“The task is to get the horse to go where the human wants it to,” Regina said, “without talking to it or using a rope, just using body language. The exercise teaches the boys that yelling at the horse or cursing won’t work. These horses can be a wonderful metaphor for these young men's interactions with the people in their lives. The boys get very fond of their assigned horses and will do things for them that they’d refuse to do for authorities. Then in a strange way, I can’t explain, the new behaviors start to generalize to important people in their lives."

We entered a metal barn with a cleanly swept floor and tack arranged on pegs. The feed buckets carried the name of each individual horse, and bridles were carefully hung on designated wall hooks.

"You have a nice operation here," I commented.

"Thanks, we try. Now if the money would just start flowing in. We've got wonderful volunteers, don't get me wrong. But the costs are incredible. Last year was a bad hay crop and the costs rose. Today I just got the insurance bill—double what it was last year. We're barely making ends meet."

At the end of the barn, a jet-black horse was rubbing noses with a goat kid over the half-door. It reminded me of a horse I had made friends with once. When I was young we didn't have the money for riding lessons, but after school, I'd ride my bike down to the farm at the end of our road. There I'd feed sugar cubes lifted from the cafeteria to an old black mare. Maybe these kids could be influenced in a positive way, just as I had been.

Regina seemed to agree. "Handling these animals also creates good work habits the boys can carry into their future careers," she said, warming to her topic. "Caring for horses builds attention to detail and responsibility. For example, the boys learn that they can't show up late to feed a horse. They discover if they don't curry their mount and walk it after a workout, the animal can become ill. The boys learn that for every action there is a reaction."

She picked up a curry brush on the floor and placed it on a shelf. "It might be helpful for you to speak to Steve Nathan, Druce's roommate while he was here." She called out to a young man measuring grain into the buckets.

"I'll leave you in Steve's good care," she said. "Let me know if I can be of further help." Her farewell handshake was the same, once up, once down. When she left the barn, the three dogs milled about her for the walk to the ranch house.

Steve was a skinny man of about twenty, with black hair shaved close to his scalp under an Oakland A's baseball cap. He had a rough homemade tattoo of an eagle on his right forearm. His knuckles featured gang tattoos of L-O-V-E on one hand and H-A-T-E on the other. We moved to two white folding chairs and sat facing each other.

"I was sorry to hear about Druce," Steve said. He was soft-spoken and looked at me directly. He removed the cap and sat open-kneed, twirling it nervously.

"The two of you shared the same room?"

"That's right. Druce came in a little after me, and my room had the only spare bunk."

"What did you think of him?"

"It doesn't seem right to speak ill of the dead."

"It might help others if you share with me what you know."

He gave a big sigh. "Druce didn't take our mission here seriously. He sold drugs—I saw him. Not that I took any of them." He looked at me anxiously.

"I wouldn't think that," I reassured him.

"And he bragged a lot. He claimed he was this big-shot burglar, that he knew how to get into houses, ya know? And he had this con he was planning to pull when he got out of here."

"Which was?"

"He said he'd find these expensive things advertised for sale on the Internet—cowboy boots, guns, jewelry—that sort of stuff. He'd call up the owners, pay them a visit, check out the stuff and case the place. Then say he'd changed his mind, only go back later and burglarize the home. And then fence what he stole. That was his plan. Talked about it all the time."

"Do you know if he ever did?"

"Steal stuff? Can't say," Steve said. "I never talked to him after he left. I've considered the temptations of all those worldly possessions, though. Boots I could use, but guns aren't allowed around here, for sure. We work mostly with the horses." He brightened. "And chickens. You want some eggs?" He seemed anxious to leave the topic of Druce Kevern.

"Sure, why not." Did that count as a police bribe? We walked to an outside refrigerator and he handed me a used carton filled with odd-sized eggs—white and brown and tan.

I was no cook, but I'd give them to Isabel as a gift. She cared for my grandfather, and that counted for a lot in my book. Maybe she'd give me lessons on how to get along with him. When I looked at it straight on, I knew I needed a few.

I said goodbye to Steve and left the House of New Directions. On the way back to the sheriff's station, I grabbed a burger at Sonic. Probably not as good for me as the food those young men were cooking up at the ranch, but I was famished. A good cop travels on her stomach.

I sat on a bench at the fast food place, watching the customers pass by—young families, teen couples. All those simple interactions of life that Druce Kevern would now never experience. The case nagged at me. It was up to me to find some rationale for his death.

The afternoon dragged once I got back at the office. I ran through more review of Marsh's files and then knuckled down to finish a speech for the Chamber of Commerce. When I came up for air, the old regulator clock on the wall said six-thirty. I shoved the rest of the paperwork into my desk, locked the door, and headed out. Ben had left hours earlier and when I pulled into HT's driveway, I remembered why.

It was HT's birthday! Isabel was planning a special party and I'd promised to help. Shoot! I was in hot water now for sure.

CHAPTER TWELVE

THE AROMA OF CHILI RELLENOS spiced the kitchen air. Isabel had been working on the mole poblano sauce for three days now. Her rigid back signaled her disapproval as she chopped onions at the kitchen counter. I set the carton of eggs from the ranch down on the counter, a silent apology for being late, and dashed up the outside stairs to the loft to change.

I meant to buy HT a gift, and that hadn't happened, either. What do you buy for a grandfather you hardly know? He got my presence. That would have to do.

I clattered down the stairs moments later. Isabel lifted the lid on a big pot of pinto beans, releasing a cloud of steam. On the counter sat a clear glass bowl filled with green salad and a three-layer chocolate cake.

I reached out one tentative finger.

Isabel glared at me and blew one damp strand of hair off her forehead. "Stay out of my kitchen. That's how you can help." Her voice clipped the words like a sharp-edged carving knife.

Ouch. I really did mean to be here sooner to help.

Ben wandered into the room. He edged too close to the cake for Isabel's comfort, but her response was softer. She rapped his arm lightly with her spoon. "Stay out of that. Go set the table."

I followed Ben into the other room. I dug the extra leaf for the dining table from under HT's bed, and Ben helped me pull the two ends of the table apart. I dropped the leaf in the opening and we pushed the table back together.

When I shook open my grandmother's cutwork tablecloth, a musty, faint lavender odor unfurled as well. There were stiff fold-lines where it had been stored, and I smoothed them with my fingers as I evened the cloth on the table.

We put out the red and white special china. HT had collected the dishes at a supermarket promotion when I was a child. He'd come home each week with a new one, and my grandmother Ellie would act surprised and give him a big hug. One time when I was seven, I bought a teacup with my allowance. She hugged us both that week in appreciation.

Those were the good times. Then my father left, bringing shame on the family. My mother and Ellie had words, and late one night we moved back to Tennessee, leaving this family behind.

The table didn't have enough seating, extended, so we collected chairs from around the house to make up a set. The extra chairs and lengthened table crowded the small dining room, but it felt good to be part of the celebration. You can never go back home, they say, but sometimes I yearned for family experiences I had missed all these years. Maybe now I could make a fresh start.

"Armor and Vanessa are coming," Isabel announced from the kitchen. "I asked Flint Tanner, too, but he had a meeting out of town."

Great! Now even Isabel was matchmaking. Forget about it. I couldn't even get along with family.

I looked at Ben. "You and Armor talking again?" Maybe I'd get my loft space back.

"Not exactly," he said. "My uncle's been invited to the birthday party because he's *HT's* friend."

Meaning that the feud was still ongoing. This should be interesting, having uncle and nephew at the same table.

That left the other invited guest. "But Vanessa is *your* friend," I teased.

Ben's ears turned red. "Isabel invited her," he mumbled.

HT strolled in from the garden with a handful of late summer asters and cosmos. He presented them to Isabel with a flourish. Then, his role in the preparation completed, he settled back in his easy chair to watch the commotion, peering around the edges of his paper with obvious satisfaction.

Isabel arranged the flowers in an old crockery vase and placed it in the center of the table. With the red china and the purple and white flowers, the setup looked like a holiday was coming. The tantalizing kitchen aromas tickled my nose again. I grew hungrier by the minute.

The phone rang. Isabel talked a few moments and then hung up. “That was Vanessa. She’s on her way. I haven't heard from Armor. He wasn't sure he'd be able to make it. Would you call him, HT?” She went back to the kitchen to check on her meal.

HT dropped his paper and picked up the phone, punching each number with a jab. “Armor? I don't care what you're doing. You get your butt over here. We're waiting on you.” He hung up the phone, frowning. “This is my birthday party and he can damn well show up.” He snapped open his paper again.

A soft knock at the door signaled Vanessa’s arrival and Ben went to greet her. The girl had reinvented herself yet again for the occasion. Tonight she had dressed in a blue shantung silk dress, with her curls pulled back in a low ponytail. She looked younger, somehow, less brittle. I liked the change.

Vanessa carried a small present wrapped in gold paper with a white lacy bow. “I'm not sure it's what he wants, but...” she said, handing it to Ben.

He led Vanessa into the house and gave the present to HT. He gestured at his companion in an awkward attempt at an introduction. “HT, this is Vanessa.”

“I know who it is.” HT set his paper aside and rose with an old-fashioned courtliness. “Hello, Vanessa, and welcome to my party.” He shook her hand formally and gestured to the couch. “Come sit a spell and tell me what's going on in your world.”

Vanessa settled down beside him like a sweet young thing. I remembered other more sulky sides of Vanessa’s personality, but HT seemed taken by her charms.

“Now what have you brought me?” Paper crackled as HT carefully untied the ribbon and set it on the table. Then he dug out his pocketknife and slit the tape holding the gift paper. Slowly he unwrapped the box and refolded the paper, setting it under the ribbon.

I wiggled with impatience. I'd have crinkled wrapping paper scattered all over the floor by now. I'd done that at Christmas, the few times we'd had a Christmas at my house. Maybe being careful came with being HT's age? If so, I wasn't sure I wanted to live that long.

"What do we have here?" HT asked, opening the box and withdrawing a small object. "A tie-tack. Just what I wanted."

He sounded genuinely pleased, and my thoughts turned to my absent mother. Before her dementia, she would have enjoyed this sort of celebration.

HT yelled into the kitchen a moment later. "When do we eat?" He echoed my own desires. I was starving, and chocolate cake beckoned. Forget about the rest of the meal.

"In a minute," Isabel said. "Wait for Armor."

HT glanced again at the black-and-white cat clock on the wall, its swinging tail marking the lateness of the hour. "He better get here soon or I'll go get him myself, so help me Hannah I will."

All of a sudden, the door burst open. Armor came in, followed by Ben's dog.

Isabel rushed from the kitchen, wiping her hands on a towel. "Get that animal out of the house!"

Ben grabbed Bitzer by the collar and dragged him outside, passing close by Armor in a pointed silence.

Isabel held out her hand to welcome Armor, but the big man dropped his crutch and grabbed her in a bear hug instead, whirling her around. "Thanks for inviting me, Isabel."

He winked at me. "There's a brown package outside the door. Bet it's got your granddad's name on it."

I retrieved the sack for him and he limped into the living room with it. "Happy birthday, HT. I brung you something." He held out a bottle of Johnny Walker Red. "Best the bar's got to offer." His loud voice and blustery energy filled the room.

Armor threw a barbed glance at Ben and then turned to engage HT in the local gossip. Isabel carried serving dishes from the kitchen and Ben rushed to help her.

When Isabel suggested that we could take our places, Armor rose first. He staggered a little as he walked to the table and sat at the head, a fork and knife propped, one in each hand. "What's. For. Dinner?"

He pronounced each word carefully, as though searching some deep recess of his mind for them.

Probably I should have minded my own business, but his pronouncement echoed tones I had heard in my mother's house when she was drinking, just before explosions began. "Maybe that's HT's place, Armor?" I suggested.

He glared at me and then shifted to the side of the table with an "Okay, sure." He gestured like a benevolent king for HT to take the head spot. I remained standing, waiting for the rest of the group to file in.

Ben joined us, sitting on the opposite side of the table, as far away from his uncle as possible. That left space next to Armor for Vanessa, who sat gingerly, scooting her chair a little away from the man.

Isabel brought the tortillas, steaming from the oven where she'd held them and took her place at the foot of the table. I sat down, too, and we did the usual napkin in the lap sort of thing, preparing to pass the bowls around.

It appeared that Armor noticed Vanessa's hesitation. He laid a clumsy hand on her shoulder. "Shoot, I don't bite. Bring your chair closer to the table, Missy."

Ben half rose and Armor punched a finger in the air. "What? I'm not good enough for your girlfriend?"

Ben whipped around the table and stared down at his uncle, his animosity boiling. "Leave her alone."

He glowered at Armor, fingers clenching and unclenching.

HT intervened. "Now Armor, Ben, I invited both of you to celebrate my birthday, not argue. Armor, you simmer down. Ben, take your place at the table." Ben slowly returned to his seat, and Armor harrumphed and settled back in his chair.

Then HT patted a seat next to him, well away from his friend. "Here, sit by me, Vanessa. Place of honor."

I let out the breath I'd been holding and sat, too.

HT looked down the table to Isabel. "What a beautiful meal you've made."

Her face brightened like sunshine reappearing on a cloudy day. "Thank you, Horace. It's all for you. Happy Birthday."

Ignoring the exchange, Armor heaped rice on his plate and grabbed for the dish of mole sauce.

"Wait a minute," I said.

He slapped my hand away. "Wait a minute," he mocked. "Who made you the timekeeper, *deputy*?"

HT touched Armor's shoulder. "Isabel wants to say grace."

"Oh, sure, sure."

"Dear Lord, bless this food and all who eat it, especially our honored Horace who is having his birthday today." Isabel's soft voice filled the quiet room.

"*Now* can we eat?" Armor asked, reaching for the rellenos. He shoveled some in the general direction of his plate. As he passed the dish to Vanessa, it tilted and some of the sauce dripped into her lap. She jumped to her feet, dabbing hurriedly at her dress.

Ben leaned across the table, shoving his uncle's chest. "Look what you've done, you clumsy—"

"Who're you calling clumsy. I'll show you clumsy." Armor jammed back his chair and leaned against the table to balance, like an old pine tree ready to topple.

Sensing the commotion, Ben's dog pushed through the front door.

It all played out in a horrified slow motion. Bitzer bumped Armor's elbow, and the man lost his balance. He tottered against the edge of the table and grabbed the tablecloth in both hands. Dishes, tablecloth, flowers, and bean pot fell to the floor with a shattering crash.

"Oh, no!" Isabel burst into tears and fled the room.

Armor stood up, looked around him at the chaos and shrugged. "Well, didn't want to come, no ways. Wouldn't have, if I'd known that spawn was here." He stalked out the door.

I followed him out on the porch. "Give me your keys, Armor."

"Don't think so."

"You're in no condition to drive. Give me your keys or I'll confiscate your vehicle. You know I can, and I will."

He tossed them at me, and then enveloped me in a big sloppy hug. "Hell, Peg, you know I ain't mad at you." He lurched into the darkness, gazing upward at the distant stars. "Nice night for a walk, anyway."

When I again entered the dining room, Vanessa had scraped most of the mole sauce off her ruined dress. “I think it's time I go home, too.” She pushed her chair back. “Thank you so much, HT, for inviting me.”

Ben stood, hesitating between staying and following her. Romance won out.

“Wait. I'll go with you.” They disappeared out the front door.

HT and I looked around the empty room while Bitzer slurped the remains of the meal off the floor. Then HT began to laugh. “I never did like that mole sauce anyhow. Too spicy for this old stomach, but I didn't want to hurt Isabel's feelings.”

He crossed his eyes at me, and suddenly I was laughing, too, at the crazy turn of events. Ben’s dog gave us a look of alarm and pursued Ben and Vanessa out the half-open door.

HT wiped his brow and got to his feet. “Come help me clean this up.”

Together we righted the chairs. I picked the flowers out of the mess and rearranged them in a mason jar I set on the counter. HT got a broom and together we picked up the broken dishes. Gradually the room returned to order.

“Now, cut me a piece of that cake so I can go make my peace with Isabel,” he said.

Leaving the room with it, he muttered under his breath, “Best birthday party, ever.”

CHAPTER THIRTEEN

THE NEXT MORNING I awoke with a big tongue in my ear, and it wasn't human. I hollered at Ben's dog to get the hell off my bed. Then I threw on some clothes and ambled downstairs barefoot. The old wooden stairs were sun-warm, and the scent of jasmine brushed the early morning sunlight.

When I opened the door to the kitchen my grandfather was at the table eating the last piece of birthday cake.

"Ben never made it back to the loft," I said.

HT winked at me. "Might be the boy found a softer place to sleep."

I'd been known to do some sleepovers, too, when I was younger. Was it being a cop or the few extra years I had on Ben that made me feel so old this morning? Not certain I wanted to travel down that perplexing road. I stole a breakfast roll from the counter and went to work.

I sat in my office, shuffling papers and reviewing the events surrounding the death of Druce Kevern. I still wondered about his connection to HT. Why would HT take on a rookie that might get him in trouble? It didn't make much sense—HT was smarter than that. Then I remembered what Regina Smith had said about everybody liking Druce. Perhaps Druce suckered my grandfather in, too.

Older cops had told me about the cases that wouldn't let them sleep, and Druce Kevern's was starting to rest heavy on my shoulders. Whatever the underlying cause, the flat truth was that Druce Kevern was dead, lying in a morgue with no one concerned enough to make burial arrangements. I felt compelled to keep digging, to discover why he died.

We were down to one working computer in the office, and it wasn't mine. I sent Ben running errands and commandeered his machine to do some Internet investigation on the underlying facts of the case.

Maybe Druce's roommate at the ranch was right about the scam that Druce had been planning to run. If so, perhaps I could follow the same path of inquiry the dead man had. People were notorious about letting old ads run on the free sites. I opened the browser and searched through the for-sale entries. Under men's cowboy boots, I narrowed the search by location, Arizona, and price, highest-to-lowest.

Two pair of boots fit my criteria. They listed for five thousand dollars each. I was in the wrong line of work. Maybe I should go into shoe auctioneering.

The owner of the first pair described the leather as "rare Australian saltwater croc." The ad noted the fine belly scales, small and rectangular. Although the boots were expensive, they were not, unfortunately, the Lucchese brand.

A second pair looked more promising. They were buffalo calf, dyed purple, featuring a twisted cone last. "Over one hundred steps in the making, guaranteed to fit like a glove. All leather with the exception of the lemonwood pegs." The Lucchese brand. The area code on the phone number listed was unfamiliar. I dialed the number, listening to it ring four times before somebody answered.

"I'm calling about the boots."

"Sorry."

"They're sold?"

"I meant to take down that ad. I have to go." The voice was familiar somehow. I'd heard it before.

The man hung up. I redialed hoping to get more information but got a busy signal. Must have the phone off the hook to discourage would-be pesky buyers like me. I ran the phone number through Google and Facebook, but nothing turned up. It might be a pre-paid cell phone. Thirty bucks would buy one at any big box store. Pay with cash, no ID required. Cops and skip tracers trying to earn an honest living hated the things, but bad guys loved their anonymous nature.

Having no luck on the boots, I moved on to the next item of potential evidence, the pistol. The computer listed zillions of antique pistols for sale—a booming market, apparently—but nothing in Arizona that looked like a pistol with a ruby in the grip, a twin to the topaz inlaid one I had in my safe.

That left the third object of possible interest, the crucifix. Abandoning the computer, I dialed the crime lab. No, they hadn't received my UPS box with the golden cross yet, and when they did, it would go to the bottom of their investigative stack. So much for inter-agency cooperation.

Maybe I could bribe them with some eggs. I knew a good source.

Regina Smith had struggled to keep the halfway house afloat, and in doing so, she allowed me to see another side of incarceration. The horses gave the kids a chance to dream about a different future. I liked that idea and hoped that I could return the crucifix to Regina soon. She'd have that, anyway, with its ties to both family and to Druce Kevern.

I rotated the problem like a three-dimensional mobile. The boots, antique pistol, and crucifix hung there in my mind's eye like ornaments twisting on invisible threads; Purple, red, gold, winking in the sun. All three items were expensive, likely to be prized by their owners. They were unique, which meant a criminal fence might not offer much for them. If the items had fallen into Druce's possession, then, would he have visited a pawnshop for ready cash?

I opened the Yellow Pages and found two shops listed in the valley. Making a circle from Mingus I could visit both in an hour. I grabbed the Photoshopped copy of Druce Kevern, together with pictures of the crucifix image and Alice Heaton's remaining dueling pistol. Not ever having seen the boots, I'd wing it there.

The clerk at the first shop hadn't seen Druce or the objects at all. I drove on to the second establishment.

The doorbell jingled as I walked in, and a middle-aged overweight guy in a plaid shirt and khaki pants greeted me from behind the counter.

"Call me Charlie, Charlie Winart," he said. "How can I help you?"

"You own this place?"

"For the past twelve years."

I explained who I was and why I was in his store.

“I'm glad to see a real law enforcement officer in Mingus after the likes of Cyrus Marsh.”

“Meaning?”

He had the grace to look a little uncomfortable. “That man gave me this real uneasy feeling. You never knew where you stood with him. Sometimes he was almost rigid—he’d cite you chapter and verse of the law you were transgressing. Other times, especially if it were a friend of his, he'd just look the other way. Made it hard to know which Cyrus you were dealing with.”

Interesting. Sometimes you never knew about people until death intervened. Then the truth came out. I was discovering that in my investigation.

I lay the picture of Druce Kevern on the counter.

Charlie poked at it with a stubby finger. “Looks dead.” He picked up the photo for a closer examination. “No, he’s not been in here, to my knowledge. Sorry.”

I collected that picture and lay down the close-up of the crucifix.

“Pretty little thing,” Charlie commented. “What’s it doing in a bunch of prickly pear?”

“A long story. Has anybody tried to hock something like it?”

“I’d remember something that special. My aunt was a practicing Catholic.” He put down the photo reluctantly. “On your own, there, I’m afraid.”

I was disappointed but accepting of his statement. The jewelry was an outlier. Then, so was everything else about this case.

As best as I could, I described the Lucchese cowboy boots advertised online. “Do you ever buy anything like that?”

“That rings a bell. Let me think a minute.” He rubbed his chin in thought, then looked at me over his reading glasses. “A guy was in last week. One of those forest people. Had this pair of bright purple cowboy boots, wanted to hock them.”

“Did you buy them?”

Charlie shook his head. “We don't deal in high-end boots. Too much trouble. Folks think they're worth more than they are. Cents on the dollar, items like those boots.”

Some folks on the Internet could be waiting a long time, then, at the prices they were advertising their merchandise. Too bad. I felt better about declining a shoe sale career.

"What did the guy wearing the boots look like?"

"Tall." He raised a hand above his head. "Maybe even taller than you." He smiled at me.

"Age?"

"Maybe sixty or so. Bushy gray beard."

So not Druce.

"I'll keep an eye out in case I see him again," he promised, "but these folks come and go around here in the summer."

I sighed and lay down the final photograph of the antique pistol. "It looks like this, only with a ruby instead of a topaz in the grip," I explained.

"No, that's *exactly* the one that's been in here. I remember that yellow stone. Let me see that picture of the dead guy again."

I lay the picture of Druce on the counter.

"No, this guy didn't bring it in. It was two kids—one looked Native American, long black hair he kept brushing out of his eyes and the other was this real doll, a looker."

Ben and Vanessa? What were they doing trying to hock one of Alice Heaton's antique pistols? I tuned back into Charlie's explanation.

"I told them I couldn't buy the gun unless they had title. And they'd have to put their thumbprints on the back of the receipt, for theft purposes, you know? Everything by the books. At that, they shoved the gun back into a paper sack and scrammed."

"How long ago were they in?"

"Beginning of last week."

So that would have been *before* Alice gave the ruby pistol to Druce.

"You don't forget a face like that young lady had. A real beaut."

I gave him my card and asked him to call me if he thought of anything else. On the drive back, I tried to figure which lead to follow.

The boots first. Charlie said the man who'd been in his shop looked homeless. How do you go about finding someone who doesn't want to be found? These indigent campers only ventured into town for necessities, their unwashed clothes tempered a dirty olive green by the elements. Tourists, offended by their smell, crossed to the other side of the road. Tal Garrett probably had a law on the books about people like that I was neglecting to enforce.

On the other hand, these Wildies, as the fire chief called them, sometimes visited the grocery store for a few items they couldn't forage for themselves or frequented a bar for a cheap drink. Armor Brancussi ran the Spirit Bar. It seemed strange to ask Armor for help after the debacle at HT's, but he was a different person when he wasn't drinking. And he was stone cold sober at the bar. *If* he'd be willing to help me. Worth a try.

That brought me to the second problem, the attempted sale of the antique pistol. Hearing that Ben had accompanied Alice's daughter Vanessa was not surprising, but the fact he'd engage in theft was. On the other hand, Ben's intelligence and common sense dimmed to a faint glowing light when Vanessa showed up. Given enough incentive, she could talk him into about anything.

This selling trip of theirs occurred before the dead man's fall, which meant Vanessa might have a scheme of her own in play. I'd collar Ben and find out what they were up to. It might have nothing to do with the man's death, but questioning my clerk could prove interesting. Nothing like intrigue to get me sniffing around.

* * * * * *

THERE WAS AN UNUSUAL CROWD on the main street of Mingus as I entered the town. I slowed and blipped the sirens once. Pulling to the side of the road, I parked the squad car and pushed through the gathering to the center.

Tal Garrett and Armor Brancussi stood chin to chin, shouting obscenities at each other. Townspeople and bikers surrounded the two. The tourists had retreated to the sidewalks, looking but pretending not to, like people passing an auto accident.

"Okay, folks, break it up. Let them have room," I said.

"You son-of-a-bitch. I know'd it was you." Armor gave Garrett a shove that knocked off his glasses and mussed his comb-over.

"Don't you push me, you bastard." Garrett grabbed Armor's crutch and jerked it out from under his arm. It fell to the pavement with a hollow clatter.

Without the crutch's support, Armor toppled to the ground. As he fell, he jerked out a foot and tripped Garrett. The man landed on top of Armor with a heavy grunt. That was all it took.

Garrett jabbed Armor's midsection, causing the man to whoosh out held breath. They rolled on the pavement, hitting and punching like kids in a schoolyard—lots of wild swings and misses.

Then Armor hit his stride and landed a good punch to Garrett's nose. The partisan crowd pushed closer, shouting encouragement to their hometown hero. And it wasn't Garrett.

I waded in to separate them, just in time to get whacked in the eye by a misdirected blow from our esteemed mayor. Ouch!

"Enough. Leave be." I yanked hard on Armor's collar, pulling him off Garrett. I jabbed my palm under his elbow and scraped him to his feet.

Someone in the crowd retrieved Armor's crutch and handed it to him as he stood there, breathing hard.

"That gol-damn varmint doesn't deserve to walk on this earth, after what he did."

Tal Garrett rose unsteadily and dabbed at his bloodied nose with a handkerchief. "He smashed my glasses," he whined. "I think my nose is broken."

Roger Heaton thrust to my side and put a steadying arm around Garrett. "I'll take him back to his office, Deputy. You can interview him there."

That was fine by me. One less combatant on the scene.

"Armor, you come with me. The rest of you—go back to your afternoons. Show's over."

The crowd dispersed with sullen disappointment. An undercurrent of anger and frustration reverberated through the departing men like rumbling thunderclouds forecasting storms ahead.

There had been increasing unrest in the town since the downturn in the economy. An unemployed person could watch only so much daytime TV, before the need to blame someone intensified. Multiplied by a hundred people, that frustration could prove tough for one law person to handle. It didn't take much to spark the flames into rage. I could only keep a close watch and pray that it didn't happen.

I shoved Armor in the back of the squad car for the short ride up to my office. His shirt was torn, and he was sniffling a little. “Want a hanky, Armor?”

“Nah, I'm fine.” He wiped his nose on his sleeve, leaving a smear of red. “Landed a few good ones, didn't I?”

“Those few good ones might cost you. Tal Garrett looks like the suing kind.”

“He ain't going to do anything. I was in the right and he know'd it. Anyway, I got plenty on him. He ain't going to bother me.”

Armor seemed confident, and I was puzzled. Exactly what was going on here?

Ben wasn't at his computer when we entered the office, and I was grateful. I wanted to talk to his guardian alone.

“Going to lock me up?” Armor asked.

“No, you old fool. Sit here and let me take a look at you.”

Armor wiggled a loose tooth with his tongue. “I've been in worse. You might want to take a look at that eye of yours, Missy.”

“Shut up.” I ignored the swelling that was threatening to shut my left eye. “What started it?”

“Well,” Armor began, and I waited for the lies to start. “I've got me this garden on the hill. Grow vegetables and such, ya know?”

I looked at him.

“Well, some other things, too, that was about ready to harvest.” He appeared distressed. “But they're gone, destroyed. Somebody poured fuel oil over the whole batch. Killed my babies. I'll crush that sumbitch.”

“You aren't crushing anybody. Why blame Garrett?”

“Had to be him. He goes up there every night to gloat over his fortune, the one he's going to make because he bribed the land commissioner. And maybe you need to ask all those store owners why they are behind him. He promised them a bonus if the deal goes through. Every single man-jack of them.”

Armor shook his head. “What a waste. What a waste.”

I got the feeling he wasn't talking about the land deal. I was in the middle of that crowd and it hadn’t been comfortable.

“Why are your biker buddies so hostile?” I asked.

Armor saddened. “Maybe it's because my vegetable garden is ruint.”

“Or could be there’s been bad blood between the bikers and the merchants?”

“Well, them motorcycle jockeys have been a bit light-fingered from time to time,” he admitted. “But mainly it's them California One-Percenters. The other ninety-nine percent of us take the blame because those shopkeepers can’t tell one from the other.”

I heard enough. “Armor, I’ll let you go this time with a warning. Stay out of trouble for a while.” I gestured impatiently. “Go. Talk to HT. He'll pound some sense into you. I've work to do.”

For a man with a bum leg, Armor made remarkable time out the front door. I watched him disappear down the sidewalk, counted to twenty, and then started the long walk the other direction to Tal Garrett's office.

* * * * * *

TAL HAD RESETTLED his mayoral image: A butterfly bandage perched on his nose and his plastered comb-over once again hid his shiny forehead. Somebody, maybe Roger, had even taped the man’s glasses together.

“Deputy, I want you to do something with Brancussi. He and his buddies are creating a dangerous environment here in town.”

A vein throbbed in his temple. Still angry.

“Garrett, he's got as much right to live here as you do.”

The man should calm down, take up a soothing hobby or two. Maybe he needed a puppy to relieve his stress.

The mayor’s face paled. The physical encounter must have shaken him, and he'd lost status, brawling in the street that way. On the other hand, Armor Brancussi made his chops in a tough motorcycle world and wouldn't back down.

That meant I had two alpha males duking it out and bystanders could suffer when something like that happened. To distract Garrett, I asked him about the kickbacks to the merchants Armor had mentioned.

“It’s only fair to share the largesse. We all live here.”

“Even Armor Brancussi?” I asked, curious.

“Well, not him, of course. The man’s an employee, not an owner. Doesn’t have two cents to rub together.”

"And you know the owner of the establishment where he works."

"Of course." Garrett's smile was forced.

I leaned back and the leather chair creaked. Time to calm the situation down, if I could. "From the way I see it, you struck the first blow."

"I just gave him a little push. He provoked me."

"And you destroyed his, err, garden," I said.

"You *know* what he was growing up there."

I suddenly found myself on the wrong side of that thin blue line and back-pedaled. "I don't know and I don't want to know at this point."

Garrett shook his finger in my face. "Tell that cripple to stay the hell off my mountain. If I catch him up there again, there won't be enough of him left to make a dust wipe for that bar of his."

His voice intensified with anger. "Need I remind you that I'm mayor of this town? If you can't keep the town under control, I'll find someone who can."

Never did like being threatened. "Like Cyrus Marsh did?" My voice rose in spite of my resolve to stay calm.

"What do you mean by that?"

"Let's say nobody in this town is perfect, and that includes you, Mr. Garrett." I softened my voice with effort. "Look, fighting in the street is no solution to anything."

He remained silent, his mouth working like a snapping turtle.

I admitted defeat, at least for now, and walked back to my office. The mood of the town was dangerous and getting more so with every passing minute, with tempers flaring.

The real estate developers like Tal Garrett and the status-quo folks like Brancussi seemed determined to destroy each other, like a ledge of underground rocks shifting unseen but treacherous.

The mining operations presented a third option. From what Flint Tanner had told me, the mining company might veto the whole deal and claim the available land for new mining operations.

I sighed. Even at my six-foot height, I was no Wild West hired gun riding in to save the community. For this town built of uncompromising factions, any sort of peace would be hard won and probably temporary.

I had barely poured a new cup of coffee to ponder the question when Roger Heaton banged through the door.

CHAPTER FOURTEEN

HAVING TAKEN CARE of the mayor, Roger was now on a quest of his own. "I've come for my pistol," he announced, stomping into my office.

"*Your* pistol?" I raised an eyebrow.

"What my wife owns, I own," Roger stated flatly, his tone leaving no room for discussion.

Actually, in this instance, the dueling pistols were an inheritance from Alice Heaton's father. Technically, that made them, or at least the remaining one, Alice's sole and separate property. But not my place to say.

"You got safe storage for the weapon?"

"I bought a gun safe at the discount store in Cottonwood. I'm the only one that knows the combination."

I retrieved the case containing the long-barreled pistol from the office safe. It felt heavy in my hand. At my desk, I opened the box and pulled out the pistol with its cleaning apparatus. I shoved the ramrod down the barrel to double-check that the weapon wasn't loaded, replaced the pistol in the case, and handed it back to Roger.

He accepted the weapon and signed the receipt with a hasty scrawl.

"How valuable is this, anyway?" I asked.

"With its special provenance, if the set was intact, perhaps half a million dollars. There are collectors who like this sort of thing. As one of a set?" He shrugged. "Maybe ten thousand."

Alice had made a mistake. If she had been patient and had gone through normal channels, she could have made enough money to satisfy both Vanessa and Druce Kevern. But of course, time was exactly what Druce didn't have.

I fished a little to see what Roger's reaction to the young man might be. "So losing that one and dividing the pair was a big loss. What do you think happened to the ruby pistol?"

"Maybe Alice gave it away. She has a soft heart. Or maybe Vanessa sold it."

Roger's response seemed too casual for something of this much value. If he'd left it there, I'd have dropped the idea. But he couldn't resist adding a coda.

"I wouldn't put it past her. Vanessa's adopted, you know. Not mine." It was a distancing comment that discounted Vanessa's value as someone worthy of his notice. Interesting that he'd refer to her that way. I wonder what that said about the relationship between father and daughter. My B.S. detector went on high alert.

"Some people grow to love their adopted children as much as biological ones," I countered.

"Some can, some can't. I fall into the 'can't' category." Roger waved his hand, dismissing the topic.

He straightened and resumed his vice mayor role. "Deputy Quincy, Tal Garrett would like Armor Brancussi arrested."

"He's welcome to file charges," I said. "But it's for a judge to decide who threw the first punch. Our mayor might be careful what he asks for."

"That buddy of your grandpa's made an enemy, accosting Garrett like that. He won't stop until Armor's behind bars. Garrett's trying to keep things under control." He gave me a smile that didn't touch his eyes. "Seems to me that's your job, but I can understand that you're having problems keeping the town orderly, being inexperienced and all."

Maybe he was trying to be supportive, but it didn't sound like it to me. First the verbal jabs from Garrett and now from this man. I bristled. "My job is to uphold the law. The sheriff's department hired me, not Tal Garrett and not you. If the sheriff doesn't like what I'm doing, *he* can fire me."

Roger held up his hands. "Hey, I'm under stress, just like you are." He walked out of the office with one parting comment. "You just have to keep the peace until summer's end. Surely you can do that."

* * * * * *

WAKING THE NEXT MORNING in the loft, I glanced over at the pile of blankets, teenage boy, and snoring dog in the corner. I'd meant to ask Ben yesterday about his and Vanessa's trip to the pawn shop. But under *official* circumstances, not like this.

I sighed. It was impossible to be neutral, to maintain separation between my personal life and my job with this arrangement. If Vanessa had anything to do with Druce's death, Ben was an accessory.

I could hear the defense attorney doing cross on my testimony: "And you slept *where,* Deputy Quincy?"

It was time to move.

I'd miss them all—even Isabel. She'd forgiven me for the fiasco at HT's birthday party and sometimes left me small gifts. I'd find a carved figurine or a switch of fragrant cedar on my nightstand when I returned from work. My mother had never had the time to do anything like that, and I didn't know quite how to take it.

The street fight between Tal Garrett and Armor Brancussi tangled personal and professional relationships even more. Armor had a hot temper when drinking, and that little marijuana patch meant a lot to him. He claimed he had an alibi at the bar, but he wouldn't be the first person to hire out a spot of violence.

Perhaps Druce's fall had been unintended. Maybe Armor had just sent a buddy up there to scare him a little. Druce could even have initiated the fight. All it would take would be a small push, an accident even, to defend one's honor.

If it turned out Armor had anything to do with Kevern's fall that would mean I'd have to arrest him. How could I do that if I slept in the same room as Ben? Armor was his guardian.

The longer I thought about it, the more awkward it became. I needed to move, to live on my own again. It was the only way I'd be able to perform my duties with a clear mind.

* * * * * *

LATER THAT MORNING, I located a solution. I was walking street patrol and spotted a "For Lease" sign in an upper story window on Main Street. On a main level door, the notice was repeated, with a phone number for Mr. Johnny Evans, The Community National Bank. The vacant apartment filled the top story of a narrow building on the road's curve. I dug my cell out of my pocket and dialed the bank.

Johnny Evans was cordial. "It's a bank foreclosure that won't be final for months. We've been trying to lease it as a vacation rental, so it's even furnished. Go take a look." He gave me the combination for the lockbox containing the key.

I stepped back a few paces and squinted up at the building. The structure had been built into the side of a mountain hillside with a walkout basement that appeared to be used for storage. Then, up half a flight was the first floor. It contained a time-share office that might be busy during the day, but probably quiet at night when I'd be there.

I angled my head to look higher. The top floor, on a level with the next street above, loomed three stories up from where I stood. It had a small balcony looking right down Main Street. That would be useful for keeping an eye on the town.

I returned to the front steps and punched in the combination on the lockbox. The front door opened to an interior set of stairs rising to the second floor. The studio apartment at the top of the stairs measured about twenty-five feet square with expansive views all the way across the valley.

A king-sized bed sat against one wall. A bright red couch and easy chair formed a small sitting area in front of it. Several lamps with mosaicked bases and a small table with three chairs completed the main room. The balcony had several wicker chairs overlooking the street. Good!

At the far end of the room was a door leading to a standard bathroom and a small alcove with a microwave/refrigerator combo. Fine with me, since I never cooked anyway. There was even a coffee maker with an old-fashioned bean grinder. Out the back door, a leaning garage shaded a minute patio. Beyond that, cracked cement stairs led to the next street. The apartment was small but serviceable.

I'd take it.

I walked over to the bank to finalize the agreement. As I opened the front door, Vanessa Heaton brushed past me without even an

"Excuse me." Johnny Evans seemed upset, too, as he searched for the paperwork for the lease. He pushed down too hard on a pencil and the lead snapped. He threw the pencil in the trash and grabbed another. That one didn't suit him either. He disappeared into the main foyer and returned with three more sharpened pencils, which he lined in a row.

Twenty minutes later he still hadn't produced a lease, although he'd washed his hands twice with the bottle of sanitizer. Must be fun working in this place.

Tired of waiting, I suggested an amount for a deposit and signed a check payable to the bank. We worked out the lease arrangements verbally and shook hands on the deal. Glad to be done with his nervous ways, I turned to leave.

"Did you talk to you grandfather about his mortgage? Remember, we have rules." Johnny waggled his forefinger at me.

"He'll be calling you soon," I lied.

What a strange duck this Johnny Evans was. I wondered what I had interrupted between him and Vanessa. An employee-boss sort of thing, perhaps. Johnny would not be the easiest of people to work for.

The next phase of my plan would be to confront HT with the news I was moving out. I'd told—well, all right, threatened—to leave before when we had argued, but he probably wouldn't like my plan.

Or maybe he would. He might be glad to get rid of the granddaughter that so reminded him of his dead wife. I planned to start packing as soon as I dealt with the Ben Yazzie issue.

When I entered the station, my clerk sat at the desk playing his computer games.

"Whoee, I see all colors of the rainbow in that shiner!" he exclaimed.

"Come into my office," I growled. "I need to talk to you."

I waited until he came in and slouched into a chair. "I went into the Easy-Ready Pawn Shop in Clarkdale yesterday."

He shifted upright as he caught the direction of the conversation. "Yeah?"

"The proprietor—" I checked my notes to be sure, "—a Mr. Charles Neal—said that two people who looked like you and Vanessa tried to sell a gun in there."

Ben swallowed and his Adam's apple bobbed. “What kind of a gun?”

“Cut the crap, Ben. What were the two of you doing?”

“We didn't steal anything.”

“I didn't say you did.”

He sighed. “It's a long story.”

“Try me.”

“We thought maybe the pawn shop would buy one of her mother's dueling pistols. Vanessa needed money fast.”

“For what? Drugs?”

“Nah. She gets all she wants from her mother's medicine cabinet.”

If Ben was telling the truth, the Heatons weren't that different from many families these days. “Okay, what then?”

“When we realized we couldn't sell the topaz pistol without title we took it back to the house. Then we tried to sell it on Craigslist.”

“But that didn't work either.”

“No. Vanessa was dumb enough to put in her home phone number and when this guy called, her mother answered the phone and told him to take a hike.”

“But he called back?”

Ben agreed. “Yeah, by then maybe Mrs. Heaton figured she'd see what he'd offer for it. So he came out to look at it. But Vanessa said he didn’t want it.”

“And that night the ruby pistol disappeared.” Suddenly things were becoming more clear. Maybe Druce had planned to meet with Alice all along. Maybe she offered him the pistol, or maybe he stole it. If his two cons of long-lost-son and interested-buyer intersected, either could be possible. But that still didn’t leave Ben in the clear.

“We didn't steal the pistol,” he said defensively. “Why would we need to? It was Vanessa’s anyway.”

I circled back around. “You said she needed money. What for?”

“I can't tell you that.”

Whether or not Druce Kevern had stolen the ruby pistol from the Heaton household, its whereabouts might aid in solving the reasons behind his death. I needed to talk to Vanessa. Would she come willingly? She didn’t think she’d broken any laws, and I had nothing to charge her with, so possibly not. But she might honor a simple request from Ben.

I held out my cell phone. “Call and get her over here. Now.”

A few moments later, Vanessa entered the station. She and Ben exchanged a quick glance as she passed his desk.

“How are you, Deputy Quincy. It's nice to see you again.” Her tone was sweetly social, almost as though she was accepting an invitation for high tea.

I didn’t break out the crumpets. “Come in and shut the door, Vanessa.”

She sat down across the desk from me. I sat there, letting the silence build. Guilty folks needed to talk. Guilty of what, I wasn't sure, but I knew that Vanessa had a tale to tell.

“Do I need a lawyer?” the girl asked.

“I don't know. Do you?”

Vanessa shook her blonde hair. “I'm not a kid. I can speak for myself.”

“So talk.”

Vanessa glanced to the outside door.

“Ben can't hear you. This is your story.”

She paused and made a face. “I'm pregnant.”

I expected a flood of tears, but the girl seemed resigned, almost pragmatic about the situation. Not the way I would have handled an unexpected pregnancy. Maybe it was this new generation, I thought, suddenly feeling eons older than the girl in front of me. “Your parents know?”

“Are you kidding?” Vanessa gave a short laugh. “My father would throw me out of the house if he didn't kill me first.”

An unfortunate choice of words. “And your mother?”

“My mother. What could she do?” There was disdain in Vanessa's voice. “She'd just want me to actually have this thing and then put it out for adoption.”

“Like she did with your brother.”

“My brother, if I even have one, is probably a junkie and a criminal.” Her tone was flat, devoid of emotion.

“And the father of your child, what about him?” I watched myself get sucked into the girl's drama. Then I drew back. I’m a cop, not some therapist.

Vanessa didn't seem to notice, lost in her own thoughts. "He wanted to keep it, like a pet or something." She laughed bitterly.

"He wouldn't pay for an abortion?"

"Why would he?" Now the tears started. "I don't want this baby. I have my life ahead of me. I *can't* be tied down."

I had to ask. "Is the father Ben?"

"Ben? Of course not, don't be ridiculous. That dork."

"That *dork* has been trying to help you. I'd be counting him as a friend."

Vanessa shrugged. "Whatever. When I take lovers, they're men, not boys." She fumbled in her purse for a tissue. "Anything else?"

"No, but stay close."

Vanessa didn't look at Ben as she stormed from the office. I hoped she would decide to talk to her mother. Vanessa was in a tough situation, no matter how you considered it. Was she still a suspect in Druce Kevern's death? I fought down my tendency to feel sorry for the girl. Of course, she had to be! I doubted Druce was the father—somehow he didn't seem Vanessa's type.

But pregnant women commit murder all the time, given the right reason. Was it sibling jealousy? Or the fact he'd stolen something that belonged to her? I'd find out what Vanessa's trigger might be, and judge then how close she might have come to killing Druce Kevern.

* * * * * *

AFTER WORK, I DIDN'T STOP inside to say hello to HT like I usually did, but climbed the outside stairs to the loft. I threw possessions in the duffle I'd brought to Mingus. It didn't take long. I ran a finger over my mother's picture and tossed that in on top.

HT caught up with me as I walked down the back stairs with the bag over my shoulder. "It looks like you're moving out. You might have told me first."

His voice was rigid with anger, triggering my own. "I don't belong here," I said. "And I don't have to tell you anything."

"Is that so?" He put an arm out to stop me.

I shook off his hand. "Don't touch me, old man."

"I'll tell you the same thing I told your mother when she left. Don't be a damn fool."

We stood eyeball to eyeball glaring at each other in the late afternoon sun.

"I'm leaving, so I can do the job I was hired to do here." I felt like I was five again, defensive, trying to skate out of trouble. "I'll be close," I promised. "I'll check on you every morning."

"I don't need anybody checking on me. You think I'm turning into some decrepit old bastard? Go, and don't ever look back, like your mother did. *Isabel* will look after me." Spittle bubbled at the corner of his mouth. "And Armor, too. Maybe we'll go smoke some medical marijuana. You going to bust me for that?"

I threw up my hands in frustration and climbed the stairs for another load. Through the window, I saw him stalking up the street to Armor's biker bar.

* * * * * *

THE FIRST HUGE RAINDROPS splatted on the uneven surface of the street as I carried the last box upstairs to the new apartment. I brewed a cup of coffee and sat down in one of the wicker chairs on the balcony to drink it.

Lightning broke the sky into jagged sections of blue-black clouds. I shivered as the temperature continued to drop and smelled the ozone from a close strike. Water dripped from the roof eaves in a solid sheet, and the view across the street blurred as the rain intensified. The wind shifted and the rain misted across the porch.

Reluctantly I moved inside to watch. I pressed my palm to the cold windowpane and left it there until I couldn't feel my fingers.

At last, the storm passed, although thunder still growled like a mountain lion caught in a slot canyon. I grabbed a jacket, locked up, and walked down the street. The tourists had left for the evening and the locals thronged the still-open bars and restaurants.

I heard the music drifting through open doors, but I walked on, pulling the collar of my jacket tighter. I was *right,* moving from HT's house. That didn't stop a bitter wind from howling through me.

I brushed tears out of my eyes. I didn't need him. I didn't need anyone to do my job properly. And that's what I intended to do.

CHAPTER FIFTEEN

I PASSED A SLEEPLESS NIGHT, and the next morning I paid HT a visit. I didn't want our parting argument to build a wall between us.

He was in the garage tinkering when I arrived. "I can use some help with this roof project."

Just like him. Ignore our fight, pretend it never happened. I wanted to apologize, again, for moving out, as much for me as for him. I was tired of feeling guilty about the move.

On the other hand, at least we were talking again. I'd make do with that for now. Together we propped the extension ladder against the house side and I held it steady while he climbed up to the third-story roof.

"Reach me up that pole, now, will you?" he called when he had climbed onto the roof. "I need to clean the trash out of this gutter."

He was up too far for me to hoist the pole up, and the roof was too high to throw it. That meant I'd have to deliver the darn thing in person. Much as I liked spending time with him, I wished I was a spectator for this experience.

"Well, come on girl. I don't have all day."

No help for it. I had to climb. I grabbed the pole and put one tentative foot on the ladder, too stubborn to admit my fear of heights.

I closed my eyes and felt blindly for each rung until I hoisted myself onto the asphalt-shingled roof. It sagged in spots where age and the shifting earth caused the foundation to settle. I handed the pole to HT and sat, feet braced against the shingles watching him work. He was as agile and sure-footed as a desert big-horned sheep as he cleaned the accumulated pine needles and sycamore leaves from the gutters. I was envious of his rooftop fearlessness.

Fair weather clouds scudded past, on the same level as my nose. Their appearance signaled a pass day on the monsoon rains. A huge black rectangle shape in Clarkdale cast a long shadow, a mile below us on the valley floor.

"Hey, what's that?" I asked.

HT looked where I pointed. "That's the slag heap from the old smelter. Wait. I can't talk to you from here." He cautiously picked his way across the old shingles and sat down beside me.

Then he opened his scarred fingertips wide, framing the slag heap far below us. "Near fifteen million tons, bigger'n twenty football fields. And it will sit there forever, that solid slab of ugly metal. Not profitable for tertiary mining. And nothing will grow on it. It just sits there, a monument to man's stupidity."

His words held disgust and at the same time, a wistful regret as though something beautiful had been lost forever. He lowered his big hands and squeezed my fingers.

"And the tailings are even worse. I'm surprised that geology boyfriend of yours, Flint Tanner didn't tell you about them. Maybe he's too ashamed to. There, over by the old Indian ruins at Tuzigoot, just acres of those orange wastelands."

I looked where he was pointing. "They look pretty to me."

"Pretty!" he exploded. "Those tailing gravels are filled with *sulfides*." He spat out the word like a curse. "You got to keep them wet down, or they fly into the air and cause the most awful acid rain you can imagine."

"Well, expensive for the mining company," I admitted. "But can't they just put a watering system on them, like highway construction crews do on new roads?"

"Nope, that's the problem. If you put too *much* water on them, they form sulfuric acid that runs into the rivers and kills what's left of the green in this beautiful valley." He shook his head at the thought of it. "We've had enough of mining up here."

It was my vintage grandpa. We'd had debates like this when I was a child. I hated the topic but warmed to the closeness it gave us.

It was my turn to counter. “Well, is Garrett's land development any better?”

“Hell, no. That crooked son-of-a-gun plans to level the better part of this little town. He's even got the bank officials eating out of his hand. Why else would they be asking me for loan payments?”

Maybe because you owe them? I dismissed my thought as uncharitable.

My thoughts leaped forward. “Okay, if mining isn’t good for the town, and new development isn’t either, then *what*? Leave the buildings to slide the rest of the way down the hill? Come on, HT, you know that’s not the solution.”

His eyes held a crafty look. “Me and some of the boys is planning a demonstration tomorrow. Right there on Main Street in front of your office. You can't miss it.”

He rose and picked up the cleaning pole. “Look out below,” he hollered and tossed it over the edge of the roof into the backyard. Then he turned around and backed down the ladder.

Leaving the high places with their elevated thinking behind, I followed him. The vague threat in HT’s voice was troubling. Whatever he was planning didn’t bode well for the law in the town, and that happened to be me.

Once on solid ground, I stood back as HT slid the ladder extensions into a compact aluminum package and we stored it in the old garage. Then I washed my hands at the outside faucet and headed toward the kitchen door.

Vanessa bumped into me as I rounded the landing. She threw me a spiteful look as she passed.

“Thanks, Isabel,” the girl called into the house, clutching a dark parcel to her chest.

More than one way to end unwanted pregnancies. Was Vanessa making the right decision? Not my business. She wasn't doing anything illegal. Yet. I’d make it my business to be around if she crossed that line.

* * * * * *

WHEN I ARRIVED AT WORK the next morning, Roger Heaton rose from a bench outside, ready to start his agenda before I even had my first cup of good coffee.

"What are you going to do about this?" he demanded.

I pulled out my ring of keys and fit one in the lock of the ancient oak door of the sheriff's annex. "What 'this' are you talking about, Roger?"

He gestured angrily up the hill toward Main Street. "Those muppets are blocking traffic and scaring the tourists. Garrett wants them gone."

I looked up the street but didn't see any fuzzy yellow and purple creatures. Before I could express the thought to Roger, he squealed off in his Lexus. Undoubtedly to attend to other important things of his boss Tal Garrett's agenda.

I dumped my stuff in the office and strolled up the street for a closer look. The creatures scaring the tourists turned out to be college-age kids marching in a tight circle in front of the post office. They held placards: "Don't let the mines ruin our land" "Impeach Tal Garrett."

Made sense to me.

Armor sat on a bench watching the action. When he spotted me, he waved a clipboard in my direction. "We're establishing a new historic district. That'll cancel out any idiot's plan to tear our town down. Want to sign?"

"Can't. Got to be impartial, Armor. You know that."

He gave me a serious look. "Time's coming when you'll have to take a stand in this town, Peg. Let people know who you are and what's important to you."

I didn't agree. The only way to be respected was not to take sides, and yet that course of action separated me from every single person who lived in Mingus. It was a familiar feeling that I'd lived with throughout childhood as I kept my mom's drinking a secret from the outside world. But that didn't mean I liked it.

Taking my head shake as a negative, Armor propositioned the next couple coming by. "Hello. Are you registered voters? This will just take a few moments of your time." They listened to his speech and took the blue ballpoint he proffered to sign the petition. He retrieved the clipboard back and marched up the street in search of more possible signers.

The placard bearers grew in number, and their noise increased with each new arrival. They chanted loudly, enthusiastically punching their signs up and down. The protest spread into the street, preventing cars from driving through town.

These kids had too much time on their hands. Why couldn't they just go skinny dipping in Oak Creek or something? Then they'd be out of my jurisdiction and the next county's problem.

A couple of Armor's motorcycle buddies joined in the parade, duck-walking their bikes around the marchers. They shook supportive fists in the air. The whole demonstration had a carnival air about it. I watched it build, alert for the moment when it might turn sour.

HT arrived and sat on the bench that Armor had vacated. He watched the commotion with a big grin on his face.

I confronted him. "HT, you started this."

"Town needed a little shaking up. Too much quiet ain't good for the soul."

"Well, stop it."

"No, *you* stop it. You're the law."

He was right. This was my town and my problem. I stopped to consider. What laws were they breaking? Loitering, for one. Assembling without a permit. A sign hit the ground. Littering.

Standing well out of the way of the sign wavers so I wouldn't get another black eye, I addressed the marchers first. "Okay, guys, get your parade out of the street. You're blocking traffic."

I pointed. "Mayor's office is that way. Get your permit there."

They conferred among themselves, lowered their signs and left.

That took care of the sign-bearers. I improvised with the motorcyclists. "Free drinks at the biker bar," I shouted.

They stopped circling and parked the bikes. Armor gave his clipboard to HT and followed the doo-ragged crowd through the batwing doors. Would he honor my statement for free drinks? I hoped so. Otherwise, my tab would be astronomical.

Without the obstructions, vehicles started moving again. I directed traffic for a while, clearing the blockage the impromptu parade had created. When the vehicle lines smoothed out, I dropped down on the bench by HT.

He gave me a nod of approval. “That'll do,” was all he said.

It was enough. The five-year-old inside me glowed at his attention. That phrase still meant a lot, coming from the only father figure I’d had in my life. But I wouldn't be telling him that.

I was pleased, too, that I’d been able to defuse the protest before it grew unruly and dangerous. Mingus was small, but any casual gathering had the potential to explode into a mob when tempers flared. I didn’t want that happening here if I could help it.

* * * * * *

LATE THAT AFTERNOON, the monsoon storms rolled in, the roiling clouds turning the skies the color of bruised eggplant. The buildings across from the sheriff’s annex blurred with the intensity of the downpour. The wind whistled around the old buildings, challenging their solidness. I didn’t worry. This structure had withstood a hundred years of turmoil and still remained standing.

As suddenly as the storm had started, it quit. The gutters still dripped a syncopated beat, but the skies freshened to turquoise. It was time for a walking patrol of the town.

On Main Street, I spotted what I'd half been watching for, a pair of bright purple cowboy boots attached to a very large man wearing a gray beard. He emerged from Armor’s bar, spotted me, and ducked into a nearby alley, moving fast. I quickened my pace and rounded the corner of the building just as the man exited the alley and disappeared into the Gulch below.

The Gulch with its twisted narrow streets had a reputation. The laborers who worked the lower paying mine jobs lived in this barrio district during the boom times. On payday, the streets echoed with celebrations that sometimes turned violent.

When the mines closed, the bikers claimed this abandoned hillside as their own. Most yards had a Harley in front and a pit bull or two in the back. That didn’t seem to concern the man with the purple boots, who disappeared over a fence and down a ravine.

When I got to the fence, I stopped and eyed the two dogs who challenged further pursuit. One let out a menacing growl, and I considered the situation. No sense wasting my uniform tearing through a yard filled with critters intent on my destruction. Panting, I walked back up the alley. If the guy lived around here, Armor would know him.

I banged through the batwing doors into the saloon. “Who was that guy just left here?”

Armor switched his attention from a Steeler's exhibition game on the big screen TV to my disheveled appearance.

I tucked a lock of hair behind one ear and tried to act professional.

“You mean the big dude with the beard? That's Jake Bean. He shows up here every summer. Lives with his kids in Phoenix in the winter in a trailer out behind their house.”

That made sense. The Papago Indians used to do that. A summer camp in the mountains and a winter camp in the desert. Maybe this guy was the same way.

“I need to talk to him.”

“He's kind of leery of law folks, Peg. But money talks.”

I reached for my wallet.

“Not for me. For *him*,” Armor said. “He usually shows up midafternoon for a beer. I'll send him up your way. He likes food. You might lay in some reinforcements from the donut shop.”

Patrick Shaw pulled out a fresh batch when I arrived at his shop and sold me a baker's dozen. I walked back to the office planning my strategy. Ben was over at the fire station for training, which meant I didn’t have to fight him for the donuts. Good thing, because I needed all of them.

I brewed a fresh pot of coffee, opened the box of donuts, and set the door ajar so the enticing aromas could float out to the street. Then I settled down to wait.

The trap was set. The question was whether the quarry would take the bait. I needed to hear the story those purple Lucchese boots could tell.

CHAPTER SIXTEEN

THE CLOCK TICKED AWAY the minutes as I tried to ignore the temptation spread before me. A sugary aroma floated up to my nose, and chocolate stripes and sprinkles made my mouth water. I touched a finger to the crème filling spilling from one center. My stomach grumbled. Jake Bean had better get here soon.

Luckily, before the hour was up, he peered cautiously around the edge of the door. Purple boots graced his very large feet.

"Come in, Mr. Bean. Have a donut."

He sat and poked at the carton.

"And some coffee?" I suggested. I cautiously rose for the coffee pot, not wanting to spook him again.

He looked up, mouth full of chocolate donut, and a maple cruller poised in one hand. Then he nodded. "Black, lots of sugar."

I poured the coffee and put in two teaspoons of sugar. I looked at him and then added two more. I set the mug in front of him.

He took a big gulp. "Just the way I like it."

His bulk spilled out over the sides of the chair. His hair was thinning on top, but the gray beard more than made up for it. It flowed down upon his chest in bristly magnificence. His eyebrows joined in the middle of his forehead and then swirled up at the ends to mingle with strandy gray locks on his temple. Deep wrinkles incised his cheeks and his cobalt eyes challenged me.

"Armor said you wanted to see me."

I debated. I could ease into this by doing the get-to-know-you thing. However, my skills at social chitchat were limited and the donuts were disappearing at an alarming rate. A direct approach might be better.

"Nice boots," I commented.

"I found 'em."

"Where?"

"Up on the hill. Guy up there didn't need them anymore."

"Why not?"

"Cause he was at the bottom of the hill." Jake Bean looked at me directly. "I ain't stupid. I knew what you wanted to see me about. Figured it would be only a matter of time."

"I almost had you at the alley there."

"Nah, you weren't even close. Did Fido and Rufous put up too big a fight?"

I ignored his jibe. "Tell me about the boots."

He stretched out a leg turning his foot this way and that. The orange cactus blooms on the sides of the boots glowed in the sunlight. "Pretty, ain't they? They fit me just fine. Finders, keepers as I see it."

"Did you kill Druce Kevern?" Might as well get it out in the open.

"That his name?" He licked pink donut frosting off one big finger. "Course not. I wouldn't be sitting here talking to you if I had."

My instinct told me he was telling the truth. Still, he might be a witness to who had been there on the hillside with Druce.

"Mr. Bean, what did you see up there that night?" I kept my tone neutral. I wasn't accusing. I needed information and he was the one to give it to me.

"It was dark. New moon, you know."

The man was a storyteller. My fingers itched for my pad to take notes, but I didn't want to stop the flow. I set my mind to remember his words so that I could transcribe them later. Then I settled back to listen.

"This guy built a campfire, a dumb-ass, touristy kind of thing. Then he took off his boots and lay down beside the fire to sleep. But like a fool, he didn't clear enough undergrowth. Fire was set to spread. I live in these woods. Don't want 'em burned down around me."

He surveyed the ruins of the baked goods and took the remaining strawberry frosted donut.

Damn. I wanted that one.

"Then what happened?" I asked.

"As I was making my way down the hill to check on the fire, this other guy came out of the shadows. I dropped down in the bushes, so's they couldn't see me, to watch."

"What did this new guy look like?"

"Hard to say. It was dark, just campfire light." He stopped for a moment and stroked his beard like a furry pet, thinking. Then, "A white guy. About medium height, I'd say. Brown hair, thinning, like mine on top." He patted his head, remembering.

I let him talk.

"Sorry, that's about it." He gave up the effort. "Just—average—is all. You'd lose him in a crowd."

"Could you hear anything they said?"

"Mutters and shouts, nothin' definite. The thunder was kicking up a bit, getting ready to rain. They circled around for a while. The new guy, he wasn't very happy. Shoved the camper guy. Then they got into a tussle, close to the cliff edge."

"Why didn't you do something?"

"Why?" He looked at me as though I were crazy. "Not my fight."

He finished one last chocolate cake donut and gave a satisfied burp. "Ah, that hit the spot."

The man had an appetite on him. Armor hadn't been kidding.

"And?" I asked.

"You mean what happened then? Well, the new guy pushed the first guy, and he went over the cliff. One minute he was there, and the next he wasn't. Life is like that, you know."

Just what I needed. A homespun philosopher. "What did the new guy do then?"

"Well, he looked down at the mining pit for a long spell. Then he picked something up off the ground. Heavy like," he said.

"Could it have been a pistol?"

"Have to be a long barrel, if it was. And then he left, and I did, too."

"But not before you took the boots," I said.

"That guy as went over the cliff wasn't needing them anymore."

"Why didn't you go down to check on him?"

"Any fool could see he was dead. Anyway…"

"…not your fight," I finished.

He flashed a mouth full of yellowed, broken teeth.

I reviewed the story in my mind. "You said you started toward the camp to put out the fire?"

"That's right. And I *did* put it out after all those people left."

"Well, what started the wildfire at the site then? Patrick Shaw's crew had to go up there to put it out."

"Don't know. It was dead cold when I left. I made sure." He got a squirrelly look on his face. "Maybe that new guy, he snuck back and started another one, to mix stuff up, like."

He stood up, towering above the desk. His eyes snaked toward the door.

I stood, too. "Look, Mr. Bean," I said. "Before you go—I'll get this statement written up and you can sign it. Won't take but just a moment."

He looked at me like I had the IQ of a banana peel. "And advertise to the world that I saw stuff I shouldn't have? No, I'll be taking my leave now."

A car backfired in the street and Jake Bean jerked. His eyes stared wildly and he reached out with an involuntary motion, too quick for me to block. His elbow slammed into the side of my head with a jolting crash and I fell.

I slumped to the floor. Then everything went dark.

* * * * * *

WHEN I SWAM BACK to consciousness, someone was standing over me, and I curled into a ball to protect myself. Had Jake Bean returned?

"Easy. Are you okay? Peg, talk to me."

I shook my head, willing the world to settle in one place and stop playing hopscotch.

Flint Tanner helped me to a chair and peered anxiously into my face. "I was walking past when I saw the open door and you on the floor. What happened?"

I searched a mind filled with pain and confusion. “I was talking to a witness for the Kevern case when he got rough and took off. Gave me a nasty going-away present, that's for sure.” I shook my head again and then regretted the action as a tsunami wave of agony pummeled my brain.

Flint poured a glass of water and steadied my hand as I drank it.

I rubbed the side of my head and felt a nasty goose egg starting. It would blend right in with my black eye from breaking up the street fight. “I should have seen it coming.”

“Don't blame yourself. Armor tells me that guy used to be a commando in the Marines.”

“Who would have guessed? He sure doesn't look like that now.”

Flint agreed. “War changes people. Civilians who have only hunted for sport turn into assassins. It twists something inside, sometimes. The suicide rate and PTSD diagnoses for Vets are off the charts.”

His eyes turned dark, and I wondered if he was speaking from personal experience. There was a lot I didn’t know about Flint Tanner.

I started to stand and the room spun.

“You’re in no shape to work. Can I give you a ride home?”

He might have a good idea there. I called dispatch and told them I was closing early. Then I locked the front door with shaky fingers and let Flint assist me to his Jeep.

He half carried me up the apartment stairs and lay me down on the bed. I dimly remembered his taking off my shoes and sliding my feet under the covers. Then he left, softly closing the door behind him.

I surrendered to the welcoming darkness, my last thought that of purple boots hightailing out the office door.

CHAPTER SEVENTEEN

I FELL INTO A DREAMLESS stupor and didn't wake until the morning sun shone in my eyes. I lay there and took inventory before I moved: Arms and legs functioning, although sore. Still a headache, but better than yesterday.

Rising, I stumbled into the bathroom, aches and pains accompanying me each step of the way. Probably a bruise forming on my rear end where I landed after Jake Bean slammed into me. I turned to inspect. Nope, not yet.

I slugged down a few aspirin and started my coffee machine. Sweat pants and a T-shirt kept me decent as I walked out onto the balcony to greet the day. I took a sip of hot coffee and sniffed an errant breeze. The morning sky was robin's-egg blue, with no hint of smoke. I didn't know whether that would please or disappoint our fire chief.

Main Street buzzed with early hours activity. Delivery vans brought fresh beer kegs to the biker bar, and contractor pickups full of materials and tools passed in a steady procession on the road below. It was a picture of small town tranquility. I brushed away the unwelcome thought of how that might all change if Tal Garrett's development plans went through.

Hoping that some fresh air would help my nagging headache, I took a walk before work, tracing a familiar path to one of the small cemeteries tucked in amongst the hills surrounding Mingus. Mining executives claimed fancier cemeteries higher up the hill with their elaborate granite markers and stone crypts. I liked this simple graveyard better. Wrought metal fences made by local ironworkers enclosed graves of Irish, Welsh, and Yugoslavian mining families.

I pulled some of the puncture vine and filaree weed off the old graves and straightened a small tombstone, black with lichen. A covey of quail chuckled in the mesquite as I sat down on a sandstone bench to take in the valley spreading a thousand feet below. A long-tailed lizard skittered over the toe of my shoe and flashed under a rock.

The Druce Kevern case haunted me more than the ghosts inhabiting these graves. If his death wasn't premeditated murder, then it probably was manslaughter. Either way, it was definitely not an accident. That meant that I should notify Sheriff Jones, which in turn meant he'd send Sanchez here to take over my case.

I weighed the need to finish what I started on the investigation with the guilt of omission and put that call to the sheriff on the list of things I should do but probably wouldn't. Not yet, anyway.

Whoever had the missing dueling pistol would be a logical suspect for Druce Kevern's death, but nobody was waving it about on the street. Roger Heaton might have fought with Druce to retrieve it, pushing him over the cliff in the process. If that was the case, where was the missing pistol?

And what about Roger's daughter, Vanessa? The unwanted pregnancy still could have been an early motive for her—the pistol that Druce stole was a source of money that she needed at the time. Or was it jealousy over a rival for her parents' affections. If she believed Druce really was a long, lost son, that might be possible—Vanessa had a cold streak I didn't trust. Still, was she capable of murder?

And there was my clerk and former loft roommate, Ben Yazzie. He sometimes watched Armor's marijuana crop up on the hill, which meant he was in the vicinity of the dead man's campsite on a regular basis. Would he defend his uncle's cash crop of marijuana against intruders? Ben would do anything for Vanessa. Maybe she asked him to…I didn't want to finish that thought, but I added him to the pool of suspects.

Trust no one, my instructors at the Academy had told us. Now I saw why. I couldn't afford to give anyone a pass. Not even my grandfather.

I turned from the unresolved death to the wider problem of the unrest in Mingus. As a sworn peace officer, I was responsible for the safety of town citizens. The conflicts among the warring factions had turned the community into a powder box with an uncertain fuse. Whatever happened in the next few weeks could influence community direction for the next century, even as the mining bonanza had, a hundred years ago.

It shouldn't be my concern, I kept reminding myself. I had a temporary appointment with the sheriff's department that ended in a few months. Leaving this town and all its conflicts would be a welcome relief. I had few possessions and could move on short notice, as I had in the past.

But I couldn't. In spite of my determination to remain aloof, HT had turned back into family. And like it or not, his financial debt loomed over me as well. I should talk to Johnny Evans at the bank to get an extension. I put that chore on the around-to-it list. It occurred to me I had too many items on that list.

The breeze cooling the sweat on my arms drew me out of the maelstrom of worries. I picked up a rake and smoothed the gravel in the walking path. Then I pulled out my cell and called the station to say I'd be late. Nobody picked up the phone.

Where the hell was Ben? He'd kept irregular hours since the dog had arrived. They'd done a lot of exploring in the hills—Ben told me he was assembling his medicine bag, vital for his training to become a Shaman. A pity he didn't live closer to the mentoring of his Navajo relatives.

I tried the number again, and it still shunted to the message, spoken in Ben's soft Navajo accent. "You've reached the sheriff's annex. Leave your name and number."

A shiver of irritation drew me upright. Ben needed to tell me if he was going to be gone. No excuse about that.

I pulled one final camphorweed from the path. Its leaves smelled like the old Vicks vapor rub my mother used to put on my chest when I was sick. I brushed the sticky sap off on my pant leg and walked back to my apartment to change clothes. When I clamored down the stairs ready for work, Isabel stood there on the sidewalk.

"What's wrong? Is HT okay?"

"Armor came by and talked HT into going to the Patch. They took a jug of moonshine with them. HT shouldn't be drinking, bad for his heart. You go see about it." Her elbows spread in frustration.

"Fine. I'll go check on him."

I gritted my teeth as I backed the cruiser out of the drive and sped up the mountain. No wonder the sheriff doubted my abilities, when I ended up babysitting every miscreant in town. And that included Armor and my grandfather—*especially* my grandfather. I understood now why my mother had refused to talk to HT for over a decade. Why was it my responsibility to pick up the pieces, now that she couldn't?

The cruiser hit eighty-five as I topped the mountain summit. A passing semi's air horn jolted me back into reality. Slamming on the brakes, I squealed into the cut-off road that Isabel described.

* * * * * *

I FOUND ARMOR AND HT at the ruined marijuana patch. They had made some half-hearted attempts to clear up the mess Tal Garrett had made destroying the plants. A hoe leaned against a pine trunk, bunches of tattered plants stacked next to it.

The two men propped each other up like two sides of the letter A, a jug clutched between them. The pungent smell of broken marijuana plants mingled with the sour smell of the kerosene. Armor held the jug up high, letting the fiery liquid pour down his throat.

I stomped on the brake, enveloping them with dust. Then I rolled down my window and glared at them. "I ought to arrest both of you."

"What for?" Armor asked. "Nothing left here to confiscate."

HT wiped dust off the mouth of the jug. "Now look what you did, Peg."

My lips tightened with disgust. "Get in. I'll drive you back."

"But what'll I do with my pickup?" HT protested.

"You're in no condition to drive. Ben can retrieve it later." I glowered at them as they stumbled into my back seat. "And don't neither of you throw up. I just cleaned this cruiser."

I managed to hit every pothole in the road on the way back to town.

"You're doing that on purpose," HT complained.

I might have been. But it hurt my aching head, too. I slowed down, hit every other one after that.

Armor drifted into a drunken stupor, his snores rattling the side window. His drool smeared the window glass I'd just cleaned that morning. Their behavior reminded me of all the drunks I had known in my life including my mother. Why had I expected my grandfather would be any different, I thought bitterly.

I pulled up to the biker bar and jerked on the emergency brake. Walking to the passenger side door, I yanked it open.

"Out," I snarled at Armor.

"Huh?" Armor dropped one foot on the curb, then the other and grabbed my arm to pull himself from the back seat.

I shoved the crutch under his arm and leaned him against a sidewalk bench. Before he could stumble into the bar, I had shoved the car into gear and peeled down the street.

Isabel met us by the back door at HT's house. She gave me a hug and whispered, "Thank you." Then she gripped HT's arm and marched him into the house, her black eyes snapping.

My headache throbbing in syncopation to the rattle of the old cruiser, I drove back to the sheriff's station.

* * * * * *

MY MOOD TURNED BLACK when I walked in the front door. Ben was on his hands and knees in a scatter of papers. He pointed to glass fragments on the floor in front of a broken window. The computer monitor was shattered and the computer tower had disappeared.

My jaw tightened. Somehow, this break-in epitomized the casual way Ben treated his work here. If my clerk had been there like he was supposed to be, this might not have happened.

I stopped short. Or, if I'd been here doing my job instead of lollygagging at a gravesite or retrieving drunken relatives off a mountainside, it wouldn't have happened, either.

I stopped blaming the world and assessed the scene in front of me. What papers had I left out? Some of Cyrus Marsh's old files that I'd been reviewing. Routine, mostly. None of my present notes on the

Druce Kevern case—I patted my pocket notebook to be sure they were safe.

"What were they looking for?" I asked Ben. He wriggled uncomfortably, and I braced for the worst.

"Maybe somebody thought we knew something, me and Vanessa."

"Spit it out. What were the two of you up to this time?"

"Vanessa was going to leave home. She needed money."

Not that I blamed her, but it seemed like Vanessa *always* needed money. "And?"

"Well, we thought it might be a good idea to sort of check on the Internet, to see if…" Ben hesitated, waiting for me to get the idea without his having to tell me.

With his deft hacking skills, Ben sometimes penetrated systems just for the fun of unlocking closed doors. He always backed out, he said, without touching anything. I believed him up to now. But this had gone too far. "Anything you found was obtained illegally," I pointed out. "You could be prosecuted!"

"Know that," he said, "Doesn't matter, anyway." He waved away my concerns. "Vanessa planned to take what we found and..."

"And use it for blackmail?" My voice hit the high C screeching range.

The seriousness of this didn't seem to register with Ben.

"I got stuff on Garrett. Want to see?" He turned to where his computer used to be and then hesitated at the sight of the empty space. Shrugged.

"We got the goods on shopkeepers, too. They weren't reporting enough sales taxes. And the owner of the biker bar is skimming liquor and selling it on the side." The words raced out of him. "And then we tried getting into the bank."

"The *bank*. What for?"

"We thought maybe if we could help HT with his loan problems, he could help Vanessa. And we almost made it. Want me to try again?"

"Don't you know what you were doing was *against the law*? Get out of here, now," I exploded.

He headed out the front door with his dog close on his heels. He stopped for one last word of advice. “Find Cyrus’s personal files. He kept dirt on everybody. A lot worse than anything we found.”

What did he mean by that? Personal files? I thought I’d seen everything the former lawman had written. Was there more? I shuffled the ruined papers and stacked them on my desk. I rapidly went over the confidential materials kept here. There weren’t many. Just a few break-in reports.

It was small consolation that a thief wouldn’t have found anything of import on the Kevern case. My list of confirmed suspects was abysmally slim. But a murderer wouldn't know that. Likely the computer was stolen for easy money. It was probably in some fence’s locker by now.

Sighing, I picked up the phone to dial Sheriff Jones with the bad news.

I hadn’t got through the first sentence when he cut me off. “What you mean is that you were careless enough to let the *sheriff's* property get burglarized.”

“They didn’t take much,” I said defensively, feeling a sudden empathy for Ben when I had yelled at him moments earlier.

“You better make a complete inventory. Expect it to be deducted from your paycheck.” Sheriff Jones’ voice lowered. “One more mistake and you are out of there and back to whatever cockamamie academy had the stupidity of graduating you.”

His phone hang-up rocked ears still numb from the body slam I'd gotten yesterday.

I limped into the restroom and slugged down some more aspirin. Jones had the right to yell. If I'd been doing my job, none of this would have happened.

As I headed to my apartment late that afternoon, the thunder rumbling overhead matched my own gray mood. Tomorrow had to be a better day. It couldn't get any worse than today, that was for sure.

Or could it?

CHAPTER EIGHTEEN

FINALLY, THE WEEKEND ARRIVED, and I intended to sleep until noon. It didn't work out quite that way.

I awoke to a pounding on the door downstairs and peered at my alarm clock. Its dial glowed in the darkness—only 4:30 a.m. I pulled on a T-shirt and jeans and stumbled downstairs. Flint Tanner stood outside the door, his hat in hand.

"What do you want?" I mumbled. I hadn't spoken to Flint since the purple boot fiasco and it was unexpected to see him here on my doorstep.

"Something I want to show you."

I yawned and rubbed my eyes. "I have to work."

"Hurry! We'll miss the sunrise. It's Saturday. You can't work on Saturday."

In a way, he was wrong. The work week ended Friday night for most people, but being the only law officer in town, I was always on call. On the other hand, now I was awake. I retrieved my purse, making sure I had my cell phone.

Flint accompanied me to his Jeep and opened my door with a flourish. He'd swept out the old Pepsi cans and the fast food wrappers. Instead, a large wicker basket rested on the back seat. A bottle of wine and some bundles that looked like food protruded from the top of the basket. Was this a *date*?

He noticed my glance. "Isabel made the picnic. The wine is my choice. A new winery here in the Valley—That's a bottle of pinot called *Mangas Colorado*." He pointed to a metal flask. "There's coffee in the thermos. Ben made that."

So the whole *crew* was in on this—even Ben? He must still be bunking in HT's loft.

I'd missed them since I moved out, even that damned dog. Maybe it was time to take a break and enjoy myself for a change. A picnic might be fun. I settled back for the ride.

As Flint drove up the mountain, chaparral turned to juniper and ponderosa pine. The sun edged over the valley rim the exact minute we reached the top of the mountain.

"Ah, made it." Flint squeezed my hand in that shared moment when the whole world turned gold in the dawning light in a silhouette worthy of Midas.

He turned off on a dirt road and stopped at a barbed wire gate. He let go of my hand and gave my shoulder a nudge. "Shotgun gets to open and close."

I pried the wire loop off the old wooden post. The wire gate sagged with the release of tension when I pulled it to the side and Flint drove the Jeep through. Then, coughing with the dust he stirred up, I relooped the gate and scrambled up into the seat. Two more gates needed the same treatment as we climbed higher on the ridge. Finally, the road dwindled to a mere cow path and Flint shifted the Wagoneer to four-wheel drive.

"We're trekking up Woodchute Mountain," Flint said. "You need to learn that Arizona has more to offer besides murderers and bad guys." He pulled to a stop in a stand of tall prairie grass. "Now we walk." He grabbed the basket and handed me an old red plaid blanket to carry.

The foot trail led us through a meadow lush with gamma grass and wild iris. We passed a small pond alive with dragon and damsel flies. "Trout?" I asked.

He studied the water. "Probably not. A seasonal stock tank—it'll dry out after the monsoon rains stop. Good place for birds, though." A black-and-white phoebe swooped over the water to catch a gnat and then landed again on top of a reed. I relaxed for the first time in days.

For the next several miles we hiked a ridge only a few feet wide with a steep drop off on either side. Then we climbed to the top of one final hill that opened out onto a panoramic view of the valley below. The jagged silhouette of the San Francisco Peaks defined the horizon fifty miles away. Even now at the end of summer, snow outlined the mountaintops like a child's uneven crayon stroke.

We spread the blanket in the shade of an old shaggy-bark juniper and dived into the basket. Isabel sent homemade tortillas filled with eggs, chilies, and chorizo that turned into amazing burritos. The chilies gave a hot explosion of flavor, as the textures blended on my tongue.

I cooled my mouth with a bite of deep red plum, catching the juices that dripped down my chin with my fingers. A hawk caught the thermals and soared higher and higher above us. I recognized the broad wings and that white stripe on the tail. Probably a black hawk. Maybe I wasn't such a greenhorn after all. Birds and wild plants fascinated me.

"Time for a geology lesson," Flint said. "Let me share my world with you."

I liked the sound of that.

He stood up and reached his long arms sideways like a da Vinci wheel. Standing that way he blocked out the sun. I wiggled my toes in my boots and leaned against a boulder to listen, and learn more about this tall, strong man.

"Once upon a time, all of this," he waved his arms around, "was under water. Undersea volcanoes formed mounds that collapsed to form calderas, and then the caldera edge shattered into a ring fracture." His hands dived in illustration.

I tried a slice of melon. It was juicier than his geology lecture. But then I'm not a geologist. Maybe he'd find cop stuff boring, too.

I batted my eyelashes in what I hoped was a "gee whiz" response. "I'm following you," I said. "So far we got the undersea volcanoes and holes and fractures and stuff."

"Right. And then the sea water seeped down into the fractures, and dissolved all those minerals and brought them right up to the bottom of the sea."

"Where they cooled again," I prompted, hoping to hurry him along. Rocks could be pretty dull—they just sat there. Whereas here we were, a man and a woman alone. I plastered another I'm-so-fascinated look on my face. Move it along, guy.

"Yes!" His fist pounded his thigh. "That cooling made the best damn mineral deposits you could ever imagine. When the earth rose again, the sea became mountains, right under your town of Mingus. By today's standards, the miners took four billion dollars of minerals out of that hillside."

I sensed his primal energy with a shiver of appreciation. I'd had lovers over the years, but nothing serious. Now this passionate man stood in front of me challenging the sun…

Flint stopped abruptly and stared at me. I realized my daydreaming might lead to complications I wasn't ready for yet.

I returned to the safer topic of mining. "And that's where you come in?"

"Right. My company wants to figure out if it's economical to open the mines again."

"But isn't that Tal Garrett's land?" I asked.

"What's above you? Free air, right?"

I nodded.

"Well, the dirt underneath isn't free. Under Arizona law, it's all claimed through mineral rights."

"So if you determine it's feasible to mine again, Garrett's development will be nixed," I said.

"Canceled. Caput. No more." He sounded very satisfied. "I'll have the final report ready for the town meeting in a couple of weeks."

That might mean the end of Garrett's plans for Mingus. But what about the environmentalists like Armor and HT who wanted this area declared a Historic District? That might top both development and mining. Rock, paper, scissors. I wondered who would be the victor this time around?

Flint looked at me, and our eyes locked for one intense moment. I touched his hand. Then my hip vibrated, but it wasn't from my own energy.

I yanked out my cell phone. The caller ID said the sheriff's department. They'd found me.

"It's a burglary-in-progress on Main Street." Melda sounded breathless, as though the happening had wakened a quiet weekend. I knew exactly how she felt.

I hesitated. The thief would be long gone by the time I returned to town.

"Sheriff Jones wanted to be sure you got the message," she added, hanging up.

Flint gestured toward the phone. "Business?"

"Business." The towering anvil clouds high above swept a dark shadow over me, and I shivered. "I need to get back to Mingus."

"Sure." Flint sounded disappointed. "We'll save the wine for a better time."

We gathered up the blanket and put the remains of the picnic back in the basket. A better time. I wondered if that would ever happen on this job.

CHAPTER NINETEEN

FLINT LEFT ME at the station with a promise to get together soon.

The burglar Melda called me about turned out to be a six-year-old shoplifter who was apprehended by his parents. Damages were paid and the kid promised to never, ever do it again. I went through that experience when I was about his age. No fun, then either.

I spent the rest of the weekend wasting time on pointless projects, pacing the small confines of the studio apartment, waiting for the weekend to be over. I was in a fine humor by the time I returned to the station Monday, only to discover Ben absent from his desk. That meant I spent my morning fielding phone calls he should have been taking. Where was the kid this time?

The first call was a resident objecting to tourists parking in front of her house. The folks she fussed about paid taxes just like she did. I didn't remind her of that. Then I received a complaint from a merchant plagued by shrinkage in his inventory. We'd had a band of gypsy Travelers in town, those construction con-artists who used black paint to "repave" driveways for gullible homeowners. While they might not be the thieves, I promised to investigate.

The door opened and HT walked in. I had avoided him since the episode at the marijuana patch, and he still looked slightly hung over.

"How you feeling?" I tried to keep the judgment out of my voice.

"A little rough around the edges," he admitted. "Been a while since I tied one on like that. I don't know what got into me."

"I don't know what got into you either. High on marijuana. Ready to drive drunk. What if you'd hit somebody?"

"Well, I didn't. Where's Ben? I need my truck."

"He's not here."

"I can see that."

"I'm in enough trouble as is," I said. "I need him here doing the work he was hired to do."

"Trouble?" HT looked concerned.

"I'm on probation with the sheriff's office."

"Because of the break-in? Isabel told me." He surveyed the room. "You need better locks on those windows, less chance of burglaries that way."

The last thing I needed right now was his buttinsky advice. I gritted my teeth. We couldn't be in the same room for five minutes without sniping at each other.

He shifted back to his own topic. "Where *is* Ben? Isabel's got a bad feeling. She sent me over to check on him."

"Well, I have a bad feeling, too. He's going to lose this job if he's not careful."

The phone rang again and I held up a finger for HT to wait while I answered it.

"There's two guys squaring off in front of my house," said Roger Heaton. You need to get out here, right now." He hung up before I could respond. He must take phone etiquette lessons from his boss, Tal Garrett.

"Sorry, HT. Got to go check out a disturbance." I welcomed the interruption. I needed to leave before this interaction with my grandfather went totally off the rails.

I stretched tight neck muscles as I drove out to the Heatons' street. HT and I needed to clear the air about his financial problems and about his attitude. He didn't have to treat me like I was five years old. We would, soon— right after all this town conflict sorted itself out.

As I turned the corner, I saw two vehicles parked nose to nose in the middle of the road. An old Ford station wagon had a mattress bungeed on the roof, and three or four little kids looking out the windows. A Volkswagen bus painted with peace signs and daisies blocked its passage.

As I pulled up, a man standing beside the VW smacked the station wagon fender with the flat of his hand. He sported a gray ponytail, ragged blue jeans, and a tie-dyed T-shirt. One of the artist types that hocked doo-dads on Main Street. A stocky man with a buzz cut stepped out from behind the station wagon and raised his fist. Trouble.

I blipped the siren to get their attention and stepped out of the cruiser. “Okay, folks, what seems to be the problem here?”

“This bum’s been living in my house, that's what,” the stocky man said. “I'm not letting him leave until he pays me back rent.”

“*Your* house, man. You left it. Didn't even lock the door. Me and my girl, we just kept it warm for you,” Ponytail sneered.

The stocky man marched up on the front porch and threw stuff in the yard. “Get your damn trash out of here.”

“Hey, those are my paintings. And that's my found art. You can't do that.” The artist grabbed a piece of iron. There was a tug of war, and the stocky man fell back on his rear.

His face turned red as he stood up. He scowled in frustration. “Me and my family heard the mines were opening up and moved back from Bisbee. We found him squatting in *our house*.” He gestured at the artist. “He’s got no right to move in like that.”

“Nobody was here. And we needed a place to crash.” The artist made a conciliatory move. “Here's one of my paintings. See? *Sunset over Hermosillo*. Gotta be worth at least most of what we owe you.” He tossed the painting on the porch and pulled open the door of the VW. “I’m outa here.” He backed the bus away from the Ford and disappeared down the hill in a charge of black smoke.

The stocky man let out a breath and offered his hand. “Thanks for coming. I'm Reginald Smith.” A woman in her forties got out of the car and he gestured toward her. “And this is my wife, Jenny.”

I shook both their hands. “I'm Deputy Peg Quincy. Welcome back to Mingus. Glad to have you. But it might be a good idea to get the lay of the land before you jump to conclusions. And you might get some better locks on those doors.” I smiled briefly at the irony of giving away the advice I had received from HT.

I reflected on the small-world of grapevine gossip in the mining community. Many of the miners were like these two. When the mines closed, they just locked front doors and left, thinking the closure would be temporary. Frying pans were dumped in sinks unwashed, beds left unmade as folks moved on.

The Smiths were fortunate their home was still standing. Some of the wooden homes sagged into the hillsides, with only a fragrant lilac bush and a grove of ailanthus trees to mark where the houses had stood.

What conflicts would surface, if the miners returned to Mingus, adding yet another faction to this already divided town?

When I returned to the station, my grandfather was sitting on the bench outside. I rolled down my window. “You still here?”

“No place else to go. Got no wheels.”

I threw up my hands in exasperation. “Get in. Let's go get your damned truck.”

The clouds built, dark and ominous as we drove up the mountain. Going to rain soon. When it did, streets would run full, and the floods would start. I was stuck right in the middle, on temporary assignment in this small town at war against itself.

* * * * * *

IT WAS ALMOST NOON when I returned to the office. Ben still wasn't there. I was starting to worry a little, too. I called Armor, Ben’s uncle, on the off chance my clerk was at the biker bar, but Armor hadn't seen him.

Then I checked in with Isabel.

“Nooo,” her soft voice came over the line. “Ben left early this morning. His dog showed up about an hour ago. He’s been mooching food here in the kitchen.”

Another bad sign. Ben never went anywhere without that dog.

“Where do you sense he might be, Isabel?” Couldn’t hurt to ask. Police departments used intuitive psychics all the time, and Isabel had a reputation beyond her abilities as an herbalist.

There was a silence. Then, “Ben is in a bad place. I see dark metal around him.”

“Anything else?”

“I sense he is in pain. You need to find him.”

A dark place. Could that be a mining shaft? If so, there were almost a hundred miles of the tunnels forming a maze under Mingus.

"Put HT on the phone." Even as aggravated as I was with my grandfather, we both cared about Ben. "What's your take on this, HT? Do we need to be concerned?"

"Maybe. Ben's usually smart enough to stay clear of trouble, but when his dog came dragging back here he was covered in dirt."

Isabel could be wrong. Surely Ben had just disappeared for a Navajo Sing or something. He'd show up with a new feather in his hair, and be just fine. Or maybe not. Should I call a general alarm just on a psychic's whim? I could just see Sheriff Jones' reaction to that.

On the other hand, the town needed something to pull it together, and a rescue drill might defuse some of the building tension. I decided to go for it.

"Let's round up the fire department volunteers," I said. "They're trained in search and rescue and they care about Ben."

My grandfather agreed. "Meet you at the fire station. I'll bring the dog. He might be a help."

The general alarm bell echoed against the rock cliffs as I drove the street toward the fire hall. Patrick Shaw, the fire chief, met me there. Offices and stores closed as people congregated at the fire station. Soon most of the volunteers had gathered. One of their own was at risk.

I scanned the faces of the townspeople in front of me as they quieted, waiting for a signal. Then I gave the directions they needed to begin.

"Ben may be hurt or unconscious so you can't rely on his responding. Take your time so we don't have to recheck the same locations. Those of you entering abandoned buildings, watch your step. Rattlers like those dim corners and rotten stairs can give way unexpectedly."

I turned the floor over to the fire chief.

"We've divided you into teams. My assistant here will check off your names and assign your search areas. Report back on the fire walkie-talkies," he said. "HT will be manning the station central communication unit."

Flint Tanner had responded to the alarm, too. After the first groups dispersed, he and I spread the plat map for the old mines on the firehouse lunchroom table. Crosshatched lines marked the narrow gauge railways that brought the ore from the mines to the smelters.

The rails ran through tunnels from the deepest mine levels horizontally to Clarkdale, several thousand feet lower on the valley floor.

Flint pointed to the spot on the map where abandoned railway tunnels surfaced near the old turntable and roundhouse. “If Isabel is talking 'black places', that might be a good spot to begin.”

I grabbed the dog’s collar and placed him into the back of the cruiser. “When we get anywhere close, Ben’s dog can locate him for us.”

If the boy was even conscious at this point. But I didn’t want to follow that sort of reasoning just yet. Best to stay hopeful.

A few moments later, we pulled the cruiser into the roundhouse yard. The track emerged from the tunnel and progressed to a locomotive-sized turntable. There, like a plate on a lazy Susan, a steam engine could be shunted on a fan of tracks towards a maintenance stall in the huge semi-circular roundhouse or rotated a hundred-eighty degrees and directed back toward the mines.

No sign of Ben. I opened the door and Bitzer leaped out. The animal sniffed a few times and then lifted his leg against a stanchion. Apparently, he didn't think Ben was here, either. I snapped on a leash and we skirted the edge of the giant turntable, the huge central gear rusty with disuse.

Flint peered through a high metal door that had frozen open. The old steam engines were long gone, but the building, its floor crisscrossed with rusty tracks of rail, had the feeling of an old barn. Light beams laddered from high windows in the roof monitor.

I touched a heavy support beam and drew back a hand covered in soot. The anthracite coal used to fuel the engines had left a bitter odor in the air. I ducked my head as a barn swallow dived out the open door from the rafters above.

My apprehension shivered through the empty silence. “Ben are you here?” My words echoed in the empty space.

A spark of color winked in the dark. I reached down and encountered soft leather of Ben's medicine pouch. The bead decoration had caught the light from the high windows. We were in the right place, then, perhaps even close. For the first time since he’d gone missing, I felt a lifting of spirit. Maybe we weren’t too late.

We searched every corner of the roundhouse, poking amidst the piles of broken metal and log supports rotten with age. If Ben had visited this spot, he wasn't here now. I offered the pouch to the dog. "Find Ben," I commanded.

He sniffed at the pouch and whined.

"Find Ben," I repeated, desperation making my voice crack.

The dog whirled and pushed past my leg. We followed his lead out of the barn and into the sunshine once more. Nose to the earth, Bitzer swiftly detoured past the turntable and followed the old rails toward the old tunnel.

A chain-link fence barricaded the tunnel, and a heavy iron gate with a padlock barred entry. Surely Ben wouldn't be behind a locked gate! But the dog's churning paws tore at the fence in his eagerness to enter. He threw himself at the gate, and the old padlock swung open. It had been closed but not latched. Someone had been here before us and not that long ago.

Flint pulled the padlock out of the chain and the ancient gate creaked open. With the dog straining at the leash, we entered the tunnel. My flashlight made rotating circles of light, catching on square iron spikes in the darkened support timbers. Flecks of mica glittered in the rocks.

Heights, and now tight spaces. I liked to be in control of my environment, and both conditions stripped that ability away from me as effortlessly as leaves in a high wind. My heart started to beat faster.

The engineers had constructed this tunnel to sustain the pounding from heavy ore cars. Surely these walls wouldn't crumble with the passage of two humans and one scrawny dog? I slowed my claustrophobic breathing with effort.

The railroad tunnel smelled dusty and unused as we first entered, but after the first fifty yards, the air turned damp and cool, as the tons of rock overhead evened out the temperatures. I shivered as my body adjusted from the summer heat outside.

And yet, even that condition was a temporary one, here below ground. Some of the tunnels under Mingus were almost a mile deep. At those depths, temperatures actually started to rise again. At the very bottom of the mine, those miners had worked in temperatures exceeding 150 degrees on a summer day like this one. They'd had a hard life, one I didn't want to share for any longer than I had to.

I ran my flash in an arc as we walked, straining to see anything that appeared human. Bitzer pulled against the leash and finally, I released him. He galloped ahead, disappearing into the darkness.

"Ben, where are you?" I hollered.

Only the echo of my words returned from the darkness. If Ben could hear, he'd respond. I shut out the implications of what that meant.

We walked farther into the tunnel, separated like nuns in a hall, one on each side hugging the wall. We passed a side tunnel. I hesitated, then continued my slow walk forward. Only one way in and out. If we didn't find Ben up ahead, we could return to search this one.

I encountered an alcove, hollowed out of the rock as a safety device for miners to avoid the trains rumbling by. I traced its outline with my light, but only a broken lantern and a bit of leather strap appeared. Ben was not there. Then I heard the dim bay of the Rez dog ahead of us and I started running, my light jigging awkwardly in front of me.

Beyond the next gradual curve, I saw a mound on the tracks near the wriggling dog. Ben? The flash gave me sketchy details as I grew closer to the unconscious boy. The light caught the edge of his shirt moving up and down. Still breathing, but unconscious. I softly touched his cheek.

Flint reached him a second after me and added the light of the second flash. Ben's leg twisted at an awkward angle, and he had scrapes on both arms. A growing bruise spread across his forehead.

Had someone hurt him or had he tripped and hit his head? Either way, he needed medical assistance, *soon*.

I switched on the walkie-talkie and tried reaching home base. No response. We'd need to return to the mouth of the tunnel to get reception. And the boy shouldn't be moved, not with a head wound like that.

I felt the walls closing in on me. Ben moaned, and I made the only possible decision I could.

"I'm as close to family as the kid's got," I said. "I'll stay here with him, and you go for help."

Flint gave me a long look. "You going to be okay?"

I brushed off his concern. "I'll be fine. Just go."

Go before I lose my nerve, I wanted to add, and bit my lip.

Flint took off at a run, and I settled awkwardly on the ground near Ben. Bitzer heaved an tired sigh and leaned against me, one paw on Ben's good leg.

Taking off my jacket, I folded it in a pillow and placed it under the boy's head. I gently moved the leg into a straighter position. It would be difficult to tell how bad the break was until the medics arrive.

Ben groaned and then tried to rise.

"Shush," I said, halting his movement. "It's Peg. You've had a fall. Help is coming soon."

"Where am I?"

"A railroad tunnel. Do you remember how you got here?"

He shook his head. "Water?" he croaked.

I unclipped the bottle at my waist and held his head while he swallowed once or twice.

By the time his head lowered to the jacket again, he lost consciousness once more.

I turned off the flash to conserve batteries and started counting my breaths to slow my rising panic. One, two—up to ten and then start again. Where was Flint? And even more important, where were the EMTs? Ben needed more help than I could give him.

* * * * * *

I LOST TRACK OF TIME, there in the darkness. Once I heard a skittering against the wall. Was it a rodent, or just the rock settling? I was too tired to care. I touched Ben once again. Still warm, still breathing. I brushed the Rez dog's soft ear and he licked my hand.

After what seemed like hours, I saw a dim spot of light down the tunnel and clicked on my own to wave a signal. It was Flint with the medical team.

I'd been hesitant to move as I sat there with Ben for fear of rousing him. Every muscle had turned stiff and creaky in the damp cold. Flint's offer of a hand up was welcome.

The EMTs worked on the young boy, talking to each other as they stabilized him and lifted him onto the stretcher.

"He's alive," one grunted. "That's good."

"Breathing is even, but that bump doesn't look healthy," another replied, swearing when he tried his communication device that didn't work either. "Time to get him back to the hospital."

They positioned the stretcher between them and started the hike back to the entrance of the tunnel. Flint put one arm around my shoulder, to steady both of us as we followed.

Out in the open, my walkie-talkie clicked alive with a staticky hiss, and I radioed home base. "We've found him, HT. He's alive but injured. They're going to take him to the emergency room in Cottonwood."

"Right you are." The relief turned his voice shaky. Then I dropped the walkie-talkie as HT, embodied, grabbed me in a bear hug.

"We couldn't miss all the excitement," he announced. "Isabel and me followed the ambulance down."

Isabel rushed to the stretcher. With a gentle hand, she brushed Ben's hair back from his forehead. She murmured and pressed a St. Christopher's medal into his hand. As they lifted the stretcher into the back of the ambulance, the dog broke loose and hopped in the van after Ben's still form. An EMT lifted him back out of the ambulance into HT's waiting arms. The ambulance turned on its light bar and U-turned for the drive to the Medical Center. Ben was in the hands of professionals.

We stopped briefly in Mingus before following the ambulance down the hill. The waiting volunteers gave a cheer at our news and stampeded to the biker bar to celebrate. Armor didn't join them. He folded his apron, passing bartending duties to one of his buddies and rode to the Medical Center with Flint and me. Family was more important than business.

I pushed the old cruiser to its limits as we swept through the hairpins down the hill. Would Ben recover? It was out of my control at this point. I hated that feeling.

CHAPTER TWENTY

WE PILED INTO THE EMERGENCY Center, joining others awaiting word on family emergencies. It seemed there was no limit on tragedy. A young family gathered in a corner, a mother and two small boys. One had fallen asleep leaning up against her, and she stroked his arm. Across from them, a teenage girl tapped her cell phone, closing out the room and her own personal feelings with social media.

I didn't have that luxury. My thoughts intent on what was happening behind the closed double doors, I paced to the entrance door and back. I counted the tiles on the floor, then the panes of glass in the windows—352 of one and 44 of the other. A ratio of eight to one. I hoped Ben's chances were better than that.

When I checked the big wall clock, only three minutes had elapsed. Isabel sat stolidly on the edge of one uncomfortable plastic chair, ignoring HT's fingers holding her own. Armor flipped through an old magazine, his eyes staring blankly at the pages. How was Ben doing? Why didn't they come for us? My mind raced through convoluted patterns of guilt and what-ifs that I didn't want to pursue to the end.

Finally, the doctor pushed through the double doors. We all stood when he approached Armor to deliver the news. "We've patched up the cuts. The bruises will have to take care of themselves."

"The leg?" He was starting his explanation with the least serious injuries, and I wanted to hurry him along a little.

"Just a strain. Nothing broken there."

"What about the head wound?" That was Flint.

The doctor looked annoyed at the interruptions. "The patient has sustained a head concussion from an undetermined source," the doctor said. "We've done X-Rays and there doesn't seem to be—"

"Can I talk to him?" I asked in my role as law enforcement officer. I needed to know what had happened to my assistant, why we found him beaten and unconscious in a locked tunnel.

"Not right now. We've sedated him to allow the swelling to come down naturally. You best go home and sleep. He won't be awake until morning. You can talk to him then." His tone was dismissive, brooking no further interference.

I didn't feel comfortable leaving Ben here by himself. If someone attempted to harm him and abandoned him there in the tunnel, they might come back for another try.

HT must have sensed my hesitation. "Hey, Peg, you look all in. Go home. Clean up, get some rest."

I started to protest, and then the weight of what had happened hit me like a weight of tunnel rocks.

"Go on, now," he said. "Me and Isabel will take the first shift."

That decided it. I dropped Flint and Armor at the biker bar. Then I headed to my apartment and took a long shower, hot as I could stand, to wash the tunnel dust from my skin.

I poured a glass of wine and walked onto the balcony. A lonely breath of wind blew through a nearby pine tree, and I sat, too exhausted to think. A thin sliver of new moon peeked through the scudding clouds overhead as a gray-and-white cat hopped onto the balcony from the roof above. I scritched its ears, feeling the tension of the day slowly ease away.

At last, I went inside the house and surrendered to my body's cry for rest. Overhead thunder rumbled closer and then faded away in the distance. I dropped into a deep sleep, my last thought a prayer for Ben's recovery.

Some hours later, I awakened to a crash in the stairwell below me. I threw on some clothes and headed downstairs. The floor glittered with shards of glass, and rain blew in a broken window. A brick lay on the floor.

Clinging to the brick was a soggy envelope. I pried it off, my heart racing. First Ben's accident and now this. I opened the wet envelope with cold fingers and pried out a limp piece of paper. The message read, "It was an accident. Let it be." No signature. The font was old-fashioned Courier type, and I remembered Vanessa's typewriter at the bank. Had she written this note? And if so, why?

Upstairs in the apartment, someone banged on the back door. I jerked around. Was the person who threw the brick returning? I crept up the stairs and located my service weapon. Standing to the side of the door, I readied the weapon. "Who's there?"

"It's Flint. Let me in. I'm getting soaked."

I peered through the spyglass and saw the man silhouetted by the streetlight, rain dripping off the brim of his cowboy hat. He held a sawed-off shotgun in one hand.

"Put your weapon on the ground," I hollered through the closed door.

When he did, I unlocked the deadbolt and the main lock. I opened the door and scooped up the sawed-off. "What's with you Western guys? You all need to carry weapons?"

"Guns are a part of who we are. Never forget that." The steel in his gray eyes matched the bluing on the barrel. His expression softened. "You've got one, too." He pointed to the weapon in my hand.

I lowered it so that it wasn't pointing at his belly button.

"I heard glass breaking. I wanted to check on you," he said.

"Nobody needs to check on me. I'm a cop." After the stress of the previous day, my emotions were raw. All I wanted was to be left alone. Yet here he was disturbing my peace.

"Look," he said. "I live behind you on the next street. I heard something. Are you going to let me in?"

"Oh." I set the shotgun on the floor of the foyer and he entered, dripping all over my rug.

"You want to get out of those wet clothes?" I asked.

"Thought you'd never ask." He broke the shotgun and placed it in a corner of the room. Then he disappeared into the bathroom.

"There's a robe on the door," I said.

It was pink. And barely covered possible, even on me. But he was wearing it when he opened the bathroom door. Looked pretty darned good. He pushed his wet hair back out of his eyes. “Got anything to drink?”

“It's two in the morning.”

“Well, you're up and I'm up and it's raining outside.”

This guy wasn't going to take a hint. He opened my refrigerator and then the cabinet above it. “I'm pouring,” he said. “Scotch or Clear Creek Ale?”

I shoved him aside. “This is *my* house, and *I'm* pouring. Uh…Scotch or Clear Creek Ale?”

“Scotch is fine. Hold the water.” He sprawled on my sofa, propping his feet on the coffee table. “Been a long day.”

I poured him a drink and another for myself. A double. I joined him on the couch and handed him one glass. Maybe if I were sociable, he'd leave soon.

I felt the warmth of his body next to me, and my annoyance turned to something different. Anticipation flickered along my backbone, and then receded, waiting.

“One of the longest days in my life,” I said honestly. “If Ben had died, I don't know what I would have done.” I realized then how much the boy meant to me.

“Who would want to hurt Ben?”

“You don’t think it was an accident, either?” I asked.

“Couldn't have been. That kid has been trailing after his grandmother's sheep for years. He wouldn't have slipped like that. Somebody pushed him. Anyway, what about that locked fence with the open lock?”

“Which means somebody has a key to that old gate,” I said.

I retrieved the soggy message from the table where I had dropped it. “Look at this.”

His eyebrows knit as he read. “They aren't talking about Ben here.”

“Maybe they are.” I explained Ben's hacking activities with Vanessa and the break-in at my office. “I have a hunch this involves Druce Kevern's death, too. I haven't pieced it all together yet, but I will.”

His big hand reached out and absently stroked my knee. “What are you going to do about it?”

“I'm not giving up, that's for damn sure!”

There was a moment of silence and he looked at me. “Neither am I.”

The silence lengthened and our eyes met. Then the pink robe gaped open, revealing some very interesting equipment.

My body tingled in response. I wasn't going to get any sleep tonight after all. I reached out my hand. “What do you say we move this conversation to my bedroom?”

Flint smiled and set down his glass. Then we walked the four feet to my studio bed.

CHAPTER TWENTY-ONE

WHEN I AWOKE the next morning, the pink robe hung neatly on the bathroom door. Next to the coffee maker was a one-word note. "Thanks," it said. There wasn't even a signature.

Thanks! That's all last night meant to Mr. Flint Tanner? All right, leave it at that, a fun evening.

I nailed a plywood patch over the broken downstairs window and headed to the hospital to see how Ben was doing. Time to go back to being a cop, where black was black and white was white, and I didn't have to worry about messy emotional nuances in between. Life was much simpler that way.

The hospital was changing shifts when I arrived, with the flurry of nurses transferring news on overnight changes. Ben had been moved from ICU to a regular ward, which was good news. When I entered the boy's room, he was awake, Bitzer curled on a blanket near his feet.

"Shush. Don't let the nurses know there's extra company," HT said from a corner chair. "I snuck the pup in."

The boy looked pale, his head swathed in bandages. "Ben," I asked, "what happened to you up there?"

"I looked for blue-green rocks for my medicine bag." His voice was hazy as he tried to remember. "Bitzer chased a ground squirrel into that roundhouse building and I followed. Must have bumped my head on something. Hurts!" He rubbed at the bandages. "The next thing I know I'm waking up here."

A blow to the head sometimes caused amnesia. We could hope that it would be short term. Soon, Ben might be able to tell us whether he'd fallen or been hit. Until then we needed to keep him safe.

The nurse arrived with green Jell-O and clear broth. "Time for you to leave." She looked pointedly at the dog, who gave her a sad look. "All of you, out."

HT and I walked into the corridor past a young doctor who gave Bitzer an absent-minded pat. At the parking lot, we parted ways. HT for his home with the dog in tow. I drove on to the sheriff's station to begin my day.

In the silent office, the clock beat a metronome rhythm, and traffic noise filtered in from the street. I missed Ben's shouts of triumph as he vanquished monsters and leaped high buildings in his video games. I even missed Bitzer padding in to give my hand a cold nudge with his nose. Ben was family, and you don't hurt family. This case had turned personal.

* * * * * *

AFTER AN HOUR staring at the walls, I locked the office and hiked up to the old copper strip mine where Druce Kevern had fallen. Maybe I wouldn't feel so frustrated if I could figure out the reason for the man's death. Thunder rumbled against the far hills as I unlocked the fence and entered the graveled field. Storms coming, soon.

The surrounding cliffs of black gabbro, stained with fingers of mineral-orange, rose a hundred feet above me. Tufts of gamma grass clung to their vertical surfaces and the twisted limbs of shaggy-bark juniper formed a rugged line high above. The scream of a golden eagle patrolling the mountain rebounded against the cliff side as I paced back and forth on the gravel, reviewing the case.

Close family members sometimes committed murder as love tumbled into hate. Who was like family to Druce Kevern other than his mother? His prison buddies. Or perhaps his associates for the short time he was at the halfway house. Neither seemed likely.

Okay then. Murder required means, motive, and opportunity. The means part was clear. Get a young man impaired enough and one push sent him toppling over the cliff. Even an angry woman could have done it.

Like Vanessa? I didn't rule her out, especially after that note that had been delivered through my downstairs window on a brick. Could she have passed as a man in the darkness of the campsite, to a man like Jake Bean hiding a distance away? Perhaps.

Motive? Druce had a reputation for dealing in drugs at the halfway house. Could the motive be robbery, someone following Druce up to his campsite, drawn by the lure of easy money or easier drugs?

Or what about Jake Bean? He could be lying about what he witnessed. He might have pushed Druce Kevern over the cliff himself to steal the boots. Bean had a veteran's PTSD unpredictability and the skills for explosive violence. My head still ached where he had hit me. I considered Jake Bean as the murderer. Could be.

I moved on to the third of the triumvirate, opportunity. Several people visited Black Mountain on a regular basis, near where Druce had camped. Armor hid his illicit marijuana patch there. Isabel went there to collect herbs and Ben at times had accompanied both of them. My mind slid uncomfortably past the last name—Ben, who had lain unconscious in a hospital bed recovering from an attack by person or persons unknown.

Roger Heaton and Tal Garrett had both motive and opportunity. They were intimately involved with this mountain area, near where their development would be built. And they'd skirted the finer aspects of the law more than once. As a blackmailer, Druce might present a threat to their current real estate plan. Roger Heaton had his own issues with Druce Kevern. Even though he'd denied it, the man might truly believe Druce to be his bastard step-son.

And then there was Flint Tanner, who seemed to show up at all the right moments, including last night. If it were Flint, that *would* complicate matters. Even though we'd been physically intimate, there were dark shadows to his past he chose not to share.

Even in death, Druce Kevern wove together the lives of many who lived here in Mingus. I grabbed a chunk of stone and heaved it at the cliff. The rock shattered, fragments raining down the steep side like an avalanche. Right now my mind was as blocked as that cliff wall stretching up into a pewter sky.

If I couldn't find a way to untie the knot of this mysterious death soon, I'd have to turn the case over to the sheriff's office and face the consequences to not telling them sooner. The eagle screamed again in defiance of the approaching storm. Braced against the rising wind, I returned to my squad car.

CHAPTER TWENTY-TWO

THE PHONE WAS RINGING when I entered the station. I picked up the receiver and immediately regretted it, as Tal Garrett's voice grated in my ear.

"I've been robbed. Come over here right now."

"Your office safe was robbed?" I asked Garrett. Surely, my grandfather hadn't returned to his old safe-cracking ways.

"No, my *house*, Quincy. My collection, my prize weapon has been stolen." He sounded almost incoherent with rage. "I returned last night to find it missing. I tried to reach you this morning but no one's answering your damn phone. Where have you been anyway?"

I got directions to his house and put the office phone on message response. Without Ben in the office to cover for me, there was no one to answer calls. The next person with an emergency would have to wait. The sheriff's department would be on me about lack of coverage, and they'd be right.

I missed Ben. He kept me centered, instinctively knowing what I needed next, whether that was a cup of good coffee or a light-hearted dig at a community foible. Working without his backup would be tough, but I was no quitter. I planned to see this summer through, and then decide whether I wanted to apply for the position permanently—if they'd consider me.

The thought stopped me. When had my self-identity shifted from a temporary hire to someone who cared about this town and its people? I'd have to contemplate that thought more.

But not now.

I unlocked the old cruiser and pushed the key into the ignition. When it had whooped and hacked its way to a syncopated rumble, I shoved it into gear and headed up the hill to see Tal Garrett.

* * * * * *

TAL GARRETT'S HOUSE had slit windows and an entrance tower that loomed like a prison guardhouse. Unlike the Heatons' restored Victorian, Garrett had swept his land clear of history and constructed a house of sharp lines that stood in stark contrast to the historic buildings in the old mining town.

I parked at the end of the cement driveway and walked to a burnished aluminum door over twelve feet high. I lifted the heavy iron door knocker and let it bounce once or twice. Then I waited in the silence of the morning.

Inside, soft footsteps approached and a diminutive man, possibly Korean, opened the door. He stared as I identified myself and asked for Garrett. Then he silently escorted me to an immense living room.

Black leather couches, arrogantly expensive and uncomfortable, perched at the sides of the tall-ceilinged room. The chrome end tables and dark gray walls echoed the rigidity of the metallic front door. It felt as sterile as a surgical suite.

Garrett paced back and forth at the end of the room, waiting impatiently for me. "Took your time getting here," he said with a tight-lipped expression. Without waiting for an answer, he continued, "It had to be that Isabel woman that stole it."

Blaming Isabel again. His arrogance grated on me.

Time to slow things down to a pace that fit me better. I claimed the only comfortable chair in the room, an immense gray leather lounger. "Nice to see you again, Garrett." I gestured to the straight-backed couch. "Join me."

Then I stretched my legs a little and tilted my neck back and forth to ease muscles. I reached in my shirt for a pad to take notes and then searched for a pen. Slowly. Patted down one pocket and then another. Ah, there it was. I smiled at him. He didn't smile back.

"Take a seat," I repeated, "Get comfortable and tell me about it. Why Isabel?"

He grimaced and perched uncomfortably on the end of one black couch. “Well, why wouldn't it be her? She dusts my weapons room every week. Every single rifle and sword. I insist upon that.”

“So what’s missing?”

“It’s a pocket knife owned by General Ulysses Grant himself.”

“Really. Valuable?”

“Well, it was to him. The people of Kentucky had given him a presentation sword, and he liked it so much he had this one made as a companion piece. It had a silver-filigreed handle, with his initials carved out in pure gold, “USG,” just like that. It fit so well in my hand. Sometimes I’d sit holding it and imagine that I…”

He stopped, his face reddening with the disclosure. “Well, anyway, if it wasn't her, then it had to be Armor Brancussi. That cripple! Had to be him if it wasn't Isabel. He'd steal anything, that thief…”

This was getting nowhere. I closed my notebook and interrupted his recitation of suspects. “Why don’t you show me where you kept it?”

“This way.” He stood and led me down the hall, his shoes making a nervous staccato on the parquet floors. At the end of the hall, he stopped in front of closed double doors. He opened them with a theatrical gesture. A motion sensor switched on a bank of floodlights.

The room contained no furniture except for a blood-red couch centered on a dark wood floor. To the left, row upon row of flintlock rifles lined the wall, each precisely mounted above the other. In front of us, swords, maces, and morning stars framed two narrow bar-lined windows.

Garrett directed my attention to the right wall. “See? That's where it…”

He went silent, his mouth working convulsively as he pointed at an object awkwardly balanced on a rack that didn’t fit its size. A ruby glinted from a finely carved grip.

“That's not my knife!”

“Doesn’t look like it,” I agreed. “When were you last in here?”

“I closed up the room when I discovered the loss, about midnight. I called your office then and left a message. Didn’t you get it this morning?”

I thought back to a message light winking in the outer foyer of the sheriff's station. Ben usually handled messages like that. My clerk who was now hospitalized and immobile. "Guess not. So you've not been in this room since last night?"

"Of course not! I just told you."

Which meant someone had stolen his knife and then returned with the ruby pistol—the one Alice Heaton had given to Druce Kevern. "Hazard a guess whose gun that might be?"

"Well, Heaton's of course. He showed it to me one time when I was over there. He told me how valuable that set was." His face paled and his hands shook. "I want to call my lawyer."

"Nobody is accusing you of anything, Garrett. Here, sit on the couch. You don't look so good."

I called to his employee to bring some water for Garrett and a chair for me. No way I was going to sit on that dragon's blood couch next to Garrett.

When the water arrived, Garrett took a nervous sip from the crystal tumbler.

"Now, start at the beginning," I said, pulling up the chair.

"There *is* no beginning," he blustered.

"No lock on this door," I observed. "You have an alarm system?"

"Of course not. This is Mingus. No crime here, or wasn't, until you came to town." He glared at me.

Great! Now I was to blame for our crime spree? I ignored his implied accusation. "I need to take that weapon into custody. If you didn't put it there, I want to find out who did."

He waved a hand at me. "It's not mine—take it. And find my missing knife while you're at it." He left abruptly, his footsteps thudding down the hall.

I whipped out my handkerchief and carefully took the antique pistol from its resting place on the wall. Its surface was shiny smooth. Someone had wiped the weapon clean. No prints appeared, not even a smudge.

I wrapped it carefully in a cloth that Garrett's employee provided and walked out to my car. I'd have the forensic lab retest the weapon, but I had a feeling we'd get no useful traces from it.

Still, once released as evidence, it could be returned to the Heatons, to rejoin the topaz inlaid weapon resting in their gun safe.

Having it back would mean the Heatons' ill-fated set would be complete, topaz and ruby reunited. Would that improve their luck? I hoped so.

I had put the cruiser in reverse to back out of the drive, when Garrett burst out the front door, waving frantically.

"Roll down your window. I just remembered something. Get your notebook out," he ordered.

I stifled my irritation. "Now what?"

"When I was at the gun show in Prescott last week, I talked about my collection to a dealer up there. Maybe *he* took my knife."

"What was his name?"

"Don't remember."

"Got his phone number?" I asked.

"Nah, he was just another dealer."

So now, we had a mythical dealer with no name and a non-existent phone number. Garrett was reaching.

But he was insistent that I believe him. "The guy wore a red hat. And his booth was located right by the restrooms. I remember that because…" He reddened.

Garrett had a prostate problem? I filed the fact away under useless but unforgettable information.

"I think the original receipt for the knife had a picture attached. I'll fax it to you. It's incredibly valuable," he added.

"Never mind," I said, remembering our lack of a working fax. "I'll pick it up at your office."

I drove back to the station and stored the ruby pistol in my safe, awaiting shipment to the forensics lab. I completed my notes with the additional information Tal Garrett had given me. Trying to find one guy in a red hat near the restrooms. It was a slight lead, but Charlie at the pawn shop said he frequented gun shows. Maybe he might have a suggestion about Garrett's mysterious guy in the red hat. I locked the office and headed down the hill to the pawnshop.

* * * * * *

THE BELL JINGLED as I entered the store. Charlie wore the same plaid shirt I had first seen him wear. I wondered if he had a closet full of them. Well, my own closet was full of khaki pants and shirts fresh from the cleaners. Everyone has his or her own kind of uniform.

"Yo, Charlie. How's business?"

"Can't complain." He walked up to greet me. "What can I do for you today, Officer Quincy?" His smile was genuine.

"Do you ever visit the gun shows in Prescott?"

"Off and on. I like to keep up on what's current. Sometimes the dealers are interested if I have an unusual piece come in."

"I'm looking for a guy wearing a red hat, with a booth parked next to the restrooms."

He laughed. "You're describing Joel Pittman. Been in this business almost as long as me. Always takes that same spot. Always wears that same red hat. Some folks get in a rut, you know." I smiled at his words. Could have been describing himself.

He fished out a card and a pencil. "Here's his number. He's semi-retired, so you might find him at his house trailer in Cherry. Tell him I sent you."

"Thanks, Charlie. I owe you one."

He pushed a candy jar my direction. "Have a mint. Or what about a used clarinet? Make you a heckuva deal."

I laughed and accepted one but not the other. Didn't want to blast my neighbors out of existence at the apartment.

Before I left the parking lot, I dialed the number Charlie gave me. Joel Pittman answered his phone right away, almost as though he were sitting next to it, waiting. I set up an appointment later that afternoon.

* * * * * *

PITTMAN'S SMALL COMMUNITY of Cherry perched high on a ridge of mountains east of Mingus, about an hour south on the I-17 freeway through Copper Canyon and then west at the Cherry Road exit toward Prescott.

I didn't pass another car on the road as I pulled into the little town of Cherry. After Mingus and its quarreling citizens, I wistfully thought about a more peaceful assignment. Wonder if they could use a cop-for-hire?

Following Pittman's directions, I took a left, then a right off the main drag, and entered a modest subdivision—some small houses intermixed with modulars on permanent foundations.

A white picket fence surrounded Joel Pittman's double-wide trailer and two desert willows shaded the front yard. Their orchid-purple blooms wafted a faint scent as I brushed past. Feeders hung along the screened-in front porch and rufus hummingbirds buzzed me aggressively as I walked past.

Joel Pittman rose from a platform rocker on the porch and opened the screen door for me. "Not much traffic up here," he said, "So I figured that had to be you. Welcome. Can I offer you some iced tea?"

"Thanks. That would be wonderful."

I dropped into a canvas sling chair that settled to accommodate me. The drink was fresh-brewed sun tea, clear and mellow with no hint of bitterness. Set a gallon jug filled with water and half a dozen teabags out in the Arizona heat for a couple of hours and let the sun do the work. Nothing finer.

Greenery lined the shelves on the screened porch: spider plants with baby shoots, ivy, a geranium, or two. "Nice plants," I said.

"Thanks. Most of them belonged to my wife." Joel looked sad.

Death or divorce, either brought pain. "I'm sorry. What happened?"

"She died almost a year ago to the day. I feel her spirit around here, sometimes. Do you think that's strange?"

"Not at all." My mind turned to the way Isabel had known Ben's whereabouts. Lots of things happen in this world we can't explain.

I set my tea down and looked at him. "I'm here about someone that may have been at the gun show last week in Prescott." I told him about Tal Garrett's claim he'd been at the show.

"Last weekend, you say?" Joel took a sip of tea. "I remember Mr. Garrett." His mouth turned down, as though he tasted something bitter. "A man like that gives a bad name to gun collectors. Most are nice people."

So Garrett was telling the truth about being at the show. Was he inventing the mysterious stranger with the Heaton's pistol or was he telling the truth about that as well?

“There may have been another man about the same time, interested in selling an antique dueling pistol?”

Joel’s eyes lit with recognition. “Yes, I remember the pistol. A nice piece. I didn't want it, though.”

“Why not?”

“They're not very re-sellable, not without a complete set. Guy wouldn't give me his name. Didn't have a bill of sale, either. No provenance on those antique weapons drops their value. I wasn't interested.”

“Remember anything about him?” I asked.

“Plain as white bread. Couldn’t pick him out of a crowd in a million years.” He looked concerned at his inability to be more specific. “Sorry I can't remember more. I know this is important to you.”

“You did the best you could. I appreciate your seeing me,” I said, getting to my feet. I gave him my card and asked him to call if he thought of anything else.

“Thanks for making the trip, Deputy. Gets lonesome here.”

As I pulled out of the yard, he was watering his wife's geraniums, one by one, with an old watering can. I wondered if my grandfather sometimes felt the same way, missing his Ellie.

To return to the office in Mingus, I could retrace my original route on the freeway or take a gravel road shortcut, the route of one of the first stage lines into the valley. I paused at the crossroads for a moment, my engine idling.

The skies above were turquoise blue, the rain over for the day, and the gravel road seemed well maintained. Rocks spun out of the tire treads as I swung the car onto the gravel trail down the hill. If a horse and buggy team could follow this route, the old cruiser should have no problems. I’d be back in the office before dark.

CHAPTER TWENTY-THREE

THE GRAVEL ROAD hairpinned back and forth, descending steeply from the mountains to the valley floor below. I shifted the cruiser into low and settled back for the ride. The narrow road lacked turnouts for passing, but I didn't see the rooster tail of traffic dust ahead or behind me. I should be fine.

Hillsides were studded with prickly pear and cholla. Century plants with enormous stalks over twenty feet tall spread blossoms like horizontal bunches of grapes, rust-red fading to a mustard gold. A desert cottontail jumped in front of the car, and I braked sharply to miss him.

The road was well graded and I made good time. At this rate, I'd be home in a half-hour. I daydreamed about sitting out on my balcony with a cool one, watching the town shut down. An ominous chunk-chunk in the drive train jerked me back to the present.

Both power steering and power brakes faded out! My hands clenched the wheel as I fought to control the car in the unresponsive manual mode.

The cruiser whipsawed back and forth, gaining speed as it raced down the steep dirt road. I shifted to low, but with all power assists gone, the car wobbled erratically, first careening close to the hillside on my left, then kissing the steep drop-off on my right. Even with my foot pressed on the brake, the speed crept inexorably higher, the engine protesting in a high-pitched squeal.

A patch of deep sand stalled the cruiser and slowed its progress. I jammed on the brakes with all my strength and the car skidded to a shuddering halt, scant inches from the edge.

I shut off the motor and sat there shaking. Just inches from my right fender, the cliff plunged several hundred feet to the gorge below. Sweat dripped into my eyes, and I thrust the drops away with unsteady fingers.

An image flashed in my rear view mirror and I swiveled around to get a better view. Another vehicle roared down the hill toward my stalled car. I half-opened the door to flag down the approaching help. Then the vehicle accelerated, streaking towards me on the too-narrow road.

That idiot driver. Didn't he see me stalled here in front of him? What was he thinking?

I slammed the door and braced for the collision. The vehicle swerved at the last minute, but not soon enough. The cruiser jolted with the slam and my head whiplashed backward. The car, beige as the cloud of dust it created, roared past too fast for me to catch the digits on the Arizona plate.

My car shook from the impact and jerked forward. Front wheels spun over open air. Finally, the rear tires caught soft dirt at the edge of the roadway and slowed the forward momentum. The cruiser came to rest, tilted at an alarming angle.

Time expanded into the crisis. From somewhere inside my head, a calm voice spoke to me. *Peg, unlock your seatbelt.* I did. The voice spoke to me again. *Listen to your breathing. Do you feel your breath? Good. Now, unlock the doors.* The locks clicked open with a satisfying ka-chunk.

Now what? Somehow I had to escape before this clunky car dropped over the cliff. I slowed my panicky breath and my brain started to function again.

Windows. I had to open all the windows in case I had to crawl out. I pushed four controls, one at a time, and heard the glass receding into door wells, groaning and complaining, but moving. Lucky so far. The jolt had apparently reset the power assist. Okay, windows open.

The car had stopped its rocking, but the worst was yet to come. *Peg, you have to crawl into the back seat.* The voice squashed my panicked objections. *When you do, you'll shift more weight to the back.*

Slowly, very slowly, I swiveled to the right and lifted my right arm to rest on the back of the bench seat. Then I twisted my torso that direction as well. Each movement was painstaking. I didn't want to set up a motion that could shift the car. Inch by inch, I shifted my weight to the center of the seat.

As I did, the car resumed its rocking motion, back and forth. I froze. The car motion stilled and again I moved, drawing both knees up and rolled over to my right to face the rear. Once more, I paused, as the car adjusted to my new weight distribution. The only way to escape was to move, and even a small jolt might send the car plunging over the edge.

I swallowed, forcing moisture into my dry mouth.

How did I get into this mess? Crawling through the narrow opening between front and back would be tough for my tall frame, but I had no choice. Mustering my courage and saying a prayer to whoever was up there, I tensed to leap to the back seat and then out the opened rear window. One, two…

Wait! This car was going to plunge like a boulder caught in an avalanche when my weight left it. I'd have seconds to scramble to safety and escape its forward trajectory.

Better think this through before I made the final move. I rehearsed the sequence in my mind, streamlining muscle motions like a bobsledder before an Olympic run: First, jump to the back seat. Then, lever through the now-open back window. Finally, use the outside of the car as a springboard and jump for the safety of the bank. It seemed simple enough, but there were no do-overs. I ran through it once more: Back seat, out window, lever off car.

Okay, then, if by some miracle I escaped the car, what next? My brain played through all the options in slow motion, while my body tensed for any movement of the car.

The drop off was steep. My fingers, already wet with sweat, would slip if I couldn't catch myself on something secure. Then I'd fall, plunging down the jagged hillside following the spiraling car into the abyss. I eyed the rock-studded scree near the car and shook my head. Nothing seemed large enough to stop my momentum.

Then I spotted a manzanita bush that clung tenaciously to the side of the road. Maybe it would hold me. Those branches were hard as iron. My best shot. I had ten seconds, tops. Enough time? I began my countdown again. One…

The car shifted slightly, becoming more unstable. I bunched my muscles and shoved myself to the back seat. Diving through the open back window, I levered off the side of the car and leaped wildly, clawing for the manzanita bush.

The car bucked under my disappearing weight, dislodging a small avalanche of rocks and dirt. Then it tilted vertical, one rear tire narrowly missing my head. With a final groan, it became airborne. I clung to the manzanita branches as the vehicle tumbled end over end, once, twice, and then hit the floor of the gulch below.

The gas tank ignited with a muffled whump and a fireball exploded upward. I unclenched my fingers from the bush and scrambled onto the roadbed, feeling the convective heat roaring up from the flames raging below. My legs failed me and I collapsed in the middle of the road, head down as I struggled to breathe.

Using one scraped palm as a fulcrum, I levered to my feet. The pant leg of my uniform held a nasty rip. My rational mind kicked in, calculating how many days until my slim paycheck could finance a new pair.

My left ankle twisted under me as I stood and pain raced up my leg. I balanced on my right foot and tried the left again, more gingerly. The leg could hold my weight, so my ankle was likely sprained, not broken.

My eyes teared, fighting against the oily smoke billowing up from the gulch. Surely someone would see the fire, wouldn't they?

Maybe not. The crash had occurred at the worst possible spot, halfway between Cherry and the valley floor, hidden from view by a bend in the road. My cell phone showed no service—not even one bar.

If I had a car, the distance to town could easily be traveled in minutes. Walking, it would take hours. That was with two good feet, my throbbing ankle reminded me. But other than the car that had sideswiped me, there had been no other traffic. I could be here all night, or longer. It was time to move.

Using an old branch as a crutch, I started the long trek to the main road. White-hot pain exploded in my ankle with each step. I set my jaw and wobbled unsteadily down the road, one step, then another. I kept my mind in neutral, trying not to think.

An engine whined on the hill above me. Had the beige car circled back for another try? I jerked and my thigh cramped, almost toppling me. Then the approaching vehicle emerged out of the dark smog created by the fire below. It was an old pickup with one primer-gray front fender—my grandfather's old truck.

HT braked the truck to a halt. He jumped out and ran toward me. “Peg, what are you doing up here? I saw that smoke, and I thought someone was a goner for sure.”

I fell into his arms and felt his welcome strength. I was no longer facing this alone. With him there, my world tilted toward positive again. He put a muscled arm around my shoulder and I limped toward the truck.

“Something happened to the power steering and brakes, HT,” I said.

Was it an accident, or had they been tampered with? With the cruiser a heap of twisted metal at the bottom of the gulch, I might never know. But the sideswipe of that tan car had been deliberate—Someone had tried to kill me.

“Never did trust that old cop car. Now Betsy here…” He patted the fender. “She just keeps running, so long as you give her a drink now and then.” He opened the passenger door and helped me onto the seat. “Some water in the canteen there.”

I drank huge gulps. Some dribbled down my chin and I wiped it away with the back of my hand. “How did you know I was here?”

“I didn't,” he said. “I was in Prescott for a new saw blade, and I got an urge to try this hill road on the way back. I haven't been on it in years.”

Sometimes you just get a lucky break. I amended that thought. Sometimes you get one hell of a lucky break.

CHAPTER TWENTY-FOUR

AS WE REACHED THE BOTTOM of the cliff road, my cell phone beeped back into service. No way would I let the mountain burn, not on my watch.

I dialed the fire chief. “Hello, Pat? There’s a car fire up on old Cherry Road.”

The fire station door ratcheted up even before he disconnected.

At the intersection, HT put on the signal to turn left toward Mingus. I clamped my hand on his arm to stop him. “I need to stop by the sheriff's office in Camp Verde.”

He gave me a level stare and then nodded. “Best get it over with.”

He switched the signal right, and soon we pulled into the sheriff's parking lot. HT squeezed my shoulder as I left the truck. “Do what you need to, Peg. I'm here waiting for you.”

I pushed through the double doors and limped down the long hall to Sheriff Jones' office. The secretary had left for the day, and for a moment, I thought I'd skate free. Then Jones’ silhouette appeared on the Venetian blinds shrouding the inner office.

I brushed a hand over my tangled braid to straighten it and took a deep breath. No way to put a positive spin on this tale. Might as well tell it true. Unlatching the security bar on the half door, I walked past the secretary's desk and entered the office.

The sheriff bent over inevitable paperwork, but he looked up as I approached. “My god, what happened? You look like you picked a fight with the wrong mountain lion.”

“I ran into a little trouble up on the hill.”

“You okay?”

“Yeah, fine.” That was cop speak translated loosely as I’m still breathing.

“Glad to hear it,” he said, dismissing the issue. “Good that you stopped by. Something I've been meaning to talk to you about.”

“I've got some bad news, though,” I blurted out.

His mouth drooped. “Yeah?”

“I wrecked the squad car on the cliff.”

The smile disappeared.

“You did *what?”*

“The power steering failed. And then the brakes failed, too.” I said.

He was still back on my first statement. “What cliff? Up at Mingus?”

“Uh, no. A little town of Cherry, on the back road.”

“What were you doing up there?” His voice rose.

“I was taking a short cut.”

“You were taking a short cut.” He started to sputter.

I talked faster, wanting to get the whole story out before I faltered. “And then a car sideswiped me and pushed me half over the cliff.”

“But you got the license plate and called it in, right?” His face screwed up tight.

“Uh, no,” I said. “But then I escaped.”

“That's good, anyway.”

“And then the car dropped over the side.”

“But you recovered your gear, right? Tell me you climbed down there and got your gear out?” He moved ahead with contingency plans. “We can send a wrecker to retrieve the car.”

“The car exploded on impact. It’s nothing but a black heap of metal.”

Silence filled the room. Then he leaped to his feet upsetting his coffee all over the papers on his desk. I scrambled to save them, and he shoved my hands away.

“Leave. Right now. You're fired!”

“What?”

He counted off on his fingers. "First, Mayor Garrett calls me daily about your misconduct up there. Second, you let the office get burglarized. Third, you have a murder committed under your nose. Which you still have not solved." He peered at me over his glasses. "You *haven't* solved it yet, have you?"

"No, but…"

"And now this wanton destruction of government property. I should have never let your grandfather talk me into this arrangement. A green rookie like you." He reached out his hand. "Your badge and gun. Now."

Silently I handed them over. Straightening my shoulders, I walked out of the office, determined not to limp.

At first, I felt lighter, now that I'd told the news. But as I climbed into the pickup, I ground my teeth. I'd almost died. And what about Ben? He was still in the hospital, an innocent bystander injured through no fault of his own.

HT backed out of the parking spot and pulled into the traffic beyond the lot. "Want to talk about it?"

"No." I let several miles of creosote pass by the side window before I blurted out, "I got fired."

"Huh," he grunted. "Figured as much. Abner's got a temper when he gets riled." HT glanced over at me and then back at the traffic ahead of him. "Going to quit looking for whoever hurt Ben?"

"No." Job or no job, I'd not rest until I found out who did this.

"Thought as much. So what's your next step?" He slowed as a car passed us. "Can't see those tan cars at all," he complained. "Must have been in my blind spot."

The tiles clicked inside my head and suddenly fell into an ordered line. "Blind spot. That's it. The original invisible man. *Johnny Evans*. He did it, HT, I know he did."

"Can you prove it?"

"Not yet. But if he's got Garrett's fancy knife, that would be a start."

"How are you going to find that out? You don't have cop authority for a search-and-seizure anymore."

My brain explored the options. "If we could get into Evans' house and even into his home safe, maybe we'd find something that would incriminate him. You could help me do that if you wanted to." I looked at him yearningly.

His hands tightened on the wheel and he stared straight ahead, as though the yellow stripe on the road was the most fascinating thing on the planet. "Nope, not going to happen."

"Come on, HT. What have we got to lose?"

"Me, maybe nothing. But you've got your life ahead of you. Prison is no picnic." His tone was bleak. "You ain't going to end up there like I did. No way I'd let that happen."

"He almost killed me. And don't forget what happened to Ben," I said. My shoulders stiffened. "If you won't help me, then I'll go it alone. Evans is not going to get away with this."

"Not so fast," he temporized. "Let me think on it. We need to see how Ben is doing—They released him this afternoon. Isabel's making apple pie, and you're invited." He patted my hand. "Things will work out, Peg, one way or another. They always do."

Not true. Life works out the way you *make* it work out. Johnny Evans was going to pay. I'd make sure of that.

CHAPTER TWENTY-FIVE

AFTER SUPPER, MY GRANDFATHER and I sat on the porch swing. After several moments of rocking back and forth, he put down a foot and stopped the motion.

"All right, I'll help you do this thing on one condition. You don't set one foot in Johnny's house."

"Whatever you say." At this point, I'd agree to anything.

Still, it seemed strange to join HT's history of breaking and entering. I wasn't a good thief. I'd gotten caught at that young age when kids begin stealing, and my mother made me return the candy bar. Her lecture must have stuck because I never tried it again.

But this was different. We weren't *taking* anything, just looking. If we discovered something that linked Evans to Druce Kevern's death, the risk was worth it, in my book.

I remembered clearly the conversation in Johnny Evan's office. "What kind of safe do you think he has?" I asked.

"If we're lucky, Johnny's using his mother's safe. The old ones are the easiest to open. We could punch it or use a come-along, but that's the mark of an amateur. I'd rather see if I can manipulate the combination." He cracked his knuckles. "That'd be a lot more fun." His eyes sparkled like an old fire horse hearing the alarm bell.

Then he remembered himself. "And you're staying *outside.*"

I hoped he'd take my nod as total agreement. "Then you'll need numbers, some likely sequences. Maybe Ben can help us there."

I didn't condone my clerk's computer hacking ability, but here was one place it might be useful. I hollered to Ben and he ambled out on the porch, a wedge of apple pie folded in his hand like a pizza slice.

The sheriff's department computer had been stolen, but I didn't think that would stop Ben. "Can you get access to the Internet?"

"Vanessa's laptop. We can go down to the Spirit Cafe and use their Wi-Fi." The pie disappeared in two enormous bites and he licked his fingers.

"Here's what I want you to do," I said. "Hack into Johnny Evans' personal information: Financial records, past employment history, birthdays, anything that has numbers attached to it."

Ben rubbed his hands together. Sanctioned hacking. He smirked.

"And then you back out of those systems, fast. I don't want a chance of anyone discovering you've been there."

"I'll be careful," he said.

"*More* careful than you were last time. Stay safe."

He touched his head, remembering. Would that be enough of a deterrent? I hoped so.

"And then we need a diversion."

"What about Vanessa?" Ben asked. "I think he likes her."

"Would she do that for us?"

"Vanessa will do anything for money." Ben's tone was sad.

"Promise her some," I said, waving away HT's objections. "We'll find some cash, somehow, or if we don't, we'll stiff her. What can she do—report us?"

Knowing Vanessa, that's probably what she would do, but I didn't care. I wanted this guy so bad I could feel his neck bones crunching beneath my fingers.

Ben got on his cell. "Vanessa? Yeah, I'm out of the hospital. They sprung me. Look, meet me at the café. Bring your laptop. We're panning for gold." He winked at me.

I winced. Nothing like encouraging youth to engage in criminal activities.

Ben hung up and started out the door. "See you later, guys."

"Be careful," I warned.

"Always, Boss."

He banged down the back stairs with the enthusiasm of youth. Had I ever been that carefree? My ankle still ached from the incident on Cherry Hill.

Melda had surely heard of my firing through the office grapevine, but she took my request without a quibble. Bless that woman. I waited while she checked the town's demographic database.

She was back in a few minutes. "The reason you couldn't find Johnny Evan's home address is because it's not under his name; still listed as his mother's address. But he lives there. Sally over in traffic confirmed that for me."

"Thanks, Melda. I owe you one."

With that information in hand, HT and I piled into his pickup to recon. The moon disappeared behind the skimming clouds, but a streetlight illuminated Johnny's house at the end of a long street in Clarkdale.

Builders had constructed most of the residences without garages, and cars lined the street. Johnny's car was right in front of his house. I slouched down on the seat and put a hand to the side of my face as we passed.

"No garage," HT said. "That makes it tougher. Back in the days when I did a job, I usually entered through the man door. Once inside, I'd hit the inside door opener, back my truck in and load at my leisure." He looked up and down the street. "Let's go round one more time."

There were no alleyways between the rows of houses, either. Iron-railed picket fences, forged by the workers at the mine, bounded most of the yards. Pointed tips like spearheads topped the pickets. They glinted in the moonlight, just the right height to impale intruders on their sharp points.

I slowed the truck to a crawl on the second time around, and HT peered over the fence into Johnny's yard. "No dog, that's good." He nodded. "Got what I need. Head for home."

HT was quiet on the way up the hill to Mingus. As we swung into his drive, he turned to me. "How'd you like to be a painter for a day? I've got some white overalls that'd about fit you, and a hat to tuck that red hair under. Be good cover for us."

"Okay by me." Shoot, it might be a new job opportunity since I wasn't working for law enforcement anymore. I wasn't sure whether I defined house painting or safecracking as my new potential career. Didn't seem to matter much at this point.

Sitting in HT's drive, we ran through the plan one final time. He gave me a hug and we parted. I drove the pickup down to my flat—I'd load some gear and pick HT up the next day.

The street in front of my apartment was dark. I scanned the street in both directions before I unlocked the door, ill at ease after the episode on the road from Cherry. Since the bank owned the apartment, Johnny Evans had the right to enter. And he had access to a master key.

Maybe he assumed that I went over the cliff with the cruiser, but I wasn't taking any chances. I lugged a wooden chair downstairs and wedged it under the knob of the outside door. I did the same for the back door.

I missed the reassuring presence of my service weapon. It usually spent the night on the stand beside my bed. I bet it was lonely in Sheriff Jones' desk.

From the corner, light glinted off Flint Tanner's shotgun. He never asked for it back after he spent the night here. Given that we weren't speaking, I never volunteered to return it, either. I'd give it back, one of these days, when we were on better terms. I shoved the shotgun under the bed, its stock positioned for a quick grab if needed.

Then having made all the precautions I could, I turned out the lights and settled down for an uneasy sleep. In my dreams, the ghosts of Mingus mocked me from their sanctuary in the mining tunnels below the street. I tossed and turned, not sure what the next day would bring.

CHAPTER TWENTY-SIX

THE NEXT MORNING, I tucked the shotgun under the front seat of the pickup before I drove over to HT's house. It wasn't the sidearm I was used to, but I'd hunted game in Tennessee—it would serve.

My mood was grim. The law enforcement training I'd had was clear—Never bluff without the intent to follow through. If it came to that, I would use the shotgun without hesitation.

The aroma of Isabel's bacon and eggs greeted me as I pulled into HT's drive, but my stomach wouldn't handle anything but coffee. It was hot and I poured a cup.

Ben pounded down the stairs from the loft and banged through the screen door with Bitzer at his heels. With a flourish, he handed me a long list of numbers culled from Johnny's computer records.

We sat at the kitchen table and went over the details of the plan. Isabel was working at the sink, but I could tell she tuned in, too.

"Vanessa will stall Johnny if it looks like Johnny's going to leave the bank," I said. Then I double-checked. "Right?"

"Right." Ben grinned.

I didn't dare ask what he'd promised her to cooperate. I hoped it wouldn't bankrupt me.

"And your job is to sit in that cafe across from the bank parking lot and watch his car."

"Got it," Ben said.

"I mean it." I frowned at him, trying to instill the sense of danger that he seemed to be ignoring. "Don't go in the bank, don't talk to Vanessa, don't do anything but sit there."

"You buying the donuts?"

"No!" I said. "Buy your own. And eat slow. Don't draw attention to yourself."

"Sure, whatever," he said. "Want to synchronize watches?"

The kid watched too many thrillers. Ah, what the heck. At least he still *wore* a watch. Most of his generation didn't. "Ten a.m. on my mark."

"Check." He clicked the stem down. And then he was gone.

HT dumped paint cans, ladders, and brushes in the truck bed and we drove down to Clarkdale. I'd been fired from my job, but there were worse things that could happen than that. Much worse.

Johnny's car had vanished from the parking spot in front of the house and HT swerved into it. I tucked my hair under the painter's cap and joined him on the sidewalk. He tipped his hat to a lady walking her dog. "Morning, ma'am. Good weather today."

I looked at him with apprehension. "HT, what are you doing?" I hissed.

"People see what they expect to see, not what's right in front of them." He handed me a paint bucket. He grasped one end of the ladder in an easy swing and gestured to me to pick up the other. "Carry it like a suitcase," he ordered.

It had begun. He opened the gate in front of the house and we moved equipment to the back yard. There we dropped the ladder and HT took a set of lock picks from his pocket.

"Where did you get those? I thought you said you had gone straight."

"Ordered a pick-set off the Internet, first thing, when I got out. Kinda missed 'em jingling in my pocket." He fumbled at the back door lock set.

"Hurry. Somebody might see us." I glanced nervously at the big trees along the lot line. HT fiddled more, and I reached around him to try the door. It opened easily. "Small town. Nobody locks their doors."

I pulled a paint rag out of my back pocket and wiped my fingerprints from the door handle. “Don't touch anything in here. We're just looking.”

“Looking, right,” HT said, prowling in after me.

The kitchen was tiny but immaculate. I used the rag to open the refrigerator door. “The bulb must be out. Shine your flash in here, HT.”

The bottles and containers, aligned in precise rows evoked Johnny Evans’ fussy personality, but otherwise, there was nothing suspicious there. I closed the refrigerator door and we moved to the living room.

Blackout drapes created a dim cave of a room. I slid one drape back cautiously. A beige couch faced a beige wall. Two beige armchairs rested on a bleached hardwood floor. The room was one of those before-and-after pictures in the home decorating magazines—the “before” shot awaiting the pops of color that decorators loved.

Drawing the curtain, I hit a light switch but the overhead light didn’t come on. I tried a floor lamp with the same result. “Is the electricity off? The refrigerator seemed to be cold inside when we opened it.”

“Nothing wrong with the electric service. The reason goes back a ways. It seems that Mrs. Evans suffered a lack of oxygen during Johnny’s delivery. She turned blind and blamed him for it. Foreswore all light in the house.”

“What you are saying is that because Mrs. Evans didn’t need light, she didn't want Johnny to have any either? That’s mean.” I switched my flash back on. “But she’s been dead over a year. Why didn’t he change things back?”

“Takes a while to step into a new way of living,” HT said. “Maybe he’d adjusted to it that way, didn’t want to change. Or it could be a way to hold on to her.”

I remembered the careful way the gun dealer in Cherry tended his wife's flowers, feeling her spirit close. Did Johnny feel that same sort of attachment to his mother, or was his feeling one of relief when she died? Love and hate often intertwined.

Standing in Johnny Evans’ space was unsettling. I didn’t want to feel sorry for this man, after what he’d done to me. “Come on, HT. Let's be done with this and get out of here.”

I searched for a possible location for a wall safe. The walls held no pictures to conceal a safe behind. Not even a bookshelf. This space was as rigid as the pencils lined up on Johnny's desk at the bank.

HT muttered to himself as his nimble hands traced every possible entry point for hidden treasure. "I had a mark hide his floor safe under the bed once. Wrenched my back something terrible getting to that one."

I walked into the first bedroom and caught the staleness of unwashed linen, the faint scent of lilacs. Mrs. Evans' room. I bent down and looked under the bed to humor HT. If the dust bunnies knew where the safe was, they weren't telling. Wrinkling my nose, I straightened up and left the room.

The next room had to be Johnny's bedroom. The furniture aligned with the wall edges as though somebody had taken a ruler to it. The closet contained three suits, all tan in color. One pair of brown lace-up oxfords rested on the floor. I bet they matched the pair he now wore.

I heard of voluntary simplicity, but Johnny Evans seemed to shun all color as well. Maybe he felt he didn't deserve it. The closet shelf above the clothes was dusted and empty. I pushed the suits aside and surveyed the wall behind. No sign of a safe door.

HT headed toward a small bathroom and I followed him. He yanked open the door of the wall medicine cabinet. Instead of a row of prescription drugs, the space behind the door hid the dial of a small safe built into the wall.

"Got that computer list from Ben?" HT asked, limbering each finger like a magician shaking blood into the digits. "I'm ready."

I focused my flashlight on the list. Ben's talent was amazing. He had uncovered social security numbers for both Johnny and his deceased mother, records for bank accounts, and insurance policies.

The list held not only Johnny's birthday but also that of his mother. That might be the place to start. Mrs. Evans struck me as a self-centered person, putting her needs and wants before those of others. If this were her safe, she would have used her own birthday as the combination, not Johnny's.

HT closed his eyes to shut out the world. "Line the dial up with zero and put my hand on it."

I did. “Try this one.” I read off the three numbers: month, day, year.

HT worked slowly, counting off each click of the dial. First right, then left, then right again, but the safe didn't open.

“All right, try this order: day, month, year.”

Again, nothing. The third combination of year, month, day also struck out. So much for that good idea. We tried Johnny’s birthdate in the same combinations. Same result. Nada.

I thought a moment. If I were blind, maybe I wouldn't go by numbers, I'd go by touch. I lined the dial back to zero and we started again. “HT, try spinning the dial 180 degrees each turn.”

He completed the last turn and the tumblers dropped. “We're in,” he announced with satisfaction.

Before he could open the safe door, footsteps echoed on the front porch. HT pushed the medicine cabinet door smoothly back into place. I switched off my flash, and we crept into the hall.

I peered around the corner. Had Johnny returned? If so, we were trapped.

“FedEx!” A brisk shout bounced from the porch.

I stiffened as the man rang the bell. Then there was the thump of a package dumped near the door and the sound of departing footsteps. Soon a truck engine rumbled to life and then disappeared into the distance.

We returned to the bathroom, and the image of the two of us, ghostly white in the mirror's reflection stared back. Then the reflection skewed to the right as I tilted the door on its hinge and we again faced the porthole safe. Would the contents be worth our risk? HT gestured for me to do the honors. Slowly I swung the door open.

The knife Garrett had described to me rested on the floor of the safe box. Bingo. Johnny Evans *had* stolen it. He was the one behind the packrat swap of the Heaton’s missing dueling pistol for Garrett’s knife, one shiny object for one even more desirable. And that action made Johnny Evans prime suspect for Druce Kevern’s death and the cover-up that followed it.

What was Evans’ connection to Druce Kevern? I wasn’t sure yet how all the pieces fit together. But one thing I did know—Ben's hacking into the bank computer with Vanessa would have terrified Johnny. He stole the office computer to destroy any evidence that Ben may have uncovered. And it explained the attack on Ben in the tunnel. My clerk was fortunate to escape with only a busted head.

My phone rang, and I turned toward the hall to answer it.

"The eagle is flying."

"Ben, speak English."

"The car. Evans is pulling out of the lot. You need to get out of there, *now*."

HT slammed the safe door and spun the dial. Then he swung the medicine cabinet back in place. We rushed through the house and dived out the back door, wiping surfaces clean of fingerprints as we went.

I reluctantly left the knife in the safe. I'd put in a call to the sheriff's anonymous tip line to be sure the chain of evidence remained clear. I wanted to nail this guy.

Grabbing the ladder and paint cans, we race-walked to the truck and dumped everything in the back. I dived into the driver's seat and cranked the ignition. The engine hesitated, then coughed to life. The truck was already in motion when HT swung in beside me. With a squeal of tires, we accelerated down the street.

I drove around the block and double-parked at the town square. That's the only way Johnny could come through here, and we'd see him when he did. We sat, catching our breath, waiting. Johnny's car did not appear, and the town streets were silent.

I drummed my fingers on the steering wheel and then checked my watch. A minute later, I checked it again. It was taking too long—Johnny should be here by now.

"HT, when did Ben call?"

"Had to be ten minutes ago."

We looked at each other.

"Vanessa sold out to the highest bidder," I said. "Johnny isn't coming here. He's heading for the Heatons. And if Vanessa called to warn her mother, Alice Heaton is in danger, too."

I jammed on the gas. "Let's see how fast this old truck can go. We have to get to Mingus before Johnny Evans does something really stupid."

CHAPTER TWENTY-SEVEN

I GROUND THE TRUCK into low for the hills and switchbacks of town. Within minutes, we had arrived at the Heaton residence.

I pulled the pickup directly behind the beige car I knew all too well from my accident on Cherry Hill. My front bumper nudged the car tight, and I yanked my emergency brake full on. No sense in making a getaway easy for the criminal.

HT and I opened our doors and climbed out quietly. Then I reached under the seat and pulled out Flint's sawed-off shotgun. In this instance, I didn't think he'd mind if I used it.

The building had a front door and one in back. Any other exits? I didn't think so. Motioning HT to cover the back of the house, I crouched by Evans' car, studying the house. I racked the shotgun and crept to the front porch. There were muffled voices inside. Softly walking up the steps, I gained access to the landing. The front door was ajar and I pushed it open.

"Come right in, Deputy Quincy. We've been expecting you."

Johnny stood behind the couch holding Alice Heaton's shoulder. He clutched the topaz dueling pistol that Roger Heaton had vowed to keep under lock and key. Topaz for good fortune? Not in this case. The weapon was pointed directly at the woman's head.

"Come any closer and I'll pull the trigger."

Johnny's face was white, but his grip on the pistol was rock steady. "This time it's primed and loaded. Unlike poor Alice here, these old guns are my friends."

I cursed Roger Heaton under my breath. If he'd locked up the pistol as he promised this wouldn't be happening.

I listened for any sounds from the back, but the house was quiet. I chanced a quick glance toward the side windows. And where was HT?

Johnny caught my motion. "Forget about backup. That rear door is locked and bolted." His grip tightened on the dueling pistol and Alice gasped.

"Drop the shotgun," he snarled, or "I'll kill her right now."

He'd pushed Druce Kevern over the cliff and seriously injured Ben. He wasn't bluffing. I slid the gun slowly to the floor in front of me, barrels facing Johnny. Then I nudged a half step toward it. How long would it take me to grab the racked shotgun and fire? Too long.

"Sit down," Johnny ordered gesturing toward one of the wingbacks.

If I sat down, it would take me even longer to reach him. I gambled he'd not push it.

"I'd rather stand." I kept my voice calm and level.

"Your choice."

So far, so good. Keep him talking. While he's talking, he's not intent on killing the hostage. Only then is there a chance to halt the inevitable.

"Why don't you just drop the pistol, Johnny, let her go?" Sometimes appealing to their better instincts worked.

"I can't do that. I need the pistol to kill her." His tone was logical, but his thought was insane.

My heart froze. "Why? Alice didn't do anything to you."

"But *Vanessa* did." He squeezed hard on Alice's shoulder and she cried out. "Vanessa broke the rules..."

"You don't have to do this," I protested. "There's still time. You haven't hurt anyone."

"You don't understand. I *want* to hurt someone. Vanessa killed my baby, my tiny unborn baby. Now it's my turn to take something from her. She needs to know how it feels."

Alice was scared but still functioning. Good. I'd need her cooperation later.

It was time to divert the attention in another direction. I addressed the man holding the gun. “Ben is better. He’s out of the hospital.”

The pistol dropped slightly. Johnny looked confused, remembering. “Ben. He poked into my private business. He had no right to do that. You understand, don't you?”

I nodded. “He made a mistake. He’s young. He won’t do it again. You were right, correcting him.”

Johnny’s eyes filled with tears. Something I’d said touched him. What?

I thought about the strange environment that HT and I had just left at this man’s house. Odds were that Johnny had been disciplined severely by that strange rigid mother. Maybe that was the key!

“It was about your mother, wasn’t it?”

My mind made one those strange leaps of connection that happen under pressure. “Tell me about the boots, Johnny.” I tried to make my voice empathic.

His tone became childlike. “I wanted cowboy boots so bad. I kept asking Mother, year after year, but she always said ‘no, too expensive.’ Those were the rules.” Johnny’s face tightened.

“But when she died, you bought some,” I guessed, monitoring the hostage reaction. Alice’s awareness had shifted. She was paying attention now and seemed less frightened. Good.

Johnny smiled through his tears. “I bought bright purple boots. *Not* too expensive. *My* turn to live. *My* rules.”

The little beige man, trying to exist in a world without his mother. Perhaps that was the way to reach him.

Alice sensed his distraction and jerked away, destroying our moment of connection.

Johnny pulled her close, his fingers biting into her skin. “Quiet! I’m talking to Deputy Quincy.”

I cursed my stubbornness in trying to handle this alone.

If I kept him talking, there was a chance that HT would call for backup. I tried to defuse the situation. “Druce stole the boots from you, and you wanted them back.”

“He had to pay.” His voice fell into a singsong cadence.

“I understand why you argued. That could happen to anybody.”

He glared at me. “Don't try to join with me. It won't work.”

Where was HT?

"But Druce Kevern fell over the cliff," I said. "He wasn't a threat anymore. Why didn't you just take the boots back?" I was interested, in spite of myself. What had been the final blow to this man's esteem?

"They were contaminated, filthy. He'd *worn* them."

"And then you took the dueling pistol he'd stolen?" I was trying to track his thought process, to knife in where there might be an opening.

"Vanessa wanted it and I wanted her. And now I'll kill her mother instead." He giggled insanely.

Alice started to sob.

Hang in there, Alice. Just hang in there.

"You know I can't stop you, Johnny," I said. The quiet voice inside said, *Wait for the opportunity and then strike.* "So then you planted the gun at Tal Garrett's house and took his knife. Why did you do that?"

"I don't like bullies. I hate that man." His voice got shrill. He quieted with visible effort and readjusted his grip once again on the frightened woman. "I thought finding the weapon there might distract you. Clumsy of me."

"No, it was a good trick," I said, pacing my breathing and speech to mirror his. "It might have worked."

Johnny's eyes narrowed, as he built up courage to move. Whatever was going to happen would be soon.

I lowered my eyes to the dim shape of the shotgun lying on the floor. I might not succeed, but I'd have to try. My knees tightened for the jump.

A slight caution of movement flickered at the window behind Johnny. It was HT with a big rock in his hand.

I stared at Alice, willing the woman to see me. Now, Alice. *Now!*

The woman swooned into a faint. At the same time, HT threw the rock through the window.

Johnny jerked around, his attention distracted for a breath by the shattering glass. I dived for the shotgun on the floor in front of me and twisted right, out of his twitch-pull reflex.

Aim for the torso, aim for the big target. I pulled one trigger. Then the other.

Johnny slumped to the floor and the dueling pistol slipped from his fingers.

A red splotch appeared on the wall behind where he had stood. It widened and then started to drip, clotted red streams that lengthened to necklaces of crimson death.

Alice moaned once and pushed herself upright. Recoiling, she crabbed away from the bloody mess that had been a human being.

My feet were unsteady as I rose and lay the spent shotgun on the floor. It had done its job, just as I had done mine.

I walked toward the fallen man and kicked the dueling pistol from his tightening fingers. There was no pulse. He was gone.

A jolt of adrenaline and then a surge of shame ran through me. I'd had a choice, and in that split second, I chose to kill Johnny Evans rather than let him live. I had taken a human life. Not the life of a game animal, but one of my own.

And worse, my choice was deliberate. Even if by some miracle if I could hit the replay button, I would do exactly the same thing again. That action initiated me into that fraternity from which there was no resigning, one that cops didn't talk to husbands and wives about because they wouldn't understand.

I called the sheriff's office and briefly explained what happened. Then I called the EMTs but I told them not to use the sirens. There was no hurry.

CHAPTER TWENTY-EIGHT

THE MOMENTS AFTER the shooting of Johnny Evans smeared together in actions that happened to someone else while I watched from a cold distance.

The EMTs arrived and after the coroner pronounced the death, left with the corpse. An investigative team took both the dueling pistol and Flint's shotgun into evidence.

The lead officer talked to HT and Alice. They both corroborated my story of self-defense. Based on what he heard, the officer released me for the time being. He said they'd be in touch to take my official statement. Fine with me. I wasn't going anywhere.

I was no longer a cop, so I didn't return to the sheriff's office with the other patrolmen. HT offered to take me home with him, but I asked him to drop me off at the Mingus sheriff's station instead. It was familiar even if I didn't belong there anymore.

Ben stood when I entered the station. We hugged each other, neither of us saying a word. I felt a cold wind blowing through a big empty hole where my insides should be.

I walked into my office and slammed the door. I still had Johnny's blood on my sleeve. I brushed at it, but it wouldn't come off.

Dispassionately, I replayed the scene in my mind. Had I done everything I could have? In the right order?

I'd protected innocent people. I'd neutralized Johnny's threat and taken the pistol into custody. I'd presented a calm and professional exterior.

And I had killed a man. I started once more and relived the scene. Rewind, replay. Rewind, replay.

The minutes dragged on. Out in the hall, the regulator clock hiccupped after every seventh beat. A fly clicked against the inside window pane trying to reach the sunshine beyond the glass.

In the foyer, Ben punched keys on the replacement computer, playing his video game. Games! My games were real. Today I'd held the moment of death in my hands, both the rush and the inevitability of it. The black hole inside me widened and deepened like a cancerous growth.

I picked up and then discarded work that had seemed important yesterday: The talk an elementary school wanted me to give on being a cop. A security request for the upcoming town meeting. The sheriff's office called, looking for me, and I told Ben to take a message.

When I'd had enough of staring aimlessly at the wall, I packed up my stuff. "I'm going for a run," I told Ben.

I changed into running gear in the restroom and exited the station. I breathed hard on the climb up the steep slope, but then I reached the meadow where Isabel and Ben had gathered herbs. On the far side of the valley, ridge after ridge of mountains turned blue and soft as they marched into the distance. The threat of storm had passed, and the row of clouds billowed like a street in the sky.

I returned to a blistering pace, climbing higher on the mountainside, feeling the welcome release of tension. I pushed myself hard and then harder still. I fought for breath as the sweat poured into my eyes and my hair dripped. A blue jay became a fierce azure streak through a ponderosa pine in front of me. A woodchuck scuttled into bear grass as I approached.

Finally, I dropped to earth near a large boulder to let my breath settle. The dying sun seeped into my tense muscles and my eyes closed. I let the soft breeze caress my tired skin. Every cell, every pore was spent.

I lay back in a hollow of meadow grass and drifted off to sleep. I didn't even start when a voice broke into my dreamless fog.

"Peg? Your granddad sent me to fetch you," Flint Tanner said.

"How did you find me?" I asked drowsily.

"Isabel knew."

He pulled me to my feet. "Come on, I'll give you a ride home."

* * * * * *

THE FOLLOWING DAYS were hard ones. At first, I stayed in my apartment, not wanting to face strangers. When its walls closed in on me, I drifted over to HT's house.

No longer employed, I alternated between playing chess with Ben and running the hills each day until I dropped from exhaustion. My sleep was troubled, and the continuing investigation into the death of Johnny Evans did not help. My bleak mood showed no signs of lifting.

The monsoons had waned, although there'd still be a shower or two before they retreated down to Baja, California, for another year. The air had dried, and a slight breeze stirred the ailanthus trees lining Main Street.

Then the morning of the town hall meeting dawned. This gathering would determine the future of the community. The hint of fall in the air signaled change for both the town and for me.

I was ready.

CHAPTER TWENTY-NINE

TAL GARRETT BARRED MY WAY as I entered the town hall for the important meeting. "What are you doing here? I thought Jones fired you."

News travels fast. I searched hard for a positive response. Couldn't find one. Settled for a lame, "Good luck with the vote today."

"Oh, I'll win. I know how to handle situations when the chips are down." Garrett brushed past me, pausing to shake hands with people on his way up to the front stage. Always working the crowds, that was Tal Garrett.

Patrick Shaw touched my shoulder as I passed. "Are you doing okay? You had a rough time up there at the Heaton house. If you want to stop by and talk, I'm a good listener." His eyes held sympathy and concern. "I mean it. Anytime."

I was briefly tempted, and then shut it down. He was just being nice, saying that. No one would understand what I was going through. I said thanks and walked to where Isabel helped other women set out refreshments.

One table had an apple pie—that had to be hers—a platter of brownies and one of homemade chocolate chip cookies. Two big urns of coffee. Nothing like the smell of coffee to set the tone for business ahead.

Win or lose, this community embraced the chance to get together in this historic structure. The citizens had debated all the important events of the town in this building. The town crier announced World War I here and shouted the end to World War II. The hall had witnessed the bonanza of that first copper rush, and folks learned of the mine closings within these walls.

"Time to start, folks." Garrett banged on the podium with a gavel. "Find a seat."

HT pointed to a vacant chair next to him and invited me to sit. "Saved it for you. I was hoping you'd come. This should be interesting."

Wooden chairs creaked and voices quieted in anticipation of the speakers ahead. The aisle down the middle of the room divided the hall like a wedding ceremony. Garrett's paid votes sat on one side; the miners and their families filled the other. Alice Heaton sat in the front row on the Garrett side, a built-in audience for Roger's real estate presentation.

Ben and Vanessa grouped close by, their heads bent over a game on Ben's cell phone. Some artists, but not too many. They ordinarily didn't turn out for this sort of thing. A number of Armor's biker friends, clad in leathers and motorcycle boots leaned against the far wall. Armor wasn't there, but it sometimes took him a little longer using his crutch.

It was a diverse bunch, but that was Mingus. In some perverse way, I was proud of the turnout. This was my town, even if I didn't feel a part of it right now.

Garrett droned on for five minutes about the history of the town and its great progress in "returning from the dead" over the last decade. A poor turn of phrase. He must have prepared his speech before the events at the Heatons.

"And now, the first presentation by our illustrious vice mayor."

Roger Heaton walked up on the stage to a smattering of applause. He pulled a pair of reading glasses from his suit coat pocket and mumbled to himself as he shuffled papers. Then he stammered through a speech about the town's need for development. He placed a big architectural rendering on a flimsy wooden easel. At one point, it tipped under his pointer, and the audience held its collective breath that it would stay upright. It did, but that didn't help the presentation much. Still dull. Finally his talk trailed off, and a hand raised in the back of the room.

"Does this fancy plan mean you'll be tearing down most of the historic Main Street buildings?"

"Well, some, possibly," Roger hedged, the sweat beading on his forehead. "We haven't gotten that far into the details."

"That's exactly what they'd do," HT muttered. "This town would be leveled."

I elbowed him. "Shhh, I want to hear this."

After fielding a few more questions, Roger sat down, with loud applause from one side of the room and heavy silence from the other.

"Next, a brief presentation by the mining representative," Garrett said.

Flint Tanner mounted the stage. I had to admit he cleaned up pretty good. He wore a pinstriped suit and power tie. His voice, deep and resonant, carried to the back of the room.

Flint gave a brief history of mining and the mine group's determination to keep the town's character intact. "What we want to do is reopen the mines on a limited basis only, to see what we can recover by tertiary methods."

A man in black leathers leaning against the back wall raised his voice. "None of that fracking stuff?"

"Absolutely not. That method of extraction is mostly used for petrochemicals. We're dealing with hard minerals here, mostly copper, but some gold and silver, too."

The miners raised a few confirming eyebrows at that. Although the mines produced millions of dollars of copper ore in the seventy years they were active, gold and silver secondary ores were of high value as well. One miner put his fingers to his mouth and emitted a loud whistle of appreciation.

Garrett had heard enough. "Thank you, thank you, Mr. Tanner," he said, walking on the platform. "A big round of applause for the young man." Even before it had died out, he nudged Flint toward the stage exit.

Then he called for a vote. "You were each given a piece of paper as you entered the hall. Two choices, two only."

Not being a voting member of the community, I didn't get one. But I noticed that HT printed in big letters, "other" at the bottom and marked it with a black "X."

"Alice, will you do us the honor of collecting the ballots?" Garrett asked.

One by one, the votes passed to the center aisle, and Alice collected them in a large basket. She walked to the front and delivered them to Roger.

The voting promised to be close and the crowd waited restlessly as the committee tallied the ballots. There was some discussion among them as they stacked paper in two piles. They counted the two stacks and then results were scribbled on a piece of paper. Alice handed it to Garrett, who still stood, commanding the platform.

He opened the slip and waited a pregnant moment. "Exactly two hundred votes for the new housing development." One side of the room clapped politely.

"And exactly two hundred votes for the mines," he announced. The other side of the room cheered.

"We have a tie. That means as mayor, I get to cast the deciding vote. And I vote for…"

"Just a gol-dern minute." The crowd stirred at the back of the room, and Armor pushed through. In one hand, he held a sheaf of papers. "You ain't doing nothing, Garrett." He pointed his finger at Flint. "No offense, but you ain't neither."

Armor walked slowly to the front of the room, leaning on his crutch. "I got the absentee proxy votes of everybody that still owns property here in Mingus. There's a lot of them absentee owners. And *they* all vote for the establishment of a National Historic District."

The crowd exploded. I heard shouts of derision, support, and unease. Men rose and crowded the center aisle. One faction started pushing the other. Bikers rammed in from the back.

Quicker than a summer thundercloud, an unruly mob was forming. The hair on the back of my neck lifted. I reached to my side for the weapon that no longer rested there.

Garrett sensed danger, too. He passed the gavel to Roger and disappeared through a side door to safety. Roger banged on the podium firmly. "I hereby send this resolution back to committee for further study. Meeting adjourned." He banged once more for good measure. "Refreshments in the back for everyone."

I turned to HT. "Did you know this would happen?"

He winked at me. "This is Mingus. We never agree on anything. You should have learned that by now." He stood up to shoulder his way into the crowd. "Follow me. I saw a brownie with my name on it."

We stood in a calm eddy of the townspeople near the refreshment table. Bikers, miners, and shopkeepers gossiped over the coleslaw and baked beans as though nothing had happened. Maybe HT was right. This *was* Mingus.

Ben went by with a plate loaded with goodies. I grabbed a lemon bar from his stash.

"Sheriff Jones called the office," my former clerk said. "He wants to talk to you."

I wove through the knots of people and stood outside the hall to return the sheriff's call.

He answered on the first ring. "Peg, I owe you an apology." He harrumphed as though something difficult was stuck in his throat. "Sometimes my temper gets the better of me."

That was for sure. But the stab of righteous anger in my belly was quenched by his next words.

"You've done fine work up there. Excellent detection, solving that murder case."

Now he thought it was fine? Two weeks ago the Druce Kevern case was cause for my termination. What was the man leading up to?

"You still there?" Taking my silence as assent, he continued. "The budget came through. You've got a replacement vehicle—an SUV. Now it's not brand new, but it'll take you places, that's for sure. What do you think about that?"

"Yeah, fine," I said.

It was too little too late. A man had died because I hadn't figured it out sooner. That was sloppy police work by a rookie who should have known better.

"No, you don't understand," he said patiently. "I want you to stay on. That's what I wanted to talk to you about that day you came to my office."

A week ago, that news would have elated me. But now, I wasn't sure. "I've got some thinking to do," I hedged.

"Take all the time you need, as long as you are back to work on Monday."

I had to get straight in my mind what I had done before I'd risk strapping on a weapon again. The stakes were just too high.

"I'll consider it," I said and hung up the phone.

CHAPTER THIRTY

I MADE MY FINAL DECISION on a day of ashes.

Armor convinced Jake Bean to relinquish the purple boots. Flint and I took them to the cement patio behind HT's workshop. The acetylene torch burped into life, and we took turns directing the tongue of fire. The old leather emitted a burnt-steak odor as each boot melted to charred black. When the ashes were cool, I scooped the remains into a small container and put the box in the back of the Jeep.

Regina waited for us at the House of New Directions. "All that young man wanted was respect. He needed just one more chance."

She slipped the small gold crucifix into a pocket with a somber expression. "Here, let me accompany you to the garden," she said. "The boys helped me dig the plot."

We walked down the path to a small fenced cemetery where owners buried the horses and pets of the ranch over the years. They built the graveyard in the shape of a horseshoe with markers identifying each plot of ground. A fruit tree grew beside each gravestone, signaling beauty in the spring and bounty in the fall.

Regina explained why she had established a cemetery for her horses. "When Custer fell at the Little Big Horn, his troops used their dead horses as the final breastwork. The animals were buried where they lay. We can do something no less for the horses here that have witnessed the battles these young men have fought in their recovery."

Regina and Flint stood as I placed the urn containing Druce Kevern's cremains and the small box with the boot ashes in the grave and covered them with the newly turned earth. I couldn't bury this young cowboy with his boots on, but they would be close to him. I said a silent prayer.

In a nearby paddock, a young mare whiffled softly. Perhaps Druce Kevern would find peace here at last. A big man with a long gray beard nodded to me from the shadow of an apple tree as we left the graveyard. Maybe the veteran could find peace here as well.

* * * * * *

LATE THAT AFTERNOON Flint and I made one final journey.

Johnny Evans had no heirs, and his mother had predeceased him. When the medical examiner asked me, I recommended cremation. Then I got special court dispensation to receive the ashes.

Flint carried the two urns and I packed a wicker basket to the steepest point on Woodchute Mountain. We tipped the containers at the same time. The ashes co-mingled, mother and son together, as the wind blew them across the high divide.

Then we walked into a now familiar meadow. Flint opened the basket and lifted out the bottle of wine and two goblets.

"A toast," he said, pouring some for each of us.

"To life," I replied, lifting my glass.

A young doe joined us silently at the edge of the meadow and then vanished into the shadows of the pine forest. The black hawk soared overhead.

Afterward, as we walked back to his Jeep, Flint put his arm around my shoulder.

"End of the rain," I observed, looking up at him. "Summer's over."

It was also the official end of my sojourn here. Or not. I leaned into Flint's solid warmth and considered the sheriff's offer of reinstatement.

I heard autumn was a special time in Mingus. Maybe I'd stick around a while longer.

AUTHOR NOTE TO READERS

I hope that you have had as much enjoyment reading this debut novel as I have had sharing it with you. Although I've set this story in the fictitious town of Mingus, the mining region of central Arizona is still alive and thriving, and the historical setting that I've provided is accurate. Packrat middens do exist for decades and there is a huge slag heap near the town of Clarkdale.

Reviews: Because an Indie novelist survives through word-of-mouth recommendations, if you enjoyed *Death in Copper Town,* please let others know about it. Tell your friends and neighbors! And please, if you will, consider posting an online review at Amazon.

Where to contact me: There will be new novels in the Pegasus Quincy Mystery Series arriving at regular intervals. Please visit my website at www.LakotaGrace.com to get news of forthcoming novels, to read my blog, or to give me feedback on my work.

If you'd like to get word of new Pegasus Quincy mysteries, behind-the-scene peeks at my writing process, and updates on a new series in progress, sign up for my monthly newsletter here.

Follow me on Amazon Author Central or BookBub to get notices of new book releases.

I'd love to hear from you.

ABOUT THE AUTHOR

Lakota Grace has called the American Southwest home for most of her life. She has a doctorate in counseling psychology and has written stories since age five.

Lakota has an abiding love for the high desert plateau and the abundance of life it supports. Quail and red-tail hawks visit her feeders; bobcats and coyotes wander by. She maintains a cautious co-existence with the scorpions and javelinas who visit her backyard.

Most of all, she enjoys getting up before dawn, watching the sun hit the red rocks, and sharpening her pencil for yet another writing session.

Made in the USA
Coppell, TX
09 August 2022